Also by Brigit Young

The Prettiest
Worth a Thousand Words

BRIGHT

BRIGIT YOUNG

Roaring Brook Press
New York

Published by Roaring Brook Press

Roaring Brook Press is a division of Holtzbrinck Publishing Holdings
Limited Partnership

120 Broadway, New York, NY 10271 • mackids.com

Stars © by Noppakorn Chaiyarak/Shutterstock

Our books may be purchased in bulk for promotional, educational, or business use.
Please contact your local bookseller or the Macmillan Corporate and Premium Sales
Department at (800) 221-7945 ext. 5442 or by email at
MacmillanSpecialMarkets@macmillan.com.

Library of Congress Cataloging-in-Publication Data

Names: Young, Brigit, author.
Title: Bright / Brigit Young.
Description: First edition. | New York : Roaring Brook Press, 2022. | Audience:
Ages 8–12. | Audience: Grades 4-6. | Summary: Marianne Blume, a self-described
'ditz,' tries out for her school's Quiz Quest team in a bid to prove she is smart.
Identifiers: LCCN 2021047595 | ISBN 9781250822116 (hardcover)
Subjects: CYAC: Middle schools—Fiction. | Schools—Fiction. | Friendship—
Fiction. | Self-esteem—Fiction. | LCGFT: Fiction.
Classification: LCC PZ7.1.Y7424 Br 2022 | DDC [Fic]—dc23
LC record available at https://lccn.loc.gov/2021047595

First edition, 2022
Book design by Angela Jun
Printed in the United States by Lakeside Book Company, Harrisonburg, Virginia

ISBN 978-1-250-82211-6 (hardcover)

1   3   5   7   9   10   8   6   4   2

For Jonathan, who sees me.

Everyone you will ever meet knows something you don't.
—BILL NYE

This is how it works
You peer inside yourself
You take the things you like
And try to love the things you took.
—REGINA SPEKTOR

1

MARIANNE BLUME DIDN'T KNOW a lot, but she knew she was stupid.

And so did Mr. Garcia.

"Alright, Ms. Blume," he said, serious as ever, giving her a look like this was her one last chance.

When the class heard him call on her, most of them tuned out, scribbling on worksheets until they could actually learn something again.

"Let's give this one a try," he went on.

Oh no. He wasn't really going to make her do this, was he?

That afternoon she'd tried a couple of her usual strategies to get him to leave her be: sighing here and there like she was having outside-the-classroom troubles, and scribbling in her notebook so it looked like she was taking notes.

"Who, *me*?" She raised her eyebrows in the doe-eyed way she'd learned meant "I know nothing."

Kylie Chen, seated in the chair next to her, snorted.

The class giggled at her snort.

Thanks, Kylie. Maybe Mr. Garcia would move on. Too much distraction.

Marianne heard Vi Cross mutter something to herself two desks over. She glanced back just in time to see Vi roll her eyes.

Marianne could see that Vi was annoyed, and she understood she'd already frustrated Mr. Garcia, but what she couldn't wrap her head around was how in any world, in any version of any universe, she was supposed to figure out the value of X.

"Hmm. Sorry. I don't know this one." She threw Mr. Garcia a big smile. The more you smiled, the more people liked you. And man, did she want Mr. Garcia to like her.

"Let's walk through it together," Mr. Garcia went on, offering no sunshine in return.

Why was he doing this? He knew she didn't—and wouldn't—know the answer.

Ms. James, Marianne's English and history teacher, would've let her off the hook. So would her math teacher from last year, Ms. Corwin, who made Marianne and a few other kids spend a couple of lunches a week in her classroom completing extra worksheets. Ms. Corwin loved to chat, so they spent most of the lunch hour gabbing with her about stuff like the best mystery shows on Netflix and what they'd do if they had a million dollars. Those teachers understood Marianne. They wouldn't put her on the spot. Even Mr.

Hedley from sixth grade, a famously grumpy science teacher, would've joked around with Marianne instead of embarrassing her. Marianne figured out early on that Mr. Hedley was like most cranky old grandpas—a softie. After a few post-class questions about his grandkids, they became the best of friends. She still stopped by Mr. Hedley's room to see if his ski champion grandson was getting closer to the Olympics.

"Okay, let's work through this together . . ." Mr. Garcia turned to the Smart Board, which was Marianne's cue to shut off her brain. Like she always said, mostly just to herself: If you don't listen, you can't not know.

Her thoughts drifted to her best friend, Skyla, and what she might be doing in her science class across the hall right then.

Mr. Garcia kept talking.

Marianne put a finger to her temple and tried to send Skyla telepathic messages: *Skylaaa, my mom will only buy me all-natural deodorant and it doesn't work. Help meee.*

He went on and on.

Marianne forced herself to think about the pair of red shoes she really wanted from the thrift store downtown. She thought of how she couldn't wait for lilac season, when the whole town smelled like a perfume shop. She thought about how weird it was that killer whales were dolphins, not whales, and how she wished she could be a killer whale right then, splashing freely in the sea instead of stuck in an uncomfortable metal chair, bent over a desk, a bright overhead light making it impossible to hide the big pimple on the side of her nose and Mr. Garcia making it impossible to hide that she hadn't taken in a single thing from his class all year.

Mr. Garcia inched closer to the end of his lecture, and she knew he'd ask her to say something soon.

She wouldn't let him pull her in, wouldn't let the class see her try to translate the numbers on the board when to her it was like trying to read a foreign language that she didn't speak.

Please move on to someone else, please move on to someone else, she prayed. *Please, Almighty Whoever in the Sky, send a tornado at this very moment.*

"And so that tells us what?" he asked.

Marianne stared at the numbers and letters before her, scrawled in Mr. Garcia's chicken-scratch handwriting.

Everyone around her knew the answer. Everyone.

She peered at Kylie's notebook. They were two fellow C-or-lower kids placed together in the front, where they "had" to pay attention. Marianne saw that even Kylie had been following along for the most part, rows of numbers dutifully copied down.

Marianne's paper contained a shimmering masterpiece of doodled pink stars.

"Well? What's your first thought, Ms. Blume?"

Marianne stared blankly. Her first thought? That in order to figure out the answer she'd have to go back in time and hear what he'd said, but first she'd have to go back in time to five math books ago, and five years before that, and further and further back, to a time she hadn't felt totally, entirely lost, and start there. And if she *did* have a time machine, she wouldn't waste it on learning math. She'd ride a woolly mammoth.

"Um. My first thought? It's . . . Why the letter X, anyway, huh?" She whipped her lip gloss out of her pocket and spread it onto her pouted lips. "It makes me think of poison labels or whatever. When they were making up algebra, why did they pick X and not L? Like love? Or—better yet—M?"

A couple of kids snickered.

Mr. Garcia glared in the direction of the misbehavior.

She was wasting his time again. Teachers *hated* wasting time. *She* hated wasting his time, but he was giving her no choice! She couldn't learn this stuff. She really couldn't.

Eventually he'd have to call on someone else. No one ever paid her too much mind for too long.

"Actually, Ms. Blume, that's an interesting point. X is conventionally used to signify the unknown, but we could use any letter, really. Let's change it to M. So. What's the next step to get us to the value of M?"

"Cool. 'The unknown,'" she said, stalling. Marianne pulled a hair tie off her wrist and twisted her long tresses into an elaborate messy bun.

She wished the class would misbehave or have conversations around her, but it was quiet. People would hear whatever she said. Her insides felt like clothes tumbling in a dryer. It was like her body remembered those years before she'd figured out how to slide by. Her cheeks remembered the heat that rose in them when she answered with the opposite of the correct answer because the question itself still perplexed her. Her shoulders remembered how high they'd risen as the other fourth and fifth graders watched her flail.

But nowadays she was a pro, bubbly and unbothered. She could get out of this.

"I'm sorry," she said, and in so many ways she was, "but I didn't hear that last part. Can you repeat it from back when you started writing?"

Mr. Garcia said nothing, but a couple of kids groaned.

"Sorry!" she said again, as sincerely as she could, though she knew that her singsongy voice probably sounded pretty fake. "I was putting on my lip gloss, and I remembered I'd left the other one at home and I started thinking of where I put it, and you know . . ."

"Yup," a girl a few seats away said, and then conversations broke out.

Class was officially disrupted.

"Ha!" Lucas Hayes called out from the back of the classroom. "Yeah, you guys know how that is!" He put on an airy, girly voice and mimicked, "Lip gloss probs!"

Marianne swiveled back toward him with a thumbs-up and a grin.

To survive the day, that was what it took. A smile. A thumbs-up. Daydream. Stall. Shrug after shrug.

Lucas threw her an air high five.

"Enough!" Mr. Garcia snapped in their direction. "How about you pick it up for us from there, Mr. Hayes?" Mr. Garcia said, finally leaving her alone.

As his attention and the class's focus left Marianne, she could feel her whole body melt back into the chair. Humiliation officially dodged.

As Mr. Garcia went on to describe the homework, Marianne picked up her favorite purple pen with a big plastic unicorn on the top of it and scribbled hearts in the corners of her papers.

After class Marianne stopped by her locker to grab her history and literature binder and spotted Skyla walking by. "Skyla!" she hollered.

Skyla motioned "one sec" and continued her chatter with a few kids from her classes that year. Back in sixth grade, Skyla had only made friends with whoever Marianne had introduced her to.

Marianne barely knew these girls. And they mostly talked about boys. Boring.

She tugged on Skyla's shirt to get her attention. "I can't go home with you today," she told her in a low voice.

Marianne had yet another meeting with the principal and her parents. Twice a year she could count on a warning about her grades. At home, her dad would yell and take something away, like her time on the iPad or nightly mint-chip ice cream. He'd say, "I just don't understand why you don't *want* to do well!" Her parents would try to help her with homework more often until they both gave up and spent that time working instead. They'd attempt hired tutoring again. It would fail and they'd decide it was too expensive, anyway.

Skyla turned away from her other friends, though it seemed to Marianne that she was still listening to their conversation out of one ear.

"Meeting with Ms. Clarke," Marianne reported. "If you wait around my parents can drive us back together?"

"No, Papa and Dad are home early today and I bet they'll make nachos and I don't want to miss it. See you tomorrow. Good luck!"

"'Kay. Bye." Marianne blew her a kiss.

Skyla blew one back and returned to her other friends— her non-best friends, who really hardly knew her, anyway.

Marianne hated having no classes with Skyla that year.

But before too long it would be high school, and she and Skyla could sign up for electives together. They could be each other's dates for Homecoming, like Marianne's big sister, Lillian, did with her best friend that year.

As she headed toward the end of the hallway to lit class, she heard Lucas Hayes cackling before she saw him.

He lingered in a crowd with his twin, Ava, and a couple of other kids, smirking at something. At some*one*.

Marianne inched closer.

Vi Cross stood before them handing out fliers and yammering on and on. Why did she keep talking? Couldn't she see that they were laughing at whatever she was saying, and not in the good way?

Marianne remembered earlier in the year when Vi had run for class president but lost to Sam Musaka after giving a truly embarrassing speech about the "carbon footprint" of the school. At one point Vi had told the kids they were a "part of the problem" and scolded "For shame!" at the whole auditorium, which caused an explosion of laughter. She would probably be president of the United States one day, but the skills necessary to become president of the eighth grade were beyond her.

Marianne made her way to the outside of the crowd and held out a hand to one of the kids to snatch a flier. They passed one over. It read:

ETHERIDGE QUIZ QUEST TEAM
IN NEED OF NEW MEMBERS

JOIN QUIZ QUEST AS IT PROCEEDS
TO REGIONAL CHAMPIONSHIPS FOR
THE FIRST TIME IN ETHERIDGE HISTORY

EXCELLENT GRADES NOT REQUIRED
BUT HIGHLY PREFERRED

MUST HAVE KNOWLEDGE OF OR INTEREST
IN GEOGRAPHY, SOCIAL STUDIES, LITERATURE,
HISTORY, CIVICS, MATHEMATICS, SCIENCE,
GRAMMAR, & MORE

SEE MR. GARCIA FOR MORE DETAILS

"Wait, so how many of us can join?" Lucas asked, obviously messing with her. "Could we all do it?"

"I'm so glad you asked!" Vi chirped. "We're short one person since Addison Schuler moved, and only four of us can compete at once, so technically we only *need* one more teammate, but we can always use extra players. We'd simply have to determine who's best suited to perform at Regionals. But others could provide assistance as swing teammates in case of illness and whatnot, and if there are enough who join, we could even add B and C teams! Honestly, whoever joins has big shoes to fill. Addison was . . . incomparable."

Marianne saw something flit across Vi's face, maybe worry or sadness, but she couldn't tell what exactly.

"The point is, it's really worth the time commitment," Vi went on. "You'll see your grades improve."

"It just sounds *soooo fun*!" Ava squealed.

"It really is!" Vi beamed.

Marianne didn't think she'd ever seen Vi Cross smile before. She had two dimples in each cheek.

"I don't know if you've ever been to Ann Arbor, but it's a pretty neat place. And, of course, if we win Regionals and make it to the Championship in Lansing . . . Well, that'll be *really* exciting," Vi went on, still oblivious to the fact that she was an object of mockery. "Have you visited the state capital before?"

"What?" Lucas fake-gasped. "The *state capital*? Is the *governor* there?"

Ava and her friends snickered. Lucas and Ava were both super good-looking. Other kids flocked to them. They laughed with wide-open mouths and their pretty eyes twinkled at any opportunity to tease.

"But!" Vi held up a finger to make another point, which caused a few other kids in the crowd to stifle even more giggles. "I know some of you here don't quite have the grades to cut it. I'm sorry, but it's just the truth. So I don't want you to get the wrong idea and think you can easily make it to Ann Arbor. Or Lansing."

The kids couldn't hold it in any longer. They let out whoops of laughter.

Vi grew quiet. She appeared to finally understand what was happening but didn't know how to stop it.

Marianne did.

She jumped in. "Wait, no, for real, guys, this sounds like fun."

Lucas and Ava howled. "Ohmygod. Please, *please* join Quiz Quest, Blume," Lucas said. "Do it."

"Seriously, I would buy a ticket to see that. I'd bring my whole family," Ava deadpanned.

"Yeah, they'll ask for the value of X and you'll say 'It's M!'" Lucas's friend Niko joked. Niko had shaggy hair that nearly covered his eyes and a broad grin that took up the rest of his face.

Jalilah Jacobs—always glamorous, always unbothered—jumped in, too. "*Yeees!* Horse in Nerdland! Love it!"

Horse. Marianne could never quite shake the nickname that had started early on in sixth grade. Sometimes, when people called her that, she performed a little "*Neigh!*"

"Hardy har har. I'm serious, guys! I could be awesome at it! Vi, test me!" Marianne turned to Vi and hoped Vi would see that if she would just jump in and participate in this little performance, then she wouldn't be the target anymore.

"Ha! Yes! Show us what you got, Blume!" To Vi, Lucas said, "What are some of the questions? Easy ones." He winked at Marianne.

Like a robot, Vi answered immediately: "Easy. Right. Okay." She cleared her throat. "He was the second president of the United States, hailing from Massachusetts. Who was he?"

"Teddy Roosevelt!" Marianne shouted with a confidence she knew would make it funnier. She unwrapped a piece of gum and threw it in her smiling mouth.

Ava shrieked. "Girl, we learned this in like third grade! It's John freaking Adams! Are you for real?"

"Please, please, tell me you know the first president. Please." Lucas clasped his hands in a prayer position.

"She'll probably be like, 'George Washington Carver!'" said Niko, to everyone's delight.

"Just don't make me try to *spell* 'Massachusetts.'" Marianne blew a big bubble and let it pop. It spread across her nose, and she pulled it back in with her tongue.

"You're too much, Blume. Good stuff." Lucas smacked her back, and he, Ava, and their friends scurried to class.

Marianne stood there facing Vi as the hallways rapidly emptied.

Vi spoke first. "That's not allowed."

"Huh?"

"Chewing gum," Vi said.

"Oh."

Actually, gum *was* allowed in the hallway, just not in class, but what was the point of getting into it with someone who didn't like her?

"Oh my God," Vi grumbled. "I'm surrounded by morons."

And she stalked off.

No *Thank you for saving me from public ridicule*?

Vi Cross may have been destined to be president someday, but Marianne would never vote for her. She'd probably outlaw gum.

Marianne spotted Jalilah jogging back to her locker. She looked like she'd forgotten something.

Marianne eyed the clock on the wall and saw she had one minute left to make it five classrooms down—plenty of time. The longer she stayed out of class, the longer she could avoid Ms. James's questions about the reading.

"Hey, you think you'd ever join?" Marianne asked Jalilah, strolling a few steps toward her and the gray-blue lockers. "Quiz Quest?"

Jalilah let out a short, loud "Ha!" Pulling out a folder, she said, "You mean if no one had to know?" She mimicked thinking about something for an instant, then answered, "Still no."

Marianne laughed, wrapping her arms around her unread textbooks. "Yeah. It sounds like torture. And, like, most of the smart kids join Academic Games or Junior Diplomats, right?"

"Yeah, the kind of smart kids who have *friends* . . ." Jalilah snarked.

"Harsh but true," Marianne agreed, waving bye to Jalilah as she hurried off.

As Marianne strode toward lit, she saw Mr. Garcia turn the corner, and she instinctively looked away.

When Marianne arrived at Ms. James's door right as the bell dinged, Ms. James smiled and asked her daily question: "Hi there! How'd you like the reading?"

And, as was their tradition, Marianne answered, "Didn't get a chance to do it this time. Sorry!"

Then Ms. James sometimes said, "Why don't you get started on it now?" or "And why is that?" or "That's a shame, I wanted to hear your thoughts" or once in a blue moon, on days she looked like she'd had less sleep, "Mm-hmm."

That day she said nothing. She didn't even hand Marianne one of her Post-it notes that read, "Hey—start reading!" or "Hey—answer at least four questions on the worksheet and we'll call it even." Marianne really appreciated those Post-it notes. Why couldn't Mr. Garcia do something private like that?

Marianne doodled little ocean waves in the margins of her book and tried to think of what she'd say in the meeting that day:

I've just been really tired.
I take total responsibility. I understand.
I'll ace the next test, I swear.

At the end of class, as everyone ran off, Ms. James walked out with Marianne toward Ms. Clarke's office and told her, "I'm joining you for your meeting today."

That was a very bad omen.

And the signs just got worse from there. When Marianne walked through the front office toward Ms. Clarke's room, she could have sworn that scary music played as if someone was about to pop out from behind a table with a horror movie mask on. Inside, a sight more worrisome than any Pennywise costume greeted her. Her dad and mom sat there silently. Her dad wore a blank expression. Marianne gave him an optimistic "Howdy!" but even that didn't perk him up. Her mom remained entirely still except for her pointer finger, which played with her wedding ring, flicking the teeny diamond half a centimeter back and forth across her skin.

Ms. Clarke looked like she was about to tell Marianne someone had died.

For a moment Marianne thought maybe someone *had*. Granny? A great-aunt or -uncle? Oh no, was it their cat, Possum? *What happened to Possum?*

"*Is Possum okay?*" Marianne asked as she walked in.

"What?" they all answered at once, each more confused than the next.

"Phew," she mumbled.

"Marianne, take a seat . . ."

As Ms. Clarke broke the news to her that midterm scores would be announced the next day and that Marianne had failed three of the four, and as she began to list Marianne's grades from the previous semester and her current point totals for the present one, and as Ms. James jumped in to say something about Marianne's "wonderful presence" in class and her one "lovely, if a tad jumbled, paper" on *The Diary of Anne Frank*, Marianne tried to do exactly what she did in math class: let her daydreams carry her away.

Lillian called it "The Drift."

"Marianne's doing the Drift again, Dad!" she'd announce when speeches about homework started.

The drifting combined with the bad grades had concerned her parents so much that they'd taken her to doctors and gotten tests done, but nope, nothing was outside the norm. Not in *that* way.

Marianne could've sworn they were almost disappointed.

"You're just *choosing* not to listen to us," her dad had reprimanded her.

"Well . . . *yeah*!" Marianne had been shocked that they hadn't known that already.

So, right then, she worked her hardest to concentrate on the strange painting on Ms. Clarke's wall that resembled a little kid's drawing of a skull filled in with paint splotches. She attempted to ponder who would get kicked off her favorite reality show and how they'd take it. But try as she might not to listen as Ms. Clarke spoke, a new, urgent warning came through loud and clear:

"If something doesn't change," Ms. Clarke told her, "you will not be graduating with your class this year. You will have to repeat the eighth grade."

2

MARIANNE'S MOM WENT TO Harvard, but you'd never know it. Not because they weren't rich (they weren't), and not because her mom wasn't smart (she was). She was a linguist and spoke five languages, including one called Berber, which wasn't even written down, only spoken. Marianne couldn't imagine that. Those kids didn't even have to learn spelling in school! No, you wouldn't know her mom went to Harvard because she never mentioned it. The only actual proof was the PhD diploma in an oak wood frame hanging on the wall in her mom's office. If Marianne had gone to Harvard, she'd point to the diploma whenever someone questioned her. And she'd pronounce it "Hahvad," with a British accent, because that felt right. *Oh, you don't think I should chew gum in the hallways?* And she'd point. *Hahvad,* she'd say.

But with Marianne's mom, the only way you could tell she went someplace fancy was from the big words she used. Words like "portend," and "elucidate," and "precipice."

And every small question had a long answer. Like, "Mom, if everyone is so mad at the president all the time, why don't we just have an election right now?"

"It's complicated," her mom's responses often began, as she pushed her reading glasses up onto her hairline. "Really, we have elections quite often. You see, you have to consider the mindset of the founders as they composed the constitution, and their previous experience of life under a monarchy . . ."

She usually lost Marianne by word five.

When Ms. Clarke told them that Marianne wouldn't graduate from the eighth grade, Marianne found herself looking at her mom and wondering if she'd ever imagined, all those years ago in Hahvad, that her youngest kid would be a grade-repeater.

A *grade-repeater*. What would she tell Skyla? Would Marianne be with the seventh graders? They'd all look littler than her. She'd be a giant to them, especially the boys. And what if she didn't graduate the next year, too, and all of a sudden she was a fully formed teenager using her driver's license to take her classmates home from the eighth grade? What happened if someone never graduated middle school? Did they just get to drop out? How did they go to college? Would colleges know she'd been held back a grade? How would she ever move to Hawaii and go to U of H with Skyla?

And so this time Marianne listened. She listened to Ms. Clarke explain that Mr. Garcia said it would be numerically impossible for Marianne to pass if she didn't score extremely high on the next quizzes and final test. She took in the information she'd known somewhere in the back of her head, that unfortunately Mr. Garcia "did not believe in the concept of extra credit, but rather 'regular credit'" and that could "present a problem for Marianne." She heard her parents get defensive and say they'd been checking Saturn Grades constantly, but still they had no idea her midterms would be so low. She listened to Ms. Clarke reply, "Ultimately, the choice to pass the grade or not is up to Marianne. I know she's been evaluated for learning differences, and the conclusion was that this is a matter of hard work, dedication, and focus. She has to show us she's serious about making a change."

Clearly, no one sitting in Ms. Clarke's office had been the kid in fourth grade who tried the math problem over and over, giving only incorrect answers, knowing the whole class wondered what was wrong with her. Was she supposed to go through that again, just to make Mr. Garcia feel like a better teacher?

No wonder he'd called on Marianne that day. He knew it was do-or-die for her.

He *could* save her if he really wanted to, though.

He must have just really hated her.

Marianne watched the April birds outside the window, moving from wide circles to V shapes and back again.

Her throat tightened and she could feel tears just itching to come out. She wouldn't let them.

Ms. Clarke pulled up Saturn Grades on her laptop and pointed to percentage breakdowns for homework, participation, and tests. Her parents asked about "the process" and "the plan."

The birds flew past the gray clouds outside the window and out of her sight.

Marianne needed them to stop talking.

"I know I can do it," she interrupted with a bold lie. "I'll participate. I'll do all the stuff I have to do."

Marianne heard her dad sigh.

"I swear," she added, holding a hand to her heart.

Was her dad wishing she were more like Lillian? If Lillian had a meeting with the principal, it would probably be to let her parents know that she was overextended by getting all As, volunteering to bring meals to old people, and winning "best human girl in Michigan" or something.

But then her dad squeezed her hand.

She squeezed back.

Memories of mandated parent-and-daughter homework time flashed through her mind. She could almost hear the cries of "You *could* get it, you're just not *focusing*!" and "I'll never need to know this stuff in real life!" and the slamming of her bedroom door.

"I'll try," she told the roomful of grown-ups, who nodded and promised they believed in her and did not understand that trying had never been enough before and that was why she'd given up in the first place.

***

After a fend-for-yourself dinner she threw together while her parents headed to Lillian's swim meet, Marianne meandered her way to the porch. The sun lingered for its last moments in the sky. She texted Skyla.

how were the nachos?

extra cheesy. how was principal c?

you wont even believe me when i tell you. porch.

She heard the door at Skyla's house swing open.

They met at their railings facing each other, and Marianne spread apart the empty branches of the lilac bush to see her friend. Skyla tucked strands of her black bob behind her ears over and over, only to have them fall in front of her face again. She'd gotten a lot taller recently, Marianne noticed, and she hunched over a little, like she wanted to be smaller again. Skyla, hazel-eyed and level-headed, had never known how beautiful or cool she was.

"Did you get my telepathic message about my deodorant?" Marianne asked her.

"Nope. Still stuck with the all-natural?" Skyla asked with an "Oh, Marianne" laugh.

"Yup."

And then Marianne told Skyla every last detail of the meeting. "It was awful. And I couldn't stop thinking about how we wouldn't be in the same year together. And how we'd never make it to Hawaii." And—Marianne wanted to add but didn't—how Skyla would leave for high school without her and make *more* new friends and pretend she didn't know the loser next door who couldn't even go to Homecoming.

Skyla lifted three fingers to make the Girl Scouts honor sign. They'd been Daisies and Brownies together back in the day. "Nothing—and I mean nothing—will stop us from opening up the Skylanne Surfing Gear/Friendship Bracelet/Organic Sugar Scrub Stand of Maui."

"Better not."

"And they said you can't just do summer school?" Skyla asked.

"I think Ms. Clarke's words were 'You could take a class or two this summer, but unfortunately you can't redo all of eighth grade over a summer.'" Marianne pictured Ms. Clarke and the dozens of worry lines in the light brown skin on her forehead, the streaks of white in her hair, and her tired smile. Marianne liked her, even though most of the times they saw each other involved some kind of punishment or warning.

After a few moments in which the only sounds around them were the chirps of the early-evening birds, Skyla asked, "Have you really been doing no homework at all?"

Marianne shrugged. "I hate it."

"No one *likes* homework." Skyla fingered the turquoise beads on her necklace, looking out at two squirrels scrambling their way up a tree.

"Well, I *hate* it," Marianne repeated.

"Squirrel fight," Skyla said as the squirrels tumbled out of the branches and onto the grass. "I just do mine during class or while I wait to get picked up," she added.

"Okay, but first I'd have to know *how* to do it." Marianne heard herself snap at Skyla a little. "And I don't." Why would Skyla talk to her like this? Like her parents? Especially right then?

"You *could*," Skyla responded, echoing her mom and dad and Lillian and Ms. James and all the other people who lived on a planet far, far away from Marianne. "You're just a little . . . behind. That's all."

"Ha. Yeah, 'a little.'" Marianne took her arm out of the branches so they blocked her view of her friend.

Did it count as "behind" when you got so confused by long division in third grade that you never caught back up? She'd never forget the month Ms. Klein introduced it. Suddenly the numbers Marianne had once known split into halves and thirds and .078s and became unrecognizable. "How could twenty-eight even *go into* two?" she'd asked. "It's so much bigger!"

"If you work on it, you'll catch up!" Skyla's voice called through the bush.

"Can we stop talking about this?" Marianne pleaded to Skyla.

Instead of answering her, Skyla skipped down her porch steps and walked up Marianne's. They sat together on the rickety swing that had been there before Marianne's parents even moved in. Marianne liked to imagine that it was a hundred years old and that families had been chatting on it forever. One summer, she and her parents had painted it light blue while Lillian was away at camp.

"It's cold," Skyla said.

Marianne snuggled up next to her. "It'll be warmer in a couple weeks."

Skyla pulled some lip gloss out of her pocket and handed it to Marianne, who spread some on her lips, too.

"The thing is," Marianne said, reopening the conversation door she'd just shut, "Mr. Garcia is impossible! Even if I could do okay, I wouldn't get enough points to catch up, and he doesn't allow extra credit. I mean, have you ever heard of anything so ridiculous? What if something awful had happened to me, like my house burned down or I got some rare illness and I couldn't get the work done? I wouldn't get the chance to do anything extra to get points? It's un-American."

"Yeah, but . . ." Skyla said, "None of that happened."

"True," Marianne admitted.

"Besides, he *is* offering extra credit this year," she added casually.

"What?!"

"Yeah, nobody has taken Addison's spot yet on the trivia team. They're desperate. It's been weeks since she left, and no one has joined."

"No surprise there," Marianne grunted. "Have you seen their publicity? It's just Vi Cross shaming everyone about their grades in the hallways."

"Totally," Skyla concurred. "I mean, Nina Anderson asked me to join, but Vi is just too . . . *intense.*"

 25

Nina who? How did Skyla suddenly know so many people Marianne didn't?

Some girl had asked Skyla to join Quiz Quest? Weird. It wasn't like Skyla was some superstar student.

They must have just asked everybody.

"And it's not really an option for you, anyways," Skyla went on, picking up her phone to check it, giggling at something, and putting it back down. "I wish you were in Ms. Fitzgerald's math class with me instead. She's nice."

It surprised Marianne how good it felt to hear Skyla say that she wanted her around. That fact used to be a given. But these days, with all of Skyla's new friends . . . Marianne wasn't always sure.

Marianne's parents pulled up in their car. Lillian jumped out of the back seat, bounded up the steps, and scrunched herself in between them, her thick dark hair still damp.

"You swam good?" Marianne asked as Lillian rubbed the top of her head like she was two years old.

"Fastest yet!" their dad answered for her, lighting up.

Marianne ignored him. She knew a talk was coming about a homework plan, and she wanted to avoid meeting her mom's and dad's eyes for as long as possible to prevent it.

Marianne gave Lillian a thumbs-up, and Skyla clapped.

"They told me about the meeting," Lillian whispered into her ear. "You got this."

Her dad ambled his way up onto the porch, but her mom

went right inside. Marianne noted the light turning on in the kitchen.

"Can we have a chat?" her dad said.

He'd caught her.

Marianne groaned and heaved her body up from the swing, moving toward the kitchen as slowly as possible.

"Byyye!" Skyla sang.

At the kitchen table sat three cups of hot cider, one for each of them, and some molasses cookies Lillian had made for her book club, Literary Lionesses. Her parents were trying to be nice, which made everything so much worse.

Normally her dad said he felt disappointed, frustrated, confused. Her mom usually said something like "I just don't want you to start thinking of yourself as 'stupid' or 'bad at school,' because that will follow you all your life . . ."

This time, they spoke softly. Her mom held her hand.

They were worried.

This was real.

Marianne nibbled on her cookie as they discussed the "game plan" and she dove happily into the Drift. She tried to test how many lyrics she could remember to "Hotel California," a song her sister knew on the guitar. She remembered how hard she'd laughed when she and Lillian had looked up the lyrics and saw the first Google result was "Why is 'Hotel California' such a bad song?" They'd decided then and there that it was their favorite ever.

"Are you humming the Eagles?" her dad interrupted his lecture to ask.

"Huh?" she answered.

Her dad was a flautist and taught music theory at the Community College of Brookdale. You'd think he'd be more excited about music.

"These cookies are really yummy," she said.

"She's shutting me out, but what else is new?" her dad grumbled to her mom.

Wow. New Nice Dad had lasted for about three minutes. Stressed Annoyed Dad was back.

A fantasy took over her mind:

Her, Marianne Blume, at a Quiz Quest tournament. Multiple cameras and a spotlight pointed at two groups of kids. A big ticking clock counted down the seconds above their heads. A person wearing a Supreme Court–style robe asked questions. In her daydream, the teams were tied. One final question and the winner would be determined.

"And now, for the gold medal," the Supreme Court judge's voice boomed, "who was the second president of the United States?"

Marianne slammed her hand on the buzzer. "John Adams!" she hollered.

"Correct!"

Gold balloons fell from the ceiling with silver confetti, blanketing her hair. Her teammates lifted her up. Vi Cross mouthed to her, "I'm sorry about the gum!" And her dad sat out there in the audience, tears streaming down his face.

"Isn't she great?" he bragged to anyone who could hear him.

"I did it!" she yelled to the crowd, her hands pumping in the air. "I'm making it to high school!"

"Marianne, did you hear me?" her dad said in real life.

"Sorry," she muttered. "Hey, Dad, Mom, what do you know about trivia competitions?"

"Hmm? You mean like *Jeopardy!*?" her mom asked, dipping a cookie in the cider.

"I dunno," she answered. "*Is* it like *Jeopardy!*? Have I ever seen it, like when I was littler? I don't think I can even *spell* 'jeopardy' . . ." she mumbled to herself. "J-e-a-p . . . Why is English like that?"

"Oh, now *that* is a long conversation," her mom said.

"I don't see how that's at all relevant to this discussion," her dad said. Within a second or two, he might literally pull out some of his receding auburn hair, Marianne could tell. "Am I missing something?" He'd reached peak frustration-without-yelling, and her mom took his hand in hers.

"It's been a long day," her mom said. "Let's finish this tomorrow, okay? I'll have a schedule and plan written up by then. In the meantime, you think on the best time-management scenario going forward, 'kay? We're in this together," her mom said.

But, of course, they weren't.

As Marianne walked upstairs to her room, she could hear their hushed voices murmuring to each other.

"She's going to grow up and remember her dad as always

aggravated with her. Is that what you want?" she heard her mom scold her dad.

"But she's better than this! She's *so bright*!" he whisper-yelled.

Why did parents think that kids didn't know they were talking about them? They could've spoken at full volume. She knew everything they'd be saying.

Before Marianne got to her door, Lillian popped out of the bathroom, scrunching her hair dry with a towel.

"You were on my mind in the pool today," Lillian said.

"Weird," Marianne teased her.

"And I was thinking, Mar can do this. It's like in swimming when your time isn't good, and it's not going to get better for a while, and you just have to keep getting in the pool. You're not gonna get faster if you're dry." Lillian put a hand on Marianne's shoulder. "Right? You have to jump in that water."

"Uh-huh," Marianne said. "Sure." And she went into her bedroom.

Marianne plugged in the white Christmas lights that hung around her walls and took in their perfect glow.

She noted the unread copy of *A Tree Grows in Brooklyn* sitting on her unused desk.

She took a seat, picked it up, and chewed on a pencil.

"Alright, Tree Book," she said. "Whaddya got?"

Page one: *Serene was a word you could put to Brooklyn, New York.*

Marianne pulled out her phone, googled *Jeopardy!*, and clicked on a video of an old episode.

Around 1200 BC in the Middle East and 600 BC in China, the Bronze Age was replaced by this metallic age.

It's the geographic-sounding name for an almond in a hard candy shell.

Idiomatically, surgery might find you "under" this, though one isn't necessarily used.

Idiomatically? An almond with a hard candy shell? What even *was* all this?

The guy asking the questions reminded her of a less smiley version of her mother. He appeared polite and straightforward, and even though Marianne knew he had the answers written down in front of him, it seemed like he knew them on his own, anyway.

He was kind of like how she pictured God.

Fact after fact after fact and she didn't know a thing, and then:

Known as Orcinus orca, *it's the largest of the aquatic mammalian family* Delphinidae.

"Killer whales," she immediately said out loud to the serious man. To no one.

"What are killer whales?" a meek-looking woman replied.

"Correct," the host said, awarding the woman points.

Funny. She'd learned that from her animal calendar. Each month had a different creature with a little paragraph about it. She'd discovered that tortoises could live to be over one hundred and fifty years old and that ravens could talk, like parrots.

She couldn't remember a word Mr. Garcia said, but she could recall all of that in a second.

 31

Marianne pulled up her text messages. The host disappeared.

She wrote to Skyla.

Hey. What if I did join quiz quest

Within a split second a response appeared:

Lolololololololol
You said it's the only time Mr. Garcia has ever offered extra credit, right?
yeah but . . . wouldnt he be mad if u joined? wouldnt u hate it?
sorry for laughing. ur serious?
just seems like it might not work?
gtg studying with julie youll figure it out with garcia lu
xoxo

What would Julie and Skyla be studying together in high school while Marianne sat at home rereading *A Tree Grows in Brooklyn*, getting talking-tos, and disappointing everybody for the second year in a row?

Luckily, it didn't take a genius to see that she had only one way out.

Marianne knew what she had to do. She had to *force* Mr. Garcia to give her those points—to give her a chance.

Marianne Blume, the stupidest girl in the eighth grade, had to join Quiz Quest.

3

THE THREE KIDS IN the room grew silent as Marianne knocked on the doorframe.

Before her sat Vi, her posture perfect, chestnut ponytail tight, expression unreadable; a tiny, solemn girl who looked at Marianne as if a platypus had just walked through the door; and a redheaded boy she thought was named Dave or something. She didn't know him, but she'd seen him in the hallways minding his own business and walking with what looked like two canes attached to his hands. He eyed Marianne with curiosity.

"Hi! Is this Quiz Quest?" Marianne looked around for Mr. Garcia, but he must not have arrived yet.

Posters and projects plastered the walls of the room, which served as a seventh-grade social studies class during school hours.

"Very funny," Vi said to Marianne before returning to her conversation with the two others. "Look, Addison insisted our problem area was science, so I've made a list—"

"It doesn't matter!" the small girl spat out in a voice so high any dogs nearby would perk up. Emphasizing each word, she squeaked, "We. Do. Not. Have. Enough. People. On. The. Team! And there is *no time left*! Unless Isaac Newton wants to join us, cross off his name and throw away your list." She grumbled something inaudible and collapsed her head into her hands.

"Do they have a ghosts policy?" the boy asked. "Maybe apparitions can join."

"Hysterical," Vi deadpanned. "I'm glad you're so relaxed, Dan. Honestly? It's good to have evidence now that you never did care about Regionals as much as the rest of us. It explains a lot, actually."

Marianne almost laughed. Vi was such a tyrant.

Marianne's mom often told her about the Catholic schools she went to growing up. She said the nuns were pretty nice overall, but that when her mom—Granny—was a kid, the nuns used to hit the children's hands with long wooden rulers when they acted out. She could totally see Vi doing that to the other kids in Quiz Quest.

The tiny girl groaned through her fingers, "This is a disaster."

Marianne strolled into the room and sat down.

"You're taking volunteers, right?" Marianne tried again.

Vi froze.

Marianne thought she may have caught the corner of the boy's mouth rising slightly in a grin. The small girl looked toward Vi like she was awaiting instructions. Vi ignored Marianne and continued explaining a "science list."

But the boy spoke to Marianne. "Do you have a pulse? Yes? Good. Then please join us."

Vi didn't acknowledge Marianne's presence. She kept talking. "It's not that we don't know our basics, but we're lacking in the expansion rounds."

"I'm no doctor, but I'm pretty sure I'm alive," Marianne joked.

"Fantastic. I'm Dan. Dan Griffin." He spoke over Vi and held out a hand across their desks for a handshake. Nodding toward the petite girl, he said, "This is Nina Anderson. Geography extraordinaire. And that"—he motioned to Vi— "is Violet Cross. Our new team captain."

"Oh, we know each other." Vi kept her eyes on some papers in front of her.

"We have Mr. Garcia together," Marianne explained. "Plus, everyone knows Vi, right?"

Vi hissed, "What's that supposed to mean?"

Marianne hadn't meant to bring up the running-for-class-president debacle, but maybe Vi thought she had. That whole fiasco had made her somewhat famous.

"You're, like, the smartest kid in school!" Marianne said, covering for herself. "So do I just sit with you guys or . . . ? Do we wait for Mr. G? Do I need paper or anything?"

"*Addison* was the smartest kid in school," Vi corrected her.

Dan sighed as if this were a refrain he'd heard before.

"It's true," Nina nearly whispered.

Vi grunted, then tossed a pencil onto the desk. "I *knew* extra credit was a terrible idea."

Marianne leaned forward and whispered, "I can hear you."

Dan covered his mouth with his hand, but she could still hear the smothered laugh.

"I'm sorry." Vi finally acknowledged her directly. "It's not personal. Truly. It's just that . . . I mean, *you know*, you're not—"

But before she could finish, Mr. Garcia walked in.

Even though he acted like an old man, Mr. Garcia was pretty young for a teacher. He only had one or two white whiskers in his short beard and none in his dark hair. And even though he dressed in button-ups and black pants, once in a while, she noticed, he wore a bright fuchsia or lime green tie, so maybe he wasn't *entirely* boring. He also wasn't entirely math. He always had a big brick of a novel on his desk. Marianne noticed that because one time it was the same book her mom was reading, some lady named Tana French, who her mom claimed "elevates the mystery genre," whatever that meant.

She just couldn't figure him out.

"Ms. Blume?" Mr. Garcia addressed her as he stood behind a table pulling folders and papers out of his bag and placing them into various stacks. "Can I help you?"

She'd had his class that day, but they hadn't spoken. Not in person, anyway. His red pen spoke for him. It had written a large, circled F on the top of her math midterm. All of her tests that day held a similar mark. For the first time it had hit her that F stood for Fail. Or maybe FAILURE. Was that why there was no E and it just went from ABCD to F? E didn't stand for anything but F did? Couldn't they find a nicer way to show you failed? Or couldn't they just be more honest about it instead and put the word—FAILURE—instead of an angry-looking letter?

It was like all of middle school had been building up to those three Failures and one D plus.

The kids in the room right then probably had perfect scores on everything.

"I heard you guys were looking for volunteers," Marianne piped up. "And it's extra credit to join?" She had to make sure of that part.

"We are. It is," Mr. Garcia responded, expressionless.

Dan jumped in, looking at Vi even as he spoke to Marianne, to say, "Yes, we are! And tomorrow is the last day to submit our final roster, so sign on the bottom line—you're in."

Nina whispered something to Vi, and Vi shook her head. What was it?

"Great!" Marianne grinned at Dan.

This would be awful.

She had to do it.

Mr. Garcia tapped a stack of papers on the wood to straighten them and said, "But this is a serious commitment."

"Got it. I'm totally in." Marianne did her best to ignore Vi's mutterings and Nina's whispering and she tried to think of what a student who was passing Mr. Garcia's classes would say.

"I'm here to learn!" She smiled at Mr. Garcia—her broadest, brightest, toothiest grin.

And he looked at her like she looked at math—with absolutely zero understanding.

"She's here for the extra credit," Vi spat out. "And I get it!" she added, in what may have been an unsuccessful attempt to soften her edges. "But look, maybe someone else will join if we spread the word enough—"

"Okay, okay, that's enough, Ms. Cross . . ." Mr. Garcia tried to stop her.

"The deadline for the roster is *tomorrow*!" Dan said. "Obviously, everyone just wants to be on Junior Diplomats or Academic Games! Can you blame them? They constantly win everything," he lamented.

"We won our way to Regionals!" Vi argued. "That's a recruitment tool right there."

Dan groaned. "There's no time, and we'll be disqualified without enough teammates! Are you serious?" He looked to Mr. Garcia for backup.

"Ms. Cross." Mr. Garcia enunciated each word like a warning. "I hear your concerns. And I promise you, I will do what's best for the team." With that, he cleared his throat and said, "Welcome, Ms. Blume." He took a seat at the teacher's desk. "Let's dive right in. Scrimmage time. Ms. Blume, you'll be with Mr. Griffin."

The three other kids jumped up. Desk legs screeched across the floor as they set up. They sat in pairs across from one another.

In a rapid flurry, folders and notebooks and buzzers came out of everyone's bags.

"Wait, so we're practicing . . . now? Right away?" Marianne hadn't thought they'd jump right in like that. She didn't even know the rules yet.

Panic hit her. Dan, who'd been so welcoming, was about to see that she had nothing to offer. Vi was about to prove who Marianne really was.

Why had she gone through with such a terrible idea?

Mr. Garcia arranged his materials on the teacher's desk. He straightened his tie. A boring navy blue one that day. "Ms. Cross will explain as we go. Feel free to merely observe for now, but, of course, you may jump in at any time. If you are prepared to answer, simply hit the buzzer."

"But if you know, you *have* to buzz before anyone else does," Nina added, speaking so quickly it would have been easy to miss a word.

After all the paper shuffling and moving of chairs, there came a sudden quiet except for the tapping of Nina's foot.

"And . . . go," Mr. Garcia said. "Name the leg bone between the knee and the hip."

Buzz.

"Femur," Vi responded right away. Then she spoke to Marianne, her expression icy. "The first goal of the game is to be the first team to hit the buzzer and answer. There are no penalties for incorrect answers. But if you're correct, the answers range from five to ten points, depending on difficulty. That was a five-pointer. And it was . . ." She turned back to Mr. Garcia to check in.

"Correct," he said.

Vi smiled a smug smile. "It was correct. So then we go to . . ."

"Extension round," Mr. Garcia announced.

"If you get one correct, you go into an 'extension round,'" Vi explained. "It's more questions on the same topic as the question you just answered correctly. For extension rounds, you can confer with your teammates."

Three more questions about anatomy.

In all their hours spent together doing math, Marianne had never seen Mr. Garcia this energetic. He spoke as rapidly as an auctioneer. Amazing. Could he love this game more than math? Or was this just what grumpy math teachers looked like when they were having fun?

"This continent makes up twenty percent of Earth's land surface."

"Africa?" Nina answered.

"Correct. Extension round."

More geography.

 40

On the third question, regarding a river in Nepal, Nina answered incorrectly.

Vi's mouth and fists tightened. Then she reported to Marianne, "If you answer an extension round question *incorrectly*"—and maybe it was in Marianne's imagination, but she thought she saw Nina shudder—"the other team gets a shot at the question. So. Your turn."

Mr. Garcia gave Dan and Marianne a shot, but no dice. Marianne had never heard of the Karnali River.

Next up came literature. Math. Civics. A question about rocks. Nothing so far about *Orcinus orcas*.

"Out of flyweight, bantamweight, and featherweight, which is the heaviest weight class in boxing?"

Nina's foot tapping sped up.

A timer beeped. "The answer is featherweight," Mr. Garcia said.

"Oh, no fair, that's like a trick question!" Marianne hollered out, speaking for the first time since they started. "Because feathers are light!" she continued, looking to the other kids for backup.

Mr. Garcia moved on.

Only Dan acknowledged her. "We're not so hot on sports," he whispered.

"Oh, and, Mr. Garcia?" Vi asked, interrupting the questions. "I forgot. In the event of a tie," she continued to Marianne, "multiple extension rounds take place until a winner is determined. But ties are rare, so . . ." She eyed

41

Marianne for a moment and then said to Mr. Garcia, "Okay, let's continue?"

"Excellent explanation," he said, tapping his cards on the table again.

Wow, Mr. Garcia loved Vi. She was the exact opposite of Marianne in every way.

"Now," he went on. "What was the name of King Arthur's sword?"

Mr. Garcia pressed a button on a timer every time he asked a question.

Marianne could see the seconds tick, tick, tick . . .

King Arthur's sword . . . Like *The Sword in the Stone*. She'd seen that movie. The sword had a name?

Buzz.

"Excalibur?" Nina answered. Nina only answered with question marks.

She got it right. More literature.

One question was about Jane Austen, and Nina answered someone named something-Brontë, and Vi snapped, "Come *on*, Nina! You *know* this!"

After that, Nina hardly answered at all.

"What is the name of the world's largest island?"

It must have been Hawaii, Marianne decided. But should she say it?

Nina wasn't answering, and she was supposed to be the places expert.

She saw Vi glance at Nina and then hit the buzzer herself.

"Greenland," Vi said. "Because Australia is a continent, doesn't count," she explained to the rest of them.

"I know that, obviously," Dan mumbled almost inaudibly.

Greenland was an island? Good thing Marianne hadn't chimed in. Man, she was hopeless. Absolutely hopeless. At least she didn't have to answer. Only Vi was responding by then.

At one point Mr. Garcia asked for the name of "the Baroque composer of the Brandenburg Concertos," and Dan reached for the buzzer but paused before hitting it, missing his chance.

Vi answered, "Bach."

"Did you know it?" Marianne whispered to him afterward.

"Yeah. Oh well." He shrugged. His shrug kind of reminded Marianne of her own. Funny.

His left arm remained somewhat immobile on the table, his fingers curled into a light fist.

Dan noticed her staring. She quickly looked away.

"I have cerebral palsy," he told her. "This side"—he motioned toward his left with a nod—"can't do too much."

"Oh. Okay," Marianne said.

He leaned toward her and whispered, "Apologies in advance—sometimes it spasms a bit."

"No problem," Marianne whispered back.

"Ahem." Vi coughed from across the table to get them back into the game.

On and on the questions went, and Marianne found

herself watching instead of listening. She noted who answered and when, and if they didn't, she was curious why not.

And then:

"Who was the first woman on a United States presidential ticket?" Mr. Garcia asked.

Oh my gosh! Marianne knew this one! She had to buzz! She actually knew something!

"HILLARY CLINTON!" She stood up, forgetting to buzz. Her bubbe *loved* Hillary and her zayde *hated* her.

"Incorrect. The answer is Geraldine Ferraro," Mr. Garcia answered.

Vi glowered.

The answer was *who*?

Marianne felt her cheeks burn.

Shrugging, she twisted a strand of hair.

Mr. Garcia kept asking questions at a rapid pace, and Marianne slumped into her seat and shut off her ears.

"Hey, no big deal. That was a tough one," Dan whispered between buzzes.

"*You* knew who it was, though, didn't you?"

"Yeah," he admitted. "But that's just because my mom gives me lots of books on women's history."

"Your mom must be cool."

"She's pretty great. Unfortunately, she has to deal with my brother, and he's just such a rigid thinker, and he—"

"Excuse me?" Nina squeaked to Mr. Garcia. "Um, I can't

really concentrate when they're having a conversation over there?"

"Sorry!" Marianne cried.

"Let's just finish this round," Mr. Garcia said.

"*You're* interrupting by pointing out *we're* interrupting," Dan muttered.

"And now *you're* interrupting!" Vi squabbled back.

Marianne saw that she was the problem kid.

But also, this was a problem *team*.

"Let's take ten, all," Mr. Garcia announced, clearing his throat and adjusting his tie.

"Great," Nina grumbled.

"And hey," Mr. Garcia added on his way out the door, coffee mug in hand, doorknob in the other, "I know it's different without Ms. Schuler here."

He meant Addison.

"But we will find our way, hmm?"

From the lowered heads of the other kids, Marianne could tell his little pep talk did not have the desired effect.

Mr. Garcia left.

No one said anything, and Marianne didn't dare glance up to see the looks they must've been sharing with one another.

Her lowered gaze fell on Nina's folder. On its cover, a beautiful woman struck a dance pose in a lavender leotard.

Allowing herself to lift her eyes, Marianne asked Nina softly, "Who's that on your folder?"

Nina pointed to herself to ensure Marianne was speaking to her.

Marianne nodded.

"Oh, her? That's Misty Copeland?" In response to Marianne's blank look, Nina explained, "The first Black principal dancer at the American Ballet Theatre? In New York?"

"Cool!" Marianne smiled at her.

They all fell silent again.

Nina raised a hand even though no teacher was present.

"What is it, Nina?" Vi asked.

"So, like . . . Could I make a motion for us to emphasize flash-card sessions the next few days? Marianne, maybe you could pick a subject you need some review in and we could all review with you? We have things to review, too," she said in Dan's direction.

"Who, me?" he asked, putting a hand to his heart.

"Addison was big on flash cards, and I think that's what pushed us over the edge at Regionals, honestly?" said Nina.

"It's pointless," Vi said, springing up from her chair. "I don't mean to sound tough, but I'm the team captain and it's my job." She turned to Marianne. "And—I'm sorry, Marianne, but you know it's true—you *do not care* about school at *all*. And if you're bringing that attitude to Quiz Quest? You'll be . . . ." She searched for a word with her hands and let them fall to her sides as she pronounced, "Deadweight."

"Whoa!" Dan jumped in. "Not nice!"

"Yeah, that's not necessary," Nina agreed.

"Who is the captain? You or me?" Vi said to Dan.

"It's Addison, actually," he answered.

"We need to hand out more fliers," Vi grumbled.

Marianne pictured the kids mocking Vi the day before. Did Vi recall it, too?

"There has to be someone else who wants to join before the registration deadline. Has to," Vi repeated, as if to convince herself. "And Marianne can totally be a swing, of course! She can be an alternate!"

"We have *one day!*" Dan grew openly exasperated. "Marianne is our fourth. Deal with it!"

"This is *Regionals*, Dan," Vi pled with him.

Marianne wondered if any of them had been friends before they joined Quiz Quest. It didn't seem like it.

Nina put her forehead down on her desk and started muttering, "Ohmygodohmygod."

"Vi, wake up," Dan said. "This school never did well in this game until Addison was here. Because she's *better* than we are. So, a big congrats to San Diego's trivia team, I guess, they'll do great now. But we wouldn't have *gotten* to Regionals without Addison, and we won't get *past* it without her, so *give up.*" He leaned back in his chair, his crutches splayed out on either side of the desk.

Ah, so that was why he didn't care that Marianne was joining the team. He could see when he had no chance at something, just like Marianne did. She could respect that.

"We are *never* giving up!" Vi spoke so intensely that Marianne spotted a little spit flying out of her mouth.

An overhead light panel flickered a bit. One of many undependable bulbs in the ceilings at school.

"Wait, I know." Nina popped her head up. "She doesn't have to answer!" In her excitement, her tone reached another level of soprano.

"Huh?" Vi said.

"Wha'?" Dan said.

"She can just sit there, kind of like she did today. Right, Marianne? Since you're new and everything and you probably won't have time to catch up. We don't want to overwhelm you, and that way we can zoom in on our stuff we have to focus on? You're our fourth, but you just . . . sit there? Right?" Nina's face brightened, pleased with herself.

"Yeah, that sounds great!" Marianne nearly cheered.

"Like an Addison placeholder?" Vi began to pace in front of the class project posters. "No, no, Nina, we need someone who will jump in there and go for it. Points-wise, I don't know if we can rack up enough wins with only three people answering. But maybe it helps more than it hurts if she's just quiet the whole time . . ." She seemed to consider it.

"Nope," Dan said. "That's not how a team works, folks." He plopped a foot on his desk. The other stayed on the floor.

"I know, I know. Everyone has something of value to add," Nina said, as if repeating someone else's words, probably Mr. Garcia's.

Vi continued to pace back and forth in the four feet between the tables.

"No, that's *literally* not how the team works," Dan said matter-of-factly. "A team will be disqualified if each member doesn't answer at least ten percent of all reported answers. And extension rounds don't count since they're collaborative."

All three girls stared at him.

"Usually it's not an issue, of course, because most teammates answer often, but . . ." Dan looked to Marianne. He didn't want to say what they were all thinking. "It's okay, it was your first scrimmage," he said instead.

Nina nibbled on a middle fingernail. The action reminded Marianne of a very smart and cute gerbil.

Vi scurried over to where Mr. Garcia had been sitting and picked up a book.

As she hurriedly flipped through it, Dan reported, "Rules are in the beginning. It's right there."

Scanning the front section of the book with a finger, Vi stopped in the middle of a page. And she swore.

So Dan was right. Marianne would have to participate. She'd need to know Geraldine Ferraro and Greenland and whatever else made up 10 percent.

"What do we do?" Vi asked the ceiling.

"We help her," Nina answered. "Simple as that. We study, study, study. No breaks. Nothing."

"Is that all necessary?" Marianne tried to ask in a casual,

relaxed way, as if the idea didn't horrify her. "What are we talking here, like drills at lunchtime, or . . . ?"

"She's here for the credit," Vi cut in, her gaze set on Dan and Nina, seemingly unable to even look at Marianne. "That means she's behind in her classes, she's probably *failing*—"

"God, can you have a little bit of positivity?" Dan asked.

"And can you not talk about me like I'm not here . . ." Marianne added faintly.

"Oh, positive like *you*?" Vi stalked toward him. "Who thinks we're going to *lose* no matter *what*?" A vein or two popped out the side of Vi's neck, Marianne saw.

"Um, Addison listened to everyone?" Nina squeaked. "That's why she was such a great captain?"

"*Well, Addison isn't here!*" Vi spat. "And trust me. Marianne Blume—and she knows this as well as I do—is the epitome of a dumb blonde, and from the sound of things, she doesn't want to put in the work to be anything *but* that!"

It was one thing to be honest, but she didn't have to be so mean.

And yet, Vi was right. Marianne could not answer 10 percent of the questions, no matter what they did.

"Can we please not use ableist language like 'dumb'?" Nina spoke up with a touch of real anger. "It means 'doesn't speak,' and it's not an insult. Please and thank you."

"Also, 'dumb blonde' is *very* sexist," Dan added, waving his pointer finger in a "tsk-tsk-tsk."

"Sorry," Vi said, her pacing finally coming to a halt. "I'm really sorry."

"They're right," Marianne said, even though to be honest she had never heard any of that before. But they definitely sounded right. "And I don't know what 'epitome' means, but I know you guys are having some issues, and I'm making it worse. I should go."

No way could she handle answering 10 percent of the questions. No way. Plus, these kids were a mess.

She picked up her backpack and headed for the door.

"Bye, Dan. Bye, Nina," she added as she walked out, her ponytail bobbing behind her, which somehow made her feel even stupider, like the stupider a girl was, the more her pony-tail bobbed. That didn't make sense, but it was how she felt. Like it made her girlier, and the girlier she was, the stupider she was.

Maybe she was sexist toward herself. Was that possible?

And was she even really blond? Compared to Vi's warm brown, Nina's black, and Dan's bright orange hair, she might have been. But she always thought her mane was more of a golden brown. One time a cousin of hers who lived in Israel had come to visit and said to her, "You have honey hair, like me," and Marianne thought about that whenever she thought of her hair.

And there she was, thinking about hair and not Bach, exactly as Vi would expect.

Whatever. She'd rather be stupid than angry all the time, like Vi.

She pulled a stick of Juicy Fruit out of her coat pocket and popped it into her mouth.

As she headed down the hallway to the school's exit, Mr. Garcia strolled out of the staff lounge.

Should she run?

"Ms. Blume."

She stopped and stood in place. She'd explain she was done ruining his team, that she'd seen what a bad idea the whole thing had been. He didn't have to worry anymore.

Marianne could picture the future. She'd do more of her homework this year, under the watchful and teary eyes of her parents, but she'd get a D, *maybe* a C minus, on the math final. It wouldn't fix her overall grade much, and it certainly wouldn't make up the points she needed to pass. Ms. Clarke would call her in again. The seventh graders she saw in the hallways every day would become her classmates.

And even as she repeated the year, she'd still have the same problem: She was a stupid partial-blonde.

"I was, um, surprised by your presence in Quiz Quest today," Mr. Garcia said.

"Yeah." Marianne twisted the hanging straps on her backpack into tight spirals. "I didn't know what it would be like . . ."

He glanced at his watch and seemed to decide he had a moment to say something further. She waited for a polite, formal version of "Don't come back."

"It's—what was it again?—*torture*, yes?" he asked.

"Huh?" She dropped the straps.

Then she remembered when she'd spoken to Jalilah—how

they'd insulted Quiz Quest together, and how Mr. Garcia had walked around the corner right after. *Had he heard them?*

"And it's, um . . . for kids with no friends? Was that it?" he added, not appearing angry, exactly, but blank-faced. She simply could not figure him out.

Okay, he'd obviously heard them.

"Jalilah said the no-friends thing, not me!" was all Marianne could think to say.

"Now, I actually think this could be good for you," Mr. Garcia said, moving right along. "Quiz Quest certainly solves some of your problems . . ."

He must have been referring to the extra credit.

"And it's true we're having a bit of a recruitment issue." She thought she caught a slight grimace flash across his face. "But also," he went on, "Quiz Quest is its own form of study. Many questions require a review of basics, and . . ." He paused. "I actually think that's *exactly* what you need."

"You do?" she asked.

Out of the corner of her eye, Marianne saw Vi stand by the door. Had she been chasing after Marianne, or was she just popping out to go to the water fountain?

Mr. Garcia half turned and motioned to Vi that he'd be with her shortly. But Vi stayed put, watching.

"And I'm happy to explain to Ms. Clarke—and your parents—the benefits of peer mentorship involved here and the discipline required by this commitment, both of which will be very beneficial to your situation, I believe." He crossed his arms and nodded his head. Was he trying to convince himself?

And what did he mean? Why did he talk like a robot reading an instruction manual?

"Obviously, you, Ms. Clarke, and I will have to come up with some form of agreement regarding what's required of you in order to stay on the team—no absences, no detentions, etc. . . ."

"Oh, don't worry," Marianne jumped in. "Ms. Clarke already told my parents if I get a detention or something, I'm toast. Ha." She tried to be funny, but Mr. Garcia rolled right along without taking note.

"But!" he said, more serious than she'd ever seen the always-serious Mr. Garcia. "You made it quite clear to Ms. Jacobs that Quiz Quest is a . . . a dungeon of torture and a friendless abyss . . ."

"I—" she protested, but he spoke over her.

"And therefore, I will need *evidence. Proof!* That you've earned the extra credit, that you are really and truly *trying.*" He took out a pencil from behind his ear and tapped it on his palm like a metronome. "Without proof of effort, I reserve the right to deny credit. This is not a participation trophy; do you understand my meaning?" Although he wasn't that much taller than her, he seemed to loom over her somehow.

"Got it, Mr. G," she said. "Garcia. Got it, Mr. Garcia," she corrected herself.

He raised his coffee mug in a "cheers" gesture and then continued toward the classroom to talk to Vi.

Marianne swore she caught Vi smirking, but before Marianne could blink, the scowl returned.

"One more minute until we start again, so don't take too long," he called back to Marianne, as if she were merely going to the bathroom.

He must have seen her backpack on. He must have known she had been leaving.

But he had confirmed that this could help her. Maybe. With *proof of effort*.

Simply joining the prodigy club at all would take a *lot* of effort, especially considering how the group got along like bees and hornets. Trying to get Vi Cross to accept her would be *brutal*. And learning even 10 percent of the answers would take a climbing-Mount-Everest level of effort. And from what her sister had told her, more and more people were dying on Mount Everest every day.

Marianne peered toward the school exit and back toward Vi and Mr. Garcia, engaged in a quiet conversation in front of the Quiz Quest door.

But wait.

Dan had said she'd need to answer 10 percent of the questions.

He didn't say she had to answer them *correctly*, did he?

In class, if you tried and tried but never got it, you were a time suck. But on Quiz Quest, you could call out answer after answer with no *follow-up*, no breaking down of what you didn't understand and why. You could call out "Teddy Roosevelt" to almost any question. As long as you did it *enough*—and carried around a stack of flash cards to show how hard you were studying—you could be seen as putting in the *effort*.

If she could show up, answer enough questions, and perform the role of Quiz Quest teammate with loads of gusto, she could prove to Mr. Garcia she deserved the credit. She could escape the confines of Anna Etheridge Middle School forever. And she could sail off into the great adventure that was high school.

She could do this.

Marianne turned on her heels, tossed her gum in the trash, and followed her teacher and Vi back into the room of a million questions.

"I'm back!" she trilled to Nina's frown, Vi's fury, and Dan's grin. "So. What's the next thing I need to learn?"

4

MARIANNE CAME HOME TO the smell of her dad's cooking and the sound of Lillian plucking a bluegrass-like song on her guitar.

Her parents had decorated their home with art and trinkets from all the traveling they had done before Lillian was born. A throw blanket from Morocco covered the couch and behind Lillian's shoulder some wooden Japanese dolls decorated a shelf.

"You're getting good," Marianne told her, plopping down next to her on the living room couch. "Not like that's a surprise," Marianne added.

Without stopping her playing, Lillian laughed her off. "I'm an amateur."

"I mean . . . obviously?" Marianne pushed Lillian's shoulder. "But so what? We should start a band," she declared. "Sister bands are the best."

"Yeah, we could be like HAIM," Lillian said, tearing

her dark blue eyes away from the notes for a moment to smile right at Marianne. Lillian had a tiny gap between her two front teeth and an uneven curve to one side of her lips. When Lillian grinned, she stood out. While Marianne had inherited a light, even spray of freckles from her mom, Lillian got their dad's smattering of random dark moles. Marianne told Lillian they looked like Marilyn Monroe beauty marks, but Lillian jokingly called them "goblin dots." Lillian never seemed to worry about being a certain kind of pretty.

"Except HAIM is a trio," Lillian added, fiddling with the strings again. "Maybe Mom and Dad need to have another baby."

"Or we could call our band Two-Thirds HAIM," Marianne said.

"And you say you're not good at math!" Lillian joked. She put the guitar down on her lap and spoke as if she'd been dying to share something. "You should see this girl at school—Harper—she's like . . . one of these people you know will be famous one day? She even performed at some venue in Detroit once. Like an actual professional musician. Her band is called Unreliable Narrator and she writes these songs from, like, the perspective of all these different characters from books."

Marianne snorted and then covered her mouth. "Sorry," she said.

"Yeah, I guess it's a little pretentious," Lillian admitted.

"She's good, though! Well, she's got that kind of . . . star charisma, you know? Anyway, I wanted to ask her to join Literary Lionesses, but I don't think she'd be into it." Lillian paused and, unable to help herself from getting back to some kind of work, picked up the guitar again and fiddled around with the tuning. As she did so, she asked Marianne, "Do you think I should? Should I just ask her anyway?"

"Doesn't hurt to ask, right?" Marianne offered. "Sounds like she likes book stuff, so why not?"

"Yeah, yeah." Lillian started to strum a country tune. "Maybe."

"Um, why not? Since when are you a wuss? Just ask her," Marianne commanded.

"Ha. I feel like a wuss a *lot* of the time, actually," Lillian mumbled, and her playing grew louder.

"Oh sure." Marianne rolled her eyes.

"She's friends with Samia, which is how I met her," Lillian said loudly over her strumming.

"Oh, how's Samia and her whole thing with Jack?"

Lillian stopped playing, and Marianne settled in for a gossip session about the many complicated social dynamics of high school. It was Marianne's weekly entertainment, a reality show just for her. Sometimes she couldn't even quite believe these people were real.

"Can I get some help in here, girls?" their dad hollered from the kitchen.

Lillian put away the guitar and they moseyed over to their

dad's side, where Lillian grabbed some measuring spoons and Marianne took over the onion chopping.

"How was your day?" Marianne asked her dad.

He came over to kiss her head as he answered, "Fine, but long."

"Same," said Lillian. "One of those days when every teacher decides to have a quiz at the same time. Don't they ever talk to one another?" Lillian poured some spices into a bowl.

"How about you, Mar?" her dad asked from inside the pantry.

"I joined Quiz Quest," Marianne reported as she chopped. She took deep breaths from her mouth because her dad had told her that you actually get the teary eyes from inhaling through the nose. Would that fact be on Quiz Quest?

"Oh . . ." her dad said. She could just imagine the faces he and Lillian were making behind her back, enjoying all the "What's going on with Marianne?" drama they liked to share in together. "Whose quest? What kind of quest are you going on?"

"It's a quest for knowledge, Dad." She couldn't chop the onion into neat lines. Halfway through, the knife got stuck and the onions slipped out of her hands. "Extra credit with Mr. Garcia. It's basically a bid to save my life."

"Not dramatic at all!" her dad teased.

"It's a shame you have him," Lillian said. "I had Ms. Fitzpatrick and she was the greatest. Everyone dreaded

Garcia's tests. What does Bubbe always say about people? He's 'a cold fish.'"

"My mother thinks everyone is a cold fish, and if they're not, then they're 'a little too much,'" her dad joked. He was always making fun of Bubbe.

"He thinks it'll be the perfect thing for me." Marianne tried to sound as bubbly as possible.

Lillian came up behind Marianne and took the knife out of her hand. "Like this." She began a rapid chop-chop-chop and in less than a minute the onion sat before them in perfect little squares.

"I was doing it fine," Marianne groaned.

"Mm-hmm," Lillian humored her. "Sure, Mar."

Their mom bounded into the kitchen with a notebook in one hand and a strap of Marianne's backpack in the other. "Ready?"

Her mom's bun held only a slim fraction of her graying brown hair. The rest of it stuck out around her temples and fell in strands onto her neck. Her glasses overtook her face.

A rush of sympathy for her mom overwhelmed Marianne. Her mom didn't want this either—homework, a failing daughter, the fights that always happened . . .

She wanted to work on her translations all day, enjoy dinner with the family, and then learn a dead language or something. But instead, she was stuck with Marianne.

"Why can't I keep helping with cooking?" Marianne heard herself saying in a harsher tone than she meant to use. "Isn't cooking actually more of a skill than whatever we're learning about the genes system?"

"Ah, the age-old street smarts versus school smarts debate . . ." her dad said as he crushed the garlic.

"The *genome*," Lillian corrected her.

"If society falls apart and *Hunger Games* happens or hurricanes take over or whatever people are always freaking out about, then I'll need to know how to cook, not find out which grandpa Lillian got her blue eyes from." Marianne wiped her hands on a kitchen towel.

"You're right! It was from Grandpa!" Lillian cheered. "See? You know a lot more than you think you do. You're so ready to quest."

"Quest?" her mom asked, walking further into the kitchen.

"Wait, right, so what is this about Quest?" her dad asked, strolling over to the scene of the onion crime. "Mr. Garcia is okay with this? I don't know if—"

Marianne tried to break it down. She told them the good parts, not the part where Mr. Garcia saw right through her. She reported that they needed another team member for Regionals and no one else was joining and how Mr. Garcia thought a review of materials was exactly what she needed. And then she went too far. "So I think probably tonight isn't a great time for us to start our study sessions," she said to her mom. "I really need to get to know the new flash cards they gave me and stuff."

"If it interrupts this study time, you're not doing it," her dad snapped. Why did he have to immediately get stern with her? Couldn't he just have a calm conversation?

"Dad, you don't get it," Marianne groaned.

"You're right, I don't." He locked eyes with her mom for a moment and then went back to cooking.

"Dad, Mr. Garcia and Ms. Clarke are going to come up with some kind of deal about attendance or something and grades and if I mess up even once I'm off the team. Okay?"

He nodded as he grabbed the can opener for the coconut milk. "Okay."

Marianne had to get better grades. The way to do that was to do her homework. The best way to do her homework was to get help. Her mom wanted to help. Yet the thought of her mom seeing how far behind she'd gotten made her feel sick. Marianne wanted to escape from her skin, turn into a wisp of the steam coming out of the rice cooker, and slip out of the window her dad had cracked open to bring in the cool air.

"Those look great, Mar," he said, pointing his head toward the onions as he prepared the chicken pan. "Thanks."

Typical Dad move, trying to soften his annoyance by giving a compliment.

"Lillian did it," Marianne felt forced to admit.

"Thanks," he said to her big sister.

And that was when Marianne lost it.

"Yeah, Lillian!" she said in her fakest voice. "Nice job! Great work! You're the best! You're the daughter I always dreamt of! We're the luckiest!"

Her dad stopped whisking.

Marianne heard her mom sigh, but she couldn't face her. She knew the expression she'd be making: disappointed, worried, rubbing the creases on her forehead like if she rubbed them hard enough she could make the Marianne problem go away.

"Nice," Lillian said. "I'm going upstairs."

Marianne immediately felt horrible. "No, wait, I'm sorry!" She grabbed her sister by her sweater sleeve and pulled her in for a hug. "That was annoying. I take it back."

Lillian's typically open and warm arms remained at her sides.

"*Really* sorry," Marianne said into Lillian's ear.

And Lillian softened, her arms embracing Marianne in return.

"You're always annoying, so it's no big deal," Lillian said.

Marianne could hear her dad's whisking slowly and steadily start up again, and her mom zipped open the backpack to investigate the homework situation.

"Annoying is a key part of the little-sister contract, if memory serves me correctly," their dad said as he smelled the sauce. He had four younger siblings, three of them girls.

Her mom threw Marianne's half-open backpack over one of her tiny shoulders and reset her mode from concerned to raring-to-go. "Come on. Let's get to work."

Marianne followed her in surrender.

Progress charts, spreadsheets, and a big whiteboard filled

her mom's study. Her mom took everything out from the backpack and piled it on her work desk.

"Ooh, *A Tree Grows in Brooklyn*! I *loved* this book!" her mom said, as if announcing to Marianne that they would never have anything in common. "How far along are you?" She lovingly flipped through the pages.

"Sentence two!"

When it was math time, Marianne felt like the oxygen had been sucked out of the room. Her mom talked her through each problem, often remarking, "Wow, I honestly hardly even remember this stuff," and then somehow finding the answer time after time. Marianne bit the insides of her mouth and squeezed her hands into fists, released them, and squeezed again.

Halfway to finding the fourth X, her mom lightly touched her knuckles. "Honey, honey, whoa," she said. "Relax."

"I can't," Marianne said. "It's *math*."

"What's so unnerving about it? Can you explain it, or—" Marianne's mom searched Marianne's face like perhaps if she looked hard enough she could uncover the problem.

Would her mom understand if she brought up the time toward the end of fifth grade when Mr. Thorne asked her for the answer to a math problem and Elliott Roth burst out, "Come on, this is a waste of time!"?

How did you explain that to someone who had always found it all so easy?

"Whatever you're thinking," her mom said, her palms still

on the tops of Marianne's fists, "I want you to try a technique with me. Don't fight away all those thoughts, okay? Just say hello to them, and then goodbye. Watch them float away. You could picture them attached to kites or balloons or—"

"How about hot-air balloons?" Marianne liked this. This was *way* more interesting than math.

"Breathe with me first . . ." her mom said, and she talked her through it again.

Elliott Roth came into Marianne's head. She said hello, then she said goodbye to him as he floated off in a hot-air balloon. He came back again, but she waved him off every time. *Goodbye, Elliott.*

"Now." Her mom picked up a pencil. "Let's try it again, shall we?"

"Okay," Marianne said.

And though her heart beat slower and her hands relaxed, Marianne knew that they could sit there and breathe and then go over worksheet after worksheet, fact after fact, chapter after chapter . . . But it was just a matter of time until her mom truly understood what Marianne was: deadweight.

***

Marianne and Skyla even had different lunch hours. At 10:30 A.M. Marianne headed to the cafeteria for the earliest lunch in the world.

"It's obviously brunch," Kylie Chen always said. "They should just call it brunch."

Sometimes, if Marianne was lucky, she would catch Skyla as her group left and Skyla's came in.

That day was a lucky one.

"Hey!"

"Hey!"

They kissed cheeks.

Marianne wanted to tell her about Quiz Quest, but she didn't just want to be talking about herself all the time, so she tried to think of something to ask Skyla about *her*. "I didn't ask—how did midterms go for *you*?"

Skyla hesitated and glanced at her friends, who continued on in without her. "I did okay. Pretty good."

"Nice!" Marianne slapped her hand. "Mazel tov! So." She leaned in toward Skyla for the big reveal. "I did it." She blew a big bubble with her gum, and it popped against her lips.

Skyla clearly didn't know what she meant.

"We're going to the salad first!" Julie shouted to Skyla as their gang of friends disappeared into the cafeteria. "Hi, Marianne!"

Marianne waved. "I joined Quiz Quest," she reminded her.

"Oh!" Skyla did a double take from her friends inside back to Marianne. "Wait, seriously?"

"Why is she getting the salad? Yeah, I'm serious. I've worked the whole thing out perfectly . . ." Marianne began.

"What do you mean?"

"It's iceberg lettuce and some old shredded carrot."

"I mean about working it out. You think it's a good thing for you? Maybe it'll teach you how to study!" Skyla's hopeful tone frustrated Marianne a little.

"No, no, no, you're way off base. Listen . . ." She liked having Skyla's attention. Skyla wasn't looking back at Julie to see if she'd left the salad bar and moved on to the warm stuff. She was finally really listening to Marianne. "I don't have to answer correctly! It's incredible! Mr. Garcia thinks a 'review of basics' is 'exactly what I need,'" she said in her best Mr. Garcia impression, "and even if I get only a little bit better than normal-me grades, I can at least pass if I get the extra credit. He says I need to give him 'proof of effort,' whatever that means, but guess what? Even though you do need to answer a certain amount of the questions in a competition, you don't have to answer *correctly*! Amazing, right? *I can be wrong!* It doesn't matter! And if I look like I'm studying, and I answer enough questions, I'll get the points I need to pass his class! I don't know why I didn't think of this before!" For a moment, Marianne felt like her bubbly self again. That person had been missing the past couple of days.

Skyla had gone icy. "You probably didn't think of it before because Addison Schuler was on their team and she's, like, amazing, and they were doing really well. And you didn't know there'd be extra credit until I told you."

"That's a weird thing to say. But . . . okay?"

Skyla turned her head slightly and scanned the cafeteria

for her friends once again. There it was. Marianne had lost her already. "I'm really hungry. I got to go."

"Whoa, what's wrong?"

"Nothing! I'm starved."

"Your face is like a mood ring and it's on maroon. I *know* you. What did I say wrong?"

"Well, Mar, you just . . ."

Marianne saw Skyla gauging whether she should say it.

Then she said, "That's a really awful thing to do."

Marianne knew what Skyla meant. And heat rushed through her from head to toe, almost like the sensation she felt when she didn't know an answer. The old, reliable voice that said "bad."

"Huh?" Marianne said. "I don't know what you mean."

Dishonesty. That was bad, too.

"Vi Cross may be a little extreme, but this *matters* to her. And I don't know the other kids on the team very well, but I'm sure this matters a lot to them, too. They've worked hard. And you're going to waltz in there—for your own benefit— and *not* try to really help them win? Probably make them *lose*? I just . . . It's . . ."

What word was Skyla not saying?

"Would it *kill* you to *try*?" Skyla admonished her.

Marianne had no response.

"I love you, but I gotta go." And Skyla walked away.

Marianne watched Skyla meet up with her friends and smile like nothing had happened.

On the way to math, she saw old Mr. Hedley.

"How's Jaylen?" she asked, trying to look more chipper than she felt. "Is his knee all healed up?"

"He's back!" Mr. Hedley lit up and leaned against his classroom's doorframe. "Can't keep that kid down for long. You hanging in there?"

"Good for Jaylen! Oh, I'm great. See ya, Mr. Hedley!"

When Marianne sat down in math with Mr. Garcia, Vi passed her a piece of paper torn out of a notebook. On it she'd written:

I heard what Mr. Garcia said. Maybe now we're on the same page. Check your email tonight for materials.

Marianne's perfect plan didn't feel so perfect anymore.

Marianne knew the word Skyla had been holding inside: *selfish.* Or something like it. Maybe something even worse.

So was she supposed to quit? But after joining, wouldn't it be selfish to quit, too? They didn't have anyone else on the team!

Skyla wanted her to "try."

What made Marianne and Skyla so different was that Skyla couldn't see that Marianne wasn't going to *try* to be *bad*—she just *knew* she couldn't do it!

Marianne pulled out her notebook as Mr. Garcia began class.

They were back to X, that unknown and impossible part of an equation that took so much work to get to. So many steps and strategies. So much computing. Just the thought of it all made her want to go to sleep.

She found herself reverting to her usual beginning-of-class thought: How could she pass the time until the bell?

No, she had to listen. She had to improve her grades. No drifting.

Mr. Garcia announced they were moving on to "using the X and Y intercepts to graph linear equations."

This was the stuff of nightmares.

She prayed he would take it easy on her now that she had joined Quiz Quest and wouldn't call on her that day. Why couldn't he be more like Mr. Hedley?

"Just try," everybody said.

But Marianne knew what happened when you tried. You failed. Usually you failed again and again, in front of everyone.

Fifth grade. Negative integers. Marianne went through the problem five times with Mr. Thorne. First, she gave a positive number. Wrong. Then she answered zero. Wrong. Then she started asking how there could be negative numbers when there weren't negative *things*, and however Mr. Thorne tried to explain the concept, it all just sounded imaginary to her. And by the fifth wrong answer, she saw how bored the rest of the class looked and how frustrated Mr. Thorne was. He even sighed. A long, tired exhale, in front of everyone. He probably felt like a bad teacher, and he wasn't, not at all. Marianne just had a bad brain. And that was one of the millions of times Marianne saw what trying did. It humiliated you.

So would it *kill* her to try, like Skyla said?

Yeah. Maybe.

And negative numbers *still* made no sense.

"I think you'll find this can actually be—dare I say it?—*fun* when applied to some real-life scenarios," Mr. Garcia went on.

Marianne twisted around to look toward Vi's seat in the middle of the room. Had that note been her version of some sort of encouragement, or a threat?

"Okay, before we dive in too much further, let's start with what's usually the most difficult: connecting the equation with the line you see on the graph. Don't worry," he responded calmly to a few complaints. "We're going to go over this again and again. If you're confused at first—you'll get there."

Marianne returned to her fantasy of herself at Quiz Quest Regionals: the spotlight on her team, the judge wearing a long black robe asking questions over a loudspeaker . . . She tried to imagine what would happen if she answered every question incorrectly, buzzing and randomly shouting out names and places she'd heard of before: "Christopher Columbus!" "The Galápagos Islands!" "Harriet Tubman!"

What would Vi do? Push her off the stage? Pull her hair? Forfeit the game to escape a loss? Would Dan still like her? Would Nina literally explode from panic? Would there be "proof of effort"?

Kylie Chen raised her hand and asked several questions at once. Mr. Garcia took the time to break them all down. Marianne saw Kylie taking notes, and she tried to do the same.

But wait, why couldn't the team win, *anyway*? In *spite* of her? Skyla hadn't thought of that.

They could. She'd seen how smart they all were. If only they could get all their problems with *one another* worked out, their brain squad could probably handle 10 percent stupidity.

No Quiz Quest that day, thank the glorious heavens. The day was almost over.

Lit class next, then she'd be free.

She'd promised her mom at the end of their homework session the night before that she'd read a chapter of *A Tree Grows in Brooklyn* before she turned the lights off.

But she hadn't. Why hadn't she? What was *wrong* with her?

And she still wasn't listening to Mr. Garcia, and she saw him notice that, and she forced herself to stare at the graph and the X and the Y and some little paragraph about correctly filling a fish tank, and then she couldn't breathe. The air she took in wouldn't reach the bottom of her lungs. It stayed in the very top of her chest right under her collarbone.

Mr. Garcia's voice morphed into a low drone like he was speaking in slow motion. The tapping of Kylie's pencil next to her amplified a thousand decibels and seemed to bang right on Marianne's eardrum.

"Bathroom!" Marianne stood up, grabbed the pass, and hurried out the door.

"Hi, Ms. Kelley!" She managed to greet the hall monitor

as she ran into a bathroom stall and rested her forehead against the graffitied door.

juan likes astrid

gemma sux

have a beautiful day beauties ☺

"That's a really awful thing to do," Skyla had said.

And maybe it was.

"I love you, but I gotta go," she had said.

And what could be truer in life than that? Skyla was going somewhere, and Marianne wasn't.

5

AFTER SCHOOL MARIANNE SAW that Lillian had sent her a video. It was of a girl with the bottom of her head shaved. She was playing guitar on the bleachers, surrounded by a small crowd. Underneath it Lillian wrote, see? harper.

Did high schoolers really sit around jamming together? Awesome.

did you request hotel california yet, Marianne wrote back.

hahaha not yet. school go ok?

Marianne wished Lillian meant how were things with her friends, like she always meant when *she* asked *Lillian* about school. But she knew that Lillian meant "How are your classes? Will you pass? Did you turn in homework? Did you even do your homework? Will you be alright, or do I have to deal with a problem sister forever?"

it was great, Marianne texted. **i actually improved so**

much they said they think i can skip right to college. I was thinking id go to brown. thats a school right?

Marianne knew Lillian wanted to go to Brown one day.

but i told them i wanted to go to periwinkle instead, Marianne kept on writing. **get it? its a color joke.**

When Lillian didn't respond, Marianne wrote, **just invite harper to your frickin book club what is wrong with you.**

After a few minutes, during which Lillian was surely living her exciting high school life and not paying attention to her little sister's texts, Lillian wrote back: **gtg. swimming then the meal charity stuff. its just you & mom for dinner. dads in the pit this week. lu.**

lu too sis.

***

The next afternoon, after a school day that had felt never-ending, Vi began practice by writing a schedule on the whiteboard. It reminded Marianne so much of her mom that she almost made the joke that she felt at home. But no one would get it.

Mr. Garcia explained that, as Vi had "adopted the mantle of leadership in the sudden absence of Ms. Schuler," she would run one practice a week.

Mr. Garcia, wearing one of his fun ties that day—neon green with purple polka dots—stood in front of an enormous poster that read, "Everyone is welcome here!" surrounded by the word "welcome" in a couple dozen languages.

"Today as you study, remember . . ." he told them. "Hitting the buzzer quickly is extremely important. If a team had encyclopedic knowledge, that would be the only purpose for practice. It would be akin to track practice—speed being the only concern. However!" and he lifted a finger in the air. "*No* teams have encyclopedic knowledge. Therefore . . ."

"I think Remington is pretty close to it," Dan muttered.

"They know everything," Nina agreed. "They really do."

"*No* team has encyclopedic knowledge," Mr. Garcia repeated.

He was so . . . *proper*. If Marianne was in charge she'd respond, "Remington has *nothin'* on us, guys! Come on! Let's kick some Remington *rear*!"

"Therefore, our concentration is always on what?" he prompted them.

"Developing our specialties," Nina, Dan, and Vi responded in a monotone chorus.

"Precisely. In the weeks ahead we'll continue to concentrate on strengthening our personal knowledge bases in the various disciplines. Vi?" He gestured for her to take the floor.

"You know the drill," Vi said, knowing full well Marianne didn't. "Science, literature, history/social studies, humanities, and math. Ideally"—and Vi shot a notable frown in Marianne's direction—"we can each specialize in at least three."

"And sometimes a sub-discipline counts," Mr. Garcia added. "For example, within the humanities, perhaps one has a real handle on art. Right, everyone?" He spoke to all of them, but it didn't take a Quiz Quest team captain to know he was really talking to Marianne. Had he seen her doodles during class? If that made him think she was an art historian, he needed help with the humanities himself . . .

"Once in a while there's some pop culture stuff, too?" Nina said directly to Marianne in one of her question-statements. "Like celebrities, if they're iconic or historical?"

Marianne was almost grateful to Nina for giving up the pretense that this discussion was for everyone and not just for her.

Marianne actually didn't care about celebrities at all, even though people acted like that was a job requirement for a stupid girl.

Marianne remembered one time when she was reading a book for English class in seventh grade, her friend's big brother said to her, "The classics, huh? Shouldn't you be reading about Ariana Grande's latest breakup instead?"

She'd just giggled, because what else could she have done?

She knew nothing about Ariana Grande.

"Cool!" She threw a thumbs-up to Nina.

She hadn't ever finished that book she'd been reading. And she couldn't remember why, because she'd actually liked it. What book had it been? *Treasure Island*. That was it.

"Hey," Dan piped up, "Have you all seen the *Jeopardy!* clip when the question is what Beyoncé and Jay-Z go by when they perform together on their album and instead of 'The Carters' she answers, 'Bey-Z'? Comedy gold."

Mr. Garcia lifted a hand to impose quiet. If she knew anything about Mr. Garcia, it was that he hated when things got derailed. "On that note, I will leave Vi to oversee practice with the hope that by the end of the hour we will have determined, um, which specialties most require our focus. I'll pop my head in around twenty after." He took one step and, as if remembering her all of a sudden, turned to Marianne and added, "Ms. Blume, I trust you'll keep our conversation the other day in mind." He raised a hand goodbye and left.

Instinctively, Marianne checked in with Vi, who gave her a knowing look.

Vi had heard that conversation.

"Marianne," Vi said, breaking up her thoughts, "I emailed you several links to flash cards. You received them, I assume?" Vi couldn't even look at her.

Marianne nodded. "It was a lot," she said honestly.

Marianne browsed the words on the "welcome" poster. *Willkommen. Chào mừng. Kaabo.*

"Like I've been saying, Addison believes science is our greatest weakness," Vi announced to the group, ignoring Marianne's response.

"But Addison's not here anymore, so . . . ?" Nina folded her arms.

"We still talk," Vi said like that was obvious, and picked up her phone as if to check for Addison.

"Right, but she's not here to see what's going on? Or our progress?" Nina fought back.

"But I update her," Vi went on.

"So she's still the team captain then, basically." Dan took a swig of Gatorade.

Vi pushed forward. "Let's get started."

"What do you think your specialties are?" Nina asked, swiveling in her chair to address Marianne.

"Yeah, what are you into?" Dan joined in.

What was she into? What did that mean?

"Physics? Biology? Astronomy? That would help us," Nina went on. "Like, the other day I totally blanked on how many moons orbit Mercury? It just doesn't stick for me." Nina chewed on a pinky fingernail, though it looked like there wasn't much left to bite.

"Don't planets have one moon?" Marianne asked. If she thought about it, she knew they didn't.

"They should," Dan said. "Keep it simple."

No, she wasn't into any of that. She was into hours spent doing crafts with Skyla. She had just started to learn how to make rugs out of old T-shirts. She liked cuddling with Possum while she listened to Lillian sing. She liked long drives to her grammy's trailer home in Battle Creek, listening to music and watching the farms go by and wondering about the people who lived there. She was into helping Lillian with her winter bake sales and making her family her special lemonade in summer, the real kind where you have to perfect the sugar and lemon balance to get it just right. Could these kids do *that*?

"Civics?" Nina continued. "I mean, we all know the term of a US senator, right? But can you recall how many representatives there are? I always get those details wrong. To be fair, it constantly changes. But I should still know it."

Vi was taking notes. Marianne wondered what on earth she could be studying right then.

"Hmm, I'm not sure," Marianne said, trying to stay casual. "Maybe we should just start some practice? See how it goes?" She knew she wouldn't get any right, and the more they grilled her on her "specialty," the worse everyone was going to feel.

"Yes, but Nina is right. We need a sense of your strongest areas, so we know where to begin," Vi said to her while still writing.

Nina and Dan looked at Marianne expectantly. Vi must have known that Marianne would draw a blank.

And Marianne couldn't admit to them that she wouldn't be answering any questions right, anyway. That wasn't the plan.

"I know some animal stuff," she said. She could only imagine how that sounded to these kids.

"Zoology?" Nina happy-squeaked. "Great!"

No, she didn't know what zoology was, but she figured it

meant "animal stuff," and so she smiled and nodded. "And I like music," she said, thinking of Lillian and her guitar.

"Nice!" Dan said, perking up a little in his chair. "What do you play?"

Marianne forced herself to grin her signature everything-is-just-peachy grin. "Nothing. Quit piano a few years ago. So much practice."

Her dad had been beyond disappointed.

But the way he'd lingered over her while she practiced, the way he made her repeat every last thing the teacher said from the lesson and then critiqued the teaching style . . . She couldn't take it anymore.

"It's just a shame," he'd said after her mom had agreed she could stop. "You were quite good."

"I keep thinking about starting up with something else," she said, surprising herself with something she hadn't even known she felt. But it was true, she realized. She felt like some instrument was out there for her, but she hadn't found it yet.

"I didn't see you answer the Brandenburg question the other day, though," Vi said, putting down her pencil and eyeing Marianne like a detective.

Marianne took a breath. "Whoops," she said in her breeziest voice, and gave a shrug. Why was Vi trying to humiliate her?

It wouldn't work.

"Andy plays French horn," Dan groused. "Whereas I'm content on the kazoo," he added.

"Andy is . . . ?" Marianne asked.

"His evil twin," Nina told her matter-of-factly.

"'Evil' is too strong a word," Dan said. "It's more like . . . he has the *potential* for evil."

"He's always trying to know more than Dan. He got into Greenfield Prep and Dan didn't, so . . ." Nina explained.

"Hey, hey, no—I would've gotten into Greenfield, too, if I had been able to study *all day* instead of PT, OT, all the extra stuff my parents *insist* on . . . Anyway, I'm glad I don't go there because it turns kids into *snobs*!" Dan punctuated the air with his pencil point.

"Hear, hear!" Marianne repeated his gesture with her pen.

"I play violin?" Nina chimed in. "Yeah, there's lots of practice. I don't mind. So would you say you're particularly interested in music history?"

Marianne's instincts kicked in. Avoid. Delay. Laugh at yourself.

"How about I observe for a bit?" she said. That sounded like something a super-smart kid would do. Scientists observed, right? "Could I see how you guys practice?"

Vi paused, perhaps suspicious, then handed out stacks of flash cards to everyone. She motioned for Marianne to move closer to the group, so Marianne took the seat next to Dan.

"Just do your best," he whispered to her.

Within a second, a rapid-fire fact-a-thon commenced.

Marianne could hardly hear a thing. They read the cards with such speed that the words seemed to whirl around the room, facts bouncing off the walls.

She watched them closely.

Vi and Nina each leaned forward on their elbows and jiggled a leg.

Marianne tried it. She even added in a lip bite, which seemed to fit.

Maybe if she could mimic their behavior she would fit in, and she could wrong-answer her way through Quiz Quest with no one the wiser.

She tried to send Skyla a telepathic message. *Skyla, do you hear me? I'm making a great thinking face. I'll show you later.*

But Skyla thought her strategy on the team was terrible. So she took the message back.

It was time to jump in to get to that 10 percent.

"Which country is home to the Burgess Shale?" Vi read off a card.

"Egypt!" Marianne randomly guessed.

"The correct answer is Canada."

She'd been to Toronto a couple of times. All she remembered was the Hockey Hall of Fame.

Mr. Garcia darted in, saw them all hard at work, and left again. Excellent. That was exactly what she needed.

"Carol Ann Duffy was the first woman to hold which position in the United Kingdom?"

"Senator!" she called out. It felt so freeing to not have to worry about being right.

"The correct answer is 'poet laureate.'"

"How would anyone know that?" she couldn't help whispering under her breath as she returned to copying Nina's posture.

Dan leaned over to her. "Hey, don't worry. I can tell how hard you're trying. And you'll get there."

Had he seen her biting her lip? Her leg jiggles? Had her fake "attentive kid listening" act worked?

And she felt that panic again, like she'd get caught, like—even worse—she knew what she was doing was wrong, she knew Skyla was right . . . but she couldn't get out of it.

But maybe the other teams would be really bad and it wouldn't matter if she brought their score down a little! Maybe they'd still win!

"Thanks," she answered Dan.

"Dan, you're yapping away again!" Nina scolded him.

"Okay, okay, sorry!"

Marianne noticed that Dan was answering about as many questions as her. Maybe she had a fellow Drifter on the team.

The fact-flying felt endless until Vi broke it up.

"Marianne, did you go over any of the flash cards I sent?" she asked.

Nina and Dan halted.

". . . There were a *lot*," Marianne repeated.

Even if Marianne *was* trying, how did Vi expect her to know all that so quickly? It's not like Nina and Dan got every answer correct, either.

"She's new," Dan defended her.

"No, it's okay," Marianne said.

"We only have a little more than a month. We're not going to win if we—" Vi slipped a pencil behind an ear and began a lecture.

"Can you please stop being so negative?" Nina shut her eyes and covered her ears. "It's not helpful!" she nearly shrieked.

"I agree," Dan said, taking off his glasses and rubbing his eyes. His skin was so light that the rubbing left red marks on his face.

Nina opened her eyes and, after seeing Vi's expression, quickly said, "Sorry. I'm sorry, Vi."

Vi stood up and nearly threw her flash cards down. "It's break time," she snapped. She got on her phone, texting and pacing once again.

"I said I'm sorry!" Nina repeated, and then muttered something under her breath, clearly mad at herself. But she'd done nothing wrong . . .

Seriously, if the teammates were scared of or angry at one another all the time, Marianne wasn't their only roadblock to gold and glory.

Marianne followed Nina out to the water fountain.

Over and over, under her breath, Nina repeated: "Carthage. Carthage, Carthage, Carthage. Lost the Punic Wars. Hamilcar lost at Zama. And who was Hannibal? I always forget Hannibal." As she said each new word, she tapped a different finger with her thumb like she was doing Morse code on her fingertips.

"You alright?" Marianne asked.

"Me?" Nina asked, raising her thick eyebrows as if woken out of a trance. "I'm fine."

Marianne wondered if—like Vi—Nina only liked fellow smarties.

"I just don't know why some of this isn't sticking," Nina sighed, wiping a little bit of water from the side of her mouth.

Marianne took a sip. When she lifted her head back up, Nina was still there. She was so small, and in her bright yellow sweater dress she reminded Marianne of a parakeet.

"You look like a beautiful bird today," Marianne told her.

"Ha! Funny. Lucky I was done drinking, or I would've spit it out." Nina blushed.

She caught a flash of braces in Nina's smile.

"And I don't know about 'beautiful,'" Nina added, covering her smile again with her fingers.

"You so are!" Marianne assured her.

The yellow against Nina's dark brown complexion was gorgeous. When Marianne wore light yellow, she looked sickly.

Why didn't people tell other people the nice things they were thinking more often? Marianne liked to do that. Everyone always seemed surprised.

"So you like ballet, huh?" Marianne asked her.

"Hmm? Oh, the Misty Copeland folder." Nina giggled nervously. "I used to be really into it. I go to the ballet with my parents sometimes? I take class, but only once a week, it's not serious . . ."

"Cool! My dad plays in the pit for some ballets," she told her.

"*Really?*" Nina jaw fell open. "I'm starstruck."

"Ha, yeah. Sometimes I had to go, and it was *so boring*," Marianne confessed. "Sorry," she added. "I never knew what was going on, so I used to make up my own stories to the shows, like I'd be like, 'That girl in the white is secretly a spy, and she's trying to find her father's long-lost enemy and get revenge!'"

"And then you'd find out that you were really watching *Swan Lake* and she was just a sad swan?" Nina joked.

They both laughed.

"Exactly," Marianne said.

They stood there for a minute, by the fountain, Nina swaying back and forth and picking at the skin around her bright pink nails.

"Should we head back?" Marianne asked her.

Nina nodded.

They walked toward the room, passing a few other classrooms with clubs or teams in them. "We haven't had any classes together, yeah?" Marianne asked. "Where'd you go to elementary?"

"Hillside?" Nina nodded a lot. Another nervous tic.

"I was at Acorn," Marianne told her. "But you know Skyla, right?" Marianne remembered Nina had asked Skyla to join Quiz Quest.

"Oh, yeah, we have history and lit together! She's so smart," Nina gushed.

"Skyla's great," Marianne said. Skyla was super smart,

 88

sure, but it was weird to hear a genius-type like Nina say it like that.

They asked each other which kids the other one knew until they got back to the classroom.

Inside, Vi and Dan were squabbling.

"She *is* trying!" Dan spat out.

"She's *not*. And she's going to be the reason we lose," Vi shot back.

Vi was right.

"Um, hello?" Nina widened her eyes as a signal for them to shut it down.

For several seconds, no one spoke. Nina scurried back to her chair. Dan and Vi stayed frozen in their positions on opposite sides of the room.

"I thought maybe when Addison left . . ." Vi ran her fingertips from her hairline to her hair tie a few times.

Marianne thought she may have heard Vi's voice crack a little. Should she rub her back? Tell her it would be alright?

"I thought maybe we could manage without her. But we can't." Vi shook her head. Her gaze hardened. "And . . ." Shifting to sharpness again, she rage-sighed through her teeth. It reminded Marianne of a big cat. "And I can *tell* that you didn't study a *single* thing I sent! I actually put a lot of thought into those materials, too, I didn't just send you"—she threw her hands in the air like she was searching for a word—"*whatever*! Like. I noticed you asked that question about X the other day? About why they chose X?

89

That's actually an interesting question, one I didn't know the answer to. So . . . that told me maybe you're an ideas person. You know?"

Marianne didn't know. She had no idea what Vi was talking about.

"She *is* trying! What else do you expect from a person? Geez!" Dan nearly yelled. But Vi ignored him and went on.

"So I thought, Okay, maybe her specialty can be science concepts, theories. I want to give you a chance. I *have* to give you a chance . . ." Vi was clearly just talking to herself now, forgetting anyone was in the room. "Even if Dan gives up, even if Marianne holds us down, we're not going to quit. So what's the answer?"

People always said that talking to yourself was "crazy." Maybe it was just a sign of being really stressed out.

Marianne couldn't fix her own brain, but maybe she could fix some of Vi's stress.

She would share her plan. So be it. Maybe they could make it work together. As a team.

"Vi, no, listen to me." Marianne took a few steps toward her and gave her an optimistic smile. "I actually did look at them . . . Some of them. I skimmed."

Vi cursed.

"Yeah, I'm here for the extra credit. I admit it. I need that, right? And you guys need a team. But here's the thing: I have to answer ten percent of the questions. But do they have to be *correct*? So *what* if I get them wrong?

You all are so good that you can win without me acing it. I'm sure of it. You got this! Just let me hang out here, and show up to the game, and we'll all get what we want!" She smiled her perkiest, sweetest smile and waited for Vi to take a breath.

"What?!" Vi shrieked.

"Um, excuse me? No, that's not going to work." Nina attacked a new fingernail. "Ohmygodohmygod."

Dan didn't say anything. Was he disappointed? It's not like *he'd* been trying, either. Had he?

"No. Absolutely not," Vi said. "I'm going to talk to Mr. Garcia. You lied to him. This isn't fair." She nearly galloped to the door.

"Wait!" Marianne jumped in front of it. "Don't! What do you mean, I lied to him?"

Vi froze and took Marianne in. She searched her face, like she was trying to gauge Marianne's sincerity. "You didn't get the message, did you?" she asked, to which Marianne could only respond by widening her eyes even further and shaking her head.

"Didn't you hear him the other day? In the hallway? 'This is not a participation trophy.'" She checked in with Marianne to see if she got it. No. She went on. "He said you need to *prove* you're really trying. Real proof. Tangible proof. Or *no credit*."

"Can you just say what you're trying to say?" Marianne pleaded. "And thanks for eavesdropping, by the way."

She could hear how whiny she sounded, but she felt like she couldn't keep up.

"*If we don't win the final trophy, you don't get the extra credit!*" Vi nearly shouted. "That's what he was saying!"

The rest of the team, including Marianne, said nothing, taking this in.

"And," Vi added, crossing her arms, "I know you need it to pass the year."

Marianne felt her peachy face turn raspberry.

"I put two and two together," Vi explained.

Marianne backed away from the door and returned to her seat.

"We have to win. *You* have to win." Vi wouldn't let up.

And Marianne drifted.

Like a zombie, she pulled out her strawberry lip gloss and spread it on her mouth, over and over, on repeat, tasting the chemicals.

She stared at a liquid-shaped stain on the tile floor. What had that person been drinking? Had they gotten in trouble for spilling it? Did Mr. Woodsman, the custodian, have to clean it up?

She felt a hand on her back.

"You okay?" she heard Nina ask.

"Yup! Fine!" She answered like someone had pressed the "I'm fine" button on a Marianne robot.

She felt all three of them crowd around her.

Marianne nodded to the floor. "Did someone die there or something?"

She couldn't see their faces, but she imagined they had no idea what she was talking about.

"I should probably go," she said breezily after a moment. Her face muscles went slack, unable to force a grin, but she kept her voice light. Leaning over slightly, she grabbed her backpack, but she couldn't make herself sit up.

If Vi was right about what Mr. Garcia meant—if Marianne had to win—it was all over.

"Aw, come on," Dan comforted her. "It's not so bad."

"You don't get it," she whispered. She squeezed the top loop on her backpack as tightly as she could.

"We can help!" Nina said.

They were so wrong. And telling them who she really was? Who she really, truly was? That might be even worse than just repeating the year.

She lifted her backpack and pulled it on her lap like a blanket. She held it close to her torso. "Nah, forget it, guys." Then she stood up to head to the door. But her legs wouldn't move. She didn't even know where to go. Home to study with Mom? What was the point?

"Again? You're leaving *again*?" Vi said from behind her. "So much drama . . ." she added under her breath.

"I told you. You don't get it," Marianne said, snapping as much as Marianne ever snapped at anyone.

"I said it the other day, guys," Vi grumbled. "She doesn't care about school at *all*. Or anything else, apparently."

"It's because I *can't*!" The strange and unpleasant sensation of anger simmered inside Marianne. "I wish I could, but I *can't!*" She finally turned toward all of them, pulling a backpack strap onto her shoulder.

"What are you even talking about?" Vi asked, throwing a look to the other kids like "Can you believe this girl?"

"We already turned in our roster . . ." Dan interrupted, kindly but nervously. "You kind of . . . *have* to do it?"

"*I can't!*" she repeated, feeling an intense urge to cover her ears and not listen, stop the conversation. She took a step toward the door.

"I told you, I told you," Vi singsonged the words. "She's exactly what I thought, and she—"

But before Vi could finish, Marianne's secret burst out, no longer trapped inside where it had stayed for so, so long.

"*I can't learn!*" Marianne closed her eyes. "*I! Can't! Learn! Try or don't try, doesn't matter, I can't do it!*"

As the words left her, she deflated. The room was so quiet that all she could hear were the skid of sneakers out in the hallway and a few voices shout a couple of verses from a hip-hop song as another kid groaned, "Please stooooop."

As the rapping faded, Vi said in a stern, clear voice, "That's impossible."

"No," Marianne assured her, "it's true."

Vi shocked Marianne by lightly pushing her back down into her seat.

"*Everyone* can learn," Vi retorted.

Was her whole life going to consist of people saying this to her over and over again until she had to prove them wrong?

"You don't— I just—" Marianne tried to explain, but instead growled, "Argh!" and dropped her head into the crease of her elbow.

"She's right?" Nina offered. "I mean, maybe not everybody can learn *everything*, but . . ."

"No." Marianne shot her head up and shooed away their words with a wave of her hands. "It's too much. You have no idea. I'm basically still in the third grade. Don't know how I even made it to that." Now that Marianne had started telling her secret, she couldn't stop. "Where are all fifty states? I dunno! How do I convert fractions into something else? I dunno! I'm not a learner. It's not me. You can try to fix my brain again and again, but trust me, 'effort' is not the answer. Never has been, never will be. Your team? With me on it? It's toast."

Vi walked right up to her, and Marianne could've sworn she was going to grab her face in her hands or shake her or something. But instead she just stared right at her, her amber eyes full of determination. "That is *ridiculous*," she insisted. "The stupidest thing I've ever heard. *Everyone* can learn. And so can you. I am going to teach you. Right now," Vi said.

Marianne forced a laugh. "Okay? Um . . . good luck. Like . . . greater women have tried before," she said to a chuckle from Dan, though she meant it. She was thinking of her mother.

"I will!" Vi said, holding a finger in the air as if she was giving a speech in front of a huge crowd. "I will teach you one thing!"

"Sure, great!" Marianne fake-celebrated. "Let's do this! Give it your best shot!"

At the suggestion of a challenge, the fear of revealing her secret left her and was replaced by a sensation of confidence. On this fact, Marianne would be correct.

"Great!"

Vi cleared her throat.

Marianne glanced at Nina and Dan and saw that Dan had joined Nina in the seat next to her. They watched Vi and Marianne like they were a movie.

"Okay," Vi said softly. Moving to the center of the front of the classroom, she tapped her flash-card stack on the table to straighten it and pulled up the first one. "One fact. One thing. Easy. Here goes: What theory states that the universe is constantly expanding?"

"I don't know."

"The big bang theory."

"Like the TV show."

"Okay, good." Vi took a beat. Then repeated: "What theory states that the universe is constantly expanding?"

Obviously, she'd *just* heard the answer. That didn't mean she'd remember it later. "The big bang theory," she answered dutifully. "That doesn't prove you can teach—"

"That was step one," Vi announced.

"Okay, but I don't understand any of it . . ."

"Exactly, Marianne," she said, resembling Mr. Garcia once again. "Great point. To remember, you have to *understand*."

"A theory of expansion?" Nina butted in. "Isn't it about the beginning of the world?"

Marianne remembered she'd heard that somewhere, too.

"We'll get there." Vi moved to the front of the room and wrote BIG BANG—EXPANSION—INFINITE on the white-board with a purple marker.

And, to Marianne's astonishment, a darkness lifted from Vi. She stood straighter. She moved about the room slowly, with a kind of grace.

"I want you to close your eyes."

Marianne glimpsed Dan and Nina in the seats right behind her. They closed their eyes, so she did, too.

"Now. Picture all the energy you can conceive of. Imagine anything in the world that ever was or ever will be, all at once, *exploding outward into the universe*."

Vi's voice and speech reminded Marianne of a narrator at a planetarium. Soothing.

"Do you see it? It's spreading out *right now*, as we speak. All energy, all matter, is still going and going and going, expand-ing outward through *infinite* space."

Marianne imagined lemonade and Possum and the desk before her and Dan's crutches and Nina's one smile and her own body floating out and away.

"Obviously, we can't feel any of it happening," Vi went

on, bringing Marianne back to reality. "If you think of time as infinite—going on forever—we're just living in a teeny, tiny, incomprehensibly small sliver of it, so we feel like we're staying still. But even so . . . We're essentially exploding outward in slow motion. It's like . . . if a firework never ended!"

Marianne tried to picture a never-ending firework, the sparks shooting out and then slowly drifting into the darkness for eternity.

She wanted to keep her eyes closed and watch them shoot to the moon and beyond, to the silent part of the universe, where everything was black.

"Right, but what does that have to do with the beginning of the world?" Nina interrupted.

Marianne opened her eyes.

"See, I told you I'm bad at astronomy," Nina murmured to no one in particular.

"Right," Vi said, breaking into a grin. Apparently, her look of worry and annoyance was not a permanent state. Her round cheeks bumped into the bottoms of her glasses, like her whole face had to move out of the way to make space for her display of happiness.

"At the beginning, there was that first explosion. Like a firework went off. The big bang theory says that after that happened, everything just kept going. So, in a way, we're *still living through the big bang now*. Isn't that *amazing*?"

"I don't get it," Marianne heard herself saying. And it

was true. There were so many holes to that idea, so much left to understand. "What was *before* the big bang? *Why* did the big bang happen? What happens when it *ends*? See, this is what I'm trying to tell you. I can't wrap my head around *anything* like this!"

Instead of scolding her, Vi said, "Marianne, that's not *not getting it*. That's just being unsatisfied. And that's *good*. Science is *all about* asking those questions." She paused. "See, I knew you might have a knack for the big theories and stuff. It requires . . . imagination."

"Um, how do you know I have an imagination?"

Vi shrugged. "I see you daydream in class. Right?"

Marianne didn't know what to say. Was that true about her? That she was a daydreamer with an imagination and a mind for big ideas?

Couldn't be.

"What's that Einstein quote about imagination?" Dan said.

Gosh, these kids really *were* a different species. They could just sit and talk for hours about all the things they knew.

"'Imagination is more important than knowledge,'" Nina answered immediately, almost robotically, like it was something people said all the time. Marianne had never heard it before.

"So . . . We don't know what happens when this big bang ends?" Marianne continued. It was funny—she *really* wanted to know.

"No. Time and space are so vast—meaning huge—that we can't conceive of it."

"Wow," Marianne said.

"Wow," Nina and Dan echoed her.

Marianne couldn't stop seeing those sparks of fireworks shooting out and on and on forever, each spark holding a person or place she knew, or a planet, or a star.

When she turned her attention back to Vi, Vi had that grin again, but it was a bit smugger. Like she'd won.

"Extension round!" Vi declared, lifting her finger up in the air again like she did every time she was taking charge, really acting like a teacher now.

"Which scientist laid the groundwork for the big bang theory by demonstrating that the universe is constantly expanding?" she asked.

"Stephen Hawking!" Dan answered immediately with a smack of the desk.

"Dan, I'm teaching Marianne," Teacher Vi chastised him. "And no."

"Fine, fine," he grumbled good-naturedly.

Marianne shook her head to show she didn't know.

"Edwin Hubble," Vi told her, leaving the dry-erase marker and returning to the desk that held her backpack and flash cards.

"Oh, the telescope guy?" Marianne asked. Her sister had a telescope in the attic that no one ever used.

"Yes, exactly!" Vi said. She picked up her backpack and

threw a strap over her shoulder. "And now you know *two* things."

Big pause.

"So, Marianne. Once again . . ." And as she asked the question, Mr. Garcia came into the room and stood against the inside of the door, observing. "What theory states that the universe is constantly expanding?"

"The big bang theory," Marianne said.

"Great," Vi answered. "You got it."

All four of them sat in silence.

"Did we make any progress today?" Mr. Garcia asked, looking from one student to another.

"We have a long way to go," Vi told him. "But I think we all learned something. Right, Marianne?"

"Yeah," Marianne admitted. "It's a start."

6

DID YOU KNOW THAT the big bang is still kind of going on, and that we don't know what happens when it ends? Marianne texted Skyla.

Over dinner, she'd asked her parents, too. Her mom, who must have known all about it already, said, "Tell me more." And she had.

yeah so cool, Skyla wrote back hours after Marianne's text.

Imagine being the telescope guy and also figuring out something like that. his mom must have been so proud lol, Marianne wrote back immediately.

No response from Skyla. Were they officially in a fight?

Skyla didn't know that Marianne—by staying—had agreed to do it. To try to win. Try to learn.

As Marianne took out the rag rug she'd begun crafting, knotting strips of marmalade orange fabric in circles over and over, Marianne recognized an old feeling—*nerves*. The kind of nerves where you didn't know what would come next. Not like dread, where you *knew* something would be horrible, but more like the feeling before the first day of a new class or a summer camp.

No one had been more nervous than Skyla before their first middle-school-era summer camp as rising sixth graders, Marianne remembered, as she weaved the orange in and out of yellow and magenta. She wanted her rug to look like a sunset melting onto her floor.

"You're going to be my only friend, I know it," Skyla had kept saying. "What if they make us swim? I hate swimming in front of other people. My nose runs whenever I lift my head out of the water. Everyone's going to want to hang out with you and you're going to be stuck with me and then you're going to be annoyed you're stuck with me."

Marianne had assured her it would be fine; they were going to make Popsicle-stick bird feeders and go on hikes, not anything stressful! Plus, Marianne would include her in everything.

And Marianne had been right. Marianne made friends and those friends were happy to have Skyla around.

On the second day of camp, after Skyla had refused to swim for the third time, Marianne pushed Skyla off the dock into the water. After the shock wore off, Skyla had laughed and laughed and never complained about swimming in public again.

The nice thing about sitting and doing a craft was that you could just relax, and think, and remember.

Why couldn't crafts earn grades at school?

Marianne finished a round of orange as Lillian propped her door open.

"Ever heard of knocking?" Marianne groaned.

"Homework done?" Lillian leaned against her doorframe.

"I could kill you," Marianne said, dropping the rug. "You're two years older than me, you're not my *au pair* or something."

"Ooh, look at you with your 'au pair' reference," Lillian said. "Fancy."

"Mom worked as an au pair after college, remember?" Marianne said disdainfully. Why did she have to prove how she knew anything fancy? "And did you ask Harper to join your boring book club yet?"

"If you'd ever actually *read* a book, you'd know they're not boring," Lillian snapped, extra angry at her for some unknown sister reason.

"You know what? That's, like, really mean." Marianne picked up her fabric again and shook her head. "You think you're so perfect . . ." She pulled a strip through another strip. "Can you just go?"

"I don't think I'm perfect!" Lillian hissed. "I just don't *give up* every time things are hard, so I've learned that *eventually* I'll be at least *okay* at stuff!"

"Yeah," Marianne grumbled, "'okay' as in Honors classes, featured in the school paper five hundred times, fastest swimmer, everyone's favorite person—"

"Ya know, you think everything comes so easy for me?" Lillian snapped. "News flash: It doesn't. I work *hard*. Ugh, you are just so—"

But before Lillian could finish, their mom appeared behind her, placing her hands on Lillian's shoulders. "Homework done?" she asked, and Lillian laughed.

Marianne slumped from her bed to the floor and crawled to her desk, moaning the whole way. Her mom and sister "Oh, Mar"ed her, and Marianne got to work. She answered her two history questions about the Revolutionary War.

Dropping the pencil and eyeing the clock, she saw that six minutes of writing had gone by. It felt like an hour.

She picked up her Quiz Quest flash cards.

Her brain felt fried.

And Skyla was mad at her. How could she concentrate?

Marianne reached for her phone.

porch? Marianne texted Skyla.

They met at the steps.

Skyla handed her a paper plate with tinfoil wrapped around it.

"Papa and I made brownies," she reported.

"What? Without me?" Marianne felt the warmth of the goodies under her hands. "Thanks," she added.

Skyla kicked a sweet gum ball with her feet and it rolled under a shrub in the yard.

"Are Jason and Luis happy about your test scores?" Marianne asked.

"Yup. I did okay," Skyla answered, zipping up her fleece and wrapping her arms around herself. "So it wasn't so bad today?"

"Not sure what 'it' is," Marianne answered.

"Sounds like you learned something?" Skyla said.

"Yeah. I learned one thing. Two, I guess."

"Cool. Now it's time for three and four, then, right?" Skyla said.

"So that's how this works, huh?" Marianne muttered.

They sat down, Marianne on the fifth step, Skyla on the bottom one. Marianne waited for Skyla to talk. But after a good thirty seconds, it became clear that Skyla was waiting for *Marianne* to talk first, probably because she'd been the one who upset Skyla in the first place. But Marianne was upset, too. She had been furious at all the *judgment*! So she wouldn't talk. She'd wait.

But what had being stubborn ever gotten her? And the comfort of Skyla's mere presence, along with the brownies, made almost all of her earlier anger dissolve. Instead of staying upset, she wanted to tell Skyla about the practice. She wanted to tell her how bad she'd felt when Dan thought she was really trying and stood up for her, how she'd just straight-up admitted the truth about herself to them, probably with words more honest than she'd ever even expressed to Skyla, and how Vi had challenged her—almost like a bet—and won. She wanted to tell her how Skyla had been at least a little bit right about how bad her plan had been and how Mr. Garcia wasn't going to give her the extra credit if the team didn't win.

"Look, I—" Marianne began.

"I don't want you to get left behind," Skyla interrupted her, her eyes facing ahead toward the empty sidewalk.

Marianne made her way down to the lowest step and hooked an arm around Skyla's.

"I want you with me next year," Skyla went on. "Like always. Please?"

Marianne nodded and nestled her head on her friend's shoulder.

As the moon rose, Marianne thought that maybe she should ask Skyla to check out the telescope in the attic together. Skyla brought it up sometimes, asking to see this or that planet, or check for constellations. But Marianne usually put it off and said, "Some other time."

Maybe this was that other time. Up there, they could count dozens of stars and wonder about the exploding world.

But before she could ask, Skyla pulled away. "I know you don't think you can really cut it at Quiz Quest, but what if you let me help you? I could test you and study with you and then it wouldn't be so hard?"

How much could Skyla really help her? Would they just sit there and do homework next to each other or something? It wasn't like Skyla was a Vi Cross type. She just did what she had to do to get good enough grades.

Plus, she didn't really want Skyla to see how far behind she'd gotten.

"Let's just not talk about this anymore, okay?" Marianne pleaded.

Skyla took a beat and then stood up. "Got it. I have to go practice clarinet, anyway. 'Night."

And she left for home without looking back.

***

Every day, Vi sent Marianne a list of topics to study. Inevitably, they were long and varied and overwhelming.

For half a week, Vi FaceTimed her and walked her through one thing a night.

"One by one," Vi said. "That's the plan."

There was no "Hey, how are you?," no talk about life or TV shows or even the team. Just a person or idea or place at a time.

The Battle of Yorktown. Mauna Loa, the largest volcano in the world. Gregor Mendel's discovery. The story of Tom Sawyer. The capital of Canada (not Toronto?!).

Marianne refused to do math. She had enough of it with her mom every time they hung up.

"Eventually we have to do it," Vi reminded her several times. "But I suppose for now," and she'd sigh, "There are enough other things to learn . . ."

Then, before they signed off, Vi commanded her to do homework before a clipped "Tomorrow, then."

Marianne couldn't tell anything about Vi from her background. All she ever saw was Vi's pale, looming face under a lamplight.

But the lessons almost, maybe, kind of worked. And before the next practices, Marianne felt a little less dread, if only because if Yorktown came up she could now report that it ended the Revolutionary War. And she could remember that because Vi had helped her picture the dirt flying from the trenches that the soldiers dug, covering them in mud and sweat. She had brought to life a story of hours and hours of hand-to-hand fighting in the wet soil.

Like her grandpa always said, "What a country!"

Marianne walked into that week's second practice to a big wave from Nina and Dan.

"Welcome back," Dan said.

"Hey, can I show you something?" Nina grabbed Marianne's phone and helped her install a flash-cards app. "This will be so much easier. Here's our account."

"You call yourselves the Etheridge Ermines?" Marianne loved it.

"Technically, we're supposed to be the Etheridge Eagles, like the sports teams here. But Addison said that was too 'conventional.' And 'ermines' look sweet, but they're ferocious. She said that was like us."

"This Addison sounds like she was a pretty big deal to you guys, huh?" Marianne asked.

"She was perfect," Nina said.

Marianne laughed, but then she saw that Nina was serious.

"Oh okay, cool!" Marianne said.

Vi threw Marianne a nod of acknowledgment but sat quietly texting.

When Mr. Garcia arrived, he asked them what they'd determined as far as specialties.

Would he ask her? She had no idea what to say. Her stomach turned and tossed like a storm. What if she said "scientific theories" or something and then he tested her on it? Could she just say, "My specialty is random facts Vi teaches me!"? That would be honest but not what he wanted.

Vi listed each person's strongest areas and ended with Marianne. "She's started with astronomy, but we'll need more time to assess her strengths."

She wished she could thank Vi.

"We have about a month," Mr. Garcia said, tapping his knuckles on the teacher's desk. "Let's get to work!"

He put her with Nina this time.

At almost inaudible levels, Nina said to her, "You're going to actually try . . . right?"

What choice did she have? She needed to pass.

And Skyla wanted this from her.

And it wasn't like anybody would see the competitions, except for the team.

And what had Lillian said to her? You couldn't get faster if you stayed dry? She had to jump in the pool.

Marianne smiled at Nina and nodded.

The questions commenced. Marianne listened for the ones she knew. Did they come up every time? Or were there always new ones? She'd have to ask Vi.

The kids buzzed faster than she could, anyway, even if she did know anything.

And then, out of the blue, a question she remembered: "Who was the second president, hailing from Massachusetts, known for—"

Before Mr. Garcia finished, Marianne buzzed in.

"John Quincy Adams!" she yelled out.

"Incorrect." Normally Mr. Garcia went right on, but he stopped and turned to Marianne: "Nice try, Ms. Blume. John Quincy Adams was this man's son."

Buzz. "John Adams," Vi answered.

Marianne had thought they were the same person. So humiliating. The other kids must have felt like Elliott Roth did all those years ago: what a waste of their time.

Expecting a standard Vi glare, Marianne kept her gaze on her fingers. The pink polish was chipping off.

When she did look up, though, Vi and Dan both gave her a thumbs-up before directing their attention back to Mr. Garcia.

"Good try!" mouthed Dan.

So they weren't angry.

Okay, she'd listen in again.

Before the round was over, Marianne had twisted her hair so much she'd created a couple of knots, and she'd gotten no

111

answers correct. If it was a competition, she wouldn't have met the threshold for a teammate.

But had she thought she'd learn five facts and suddenly do a good job? So silly.

When Mr. Garcia called a break and left the room, Vi immediately turned to her.

"How's homework going?" Vi asked.

"What do you mean?" Was Vi serious, or was this another setup for a put-down?

"Are you getting the work done?"

At the thought of homework sessions with her mom, guilt overwhelmed her. Her mom sat with her through each painstaking math problem or critical-thinking question and talked it over with her, watched her write it all down, and never gave up even when they were on algebra problem number twenty and Marianne begged her nonstop to let her finish it in the morning.

"It's fine?"

"Hmm," Vi said, whipping out her phone and texting someone something. "Not convincing. That knowledge will help you. You have to spend every waking moment on it."

"Eh, practices are enough," Dan said. "We'll give it a shot, right? It's all we can do."

"Lazy," Vi shot at him. "That's lazy."

"*Lazy?*" Dan looked extremely offended. "I'm just a realist," he huffed.

Vi let out a disbelieving laugh. "And now you're just sort of lying to yourself."

"Do you think your hero Addison would put down her teammates like that?" Dan rolled his eyes.

"She's not my hero," Vi said carefully, like she was trying to control herself.

Dan stood up and stretched his back. Marianne thought she noticed one of the arm spasms he'd told her about when they first met, but she couldn't be sure.

"You're obsessed with her," he went on.

"Dan, stop," Nina pleaded.

Dan turned to Nina. "Why are you so afraid of her?"

"I'm not!" Nina insisted.

"She's not *scared* of me." Vi picked up her phone and looked like she was texting again.

"Well, she's not having *fun*, either," Dan fought back. "None of us are. And you're going to call me *lazy*?" He shook his head. "You have no idea what a *single day* is like for me at this school," he said under his breath.

"God, Dan," Vi snapped. "If you don't care about this team or want to be on it, then just leave, okay?"

"Okay!" Dan hastened toward the door, his forearm crutches supporting him as he stalked away on his tiptoes.

"No!" Nina cried. "Come on! We can't have someone quit every practice!"

"Tell that to *her*!" Dan argued. He spoke to Vi: "I never

saw this side of you—not really—until you became captain. You are the only person in the world who can *suck the joy out of trivia*." He turned to leave.

"Wait!" Marianne hollered. "Dan, stop."

He did. He leaned harder onto one of his crutches and listened to her.

"You guys *are* going to lose if you don't stop all this fighting, whether you teach me anything or not!" As she said it, she knew she was right. If they stayed like this? Squabbling all the time? Their chances at Regionals and States were close to zero.

"Oh, that I know," Dan said.

"Do you?" Marianne asked.

She'd spent a whole week altering her entire life to try to get the extra credit to get to high school, and these prodigies were just going to throw it away with their useless bickering.

"Vi, Dan's right," Marianne said.

Before Vi could protest, she continued.

"You have to be . . . Well . . . A little bit . . ." Was she scared of Vi, too? She could hardly get the word out. "*Nicer.*"

"Addison was nice." Nina stared off into the distance, wrapped up in memory.

"And you all have to *get over Addison*," Marianne went on.

It felt so good to talk about something that wasn't academic. *This* kind of stuff was so clear, so obvious. *Anyone* could see it and understand it.

"You don't know what you're talking about," Vi said,

placing her phone down beside her papers and rearranging them. "Mr. Garcia will be back soon. Dan." Her stern face fixed itself on him. "Come back."

Dan looked back to Marianne. "Go on," he said. "I want to hear more from *her*," he told Vi, nodding to Marianne.

"I'm really sorry things turned out this way," Marianne said, and oh man, was she . . . "But Addison is gone. She's not going to Ann Arbor. You're stuck with me, right? And you're stuck with each other. So . . ." She searched her brain for anything she knew about bonding.

Daisy Troop 23098. The violet petal. "Be a sister to every scout."

She and Skyla had run that meeting with Marianne's mom in first grade. They'd taped papers on one another's backs and had to go around writing nice things about one another on the paper. Then each girl took the paper off at the end and saw what girls had written. Pretty much everybody's said "nice," "fun," "pretty," and random descriptions like "brown hair" or "tall." But it felt good. Marianne smiled at the thought.

"Yes?" Vi interrupted her daydreaming. Or was it strategizing?

"Everyone? Say one thing you like about each other," Marianne declared. "Right now."

She stomped her foot to show she meant business.

Out of the corner of her eye she saw Mr. Garcia return, standing just outside the window frame of the door.

"Ridiculous," Vi groused.

"I don't think *that's* the answer here . . ." Dan mumbled.

"Just do it. Just be nice! Just stop fighting over who is bad or why and give each other a *break*!" Marianne said. "Just—"

"Dan, you have the widest frame of reference of anyone I know." The words tumbled out of Nina in a rush.

Marianne only sort of knew what a wide frame of reference meant, but it sounded like a way of saying he was extra smart, which he was.

"Out of any of us, you'd probably do the best on *Jeopardy!*," Nina clarified. "And I really believe that."

Dan took a beat and said, "Why, thank you." He stepped further back into the room. "And you have one of the best memories on the planet. Once you hear something, you know it. I envy that. I have to study lists of Best Picture Oscar winners for days to really get anywhere. I'm building a hundred memory castles. The battles of the Civil War took me an embarrassing amount of time. Andy mocks me relentlessly for it."

Nina seemed to turn inside herself out of embarrassment. "Thanks. I've always been like that. I don't know why."

Marianne nodded toward Vi.

To Nina and Dan, she mouthed, "Vi."

They hesitated.

"Vi, you're like . . . the most organized person I've ever met?" Nina said, taking a step or two toward her.

"That's what I was going to say," Dan agreed. "My mom

should probably hire you to go through the stuff in our basement. She's got hoarding issues."

Vi didn't say a word. She took off her glasses and wiped the lenses on her shirt.

"Are we done?" Vi said.

Marianne heard a grunt from Dan.

"I didn't hear *you* say anything," he said. "And I like this game," he added, sounding surprised.

Mr. Garcia continued to stand outside, watching. Marianne wondered if he could hear them and if he'd be upset with Marianne for distracting his team.

But they were on to something, she could feel it, and she couldn't stop.

"I know I don't know you guys that well yet. But Dan, you're funny, you're sweet, I like you a lot," Marianne said. "Being smarter than any other guy in school is like the fifth coolest thing about you. Nina, you seem like you're really sensitive and you think about people's feelings, which is really nice." She wanted to add that it was especially nice in this ruthless Quiz Quest environment, but she kept that to herself. "Plus, that geography brain thing you have going on really is incredible. And I'd love to see you do ballet, because I bet it's super beautiful." Marianne couldn't stop. She could've said even more. She could tell these kids really needed to hear this. "And, Vi, you're a future president-of-everything. A boss lady. One of those women with those business suits that walks around New York City on her phone telling everybody what to do and they just do it. Powerful!" Marianne could tell Vi would think she sounded silly, but she didn't care. Everything she'd said was true.

"Agreed—extremely powerful," Dan chimed in.

"Thanks, Marianne!" Nina beamed.

"You're welcome," Marianne said. "Come on in, Mr. G!" she yelled out.

Dan scooted out of his way as he entered.

Mr. Garcia glanced from kid to kid. "Are we ready for a little scrimmage?"

"Sure, why not? Let's give it a whirl," Dan answered.

Marianne clapped. She couldn't help it.

"Go, team!" she shouted, finally letting out the words she thought Mr. Garcia should say. "Remington has *nothing* on us!"

Dan laughed and sat back down.

"That's the spirit," Mr. Garcia said, and he gave Marianne what may have been their first shared smile.

It was so funny how after a lot of hard days, every even somewhat-good day felt like a holiday.

As practice ended, Marianne booked it to her mom's car parked outside. They had a lot of homework to do. But mostly she wanted to tell her how she'd taught some of the Quiz Quest kids to work together a little better as a team.

The late-afternoon sky was an ominous gray.

Before she could open the car door, Marianne heard someone call her name.

Vi jogged up behind her, her backpack so heavy it didn't even bounce up and down against her back. It was like an anchor.

Vi stopped Marianne before she got to her mom's car.

"I'm not obsessed with Addison," Vi said.

Marianne didn't know what to say. It certainly seemed like she was. But it also wasn't really Marianne's business.

"She was my only friend," Vi continued, her glasses fogging up a bit in the cold mist. "And I mean that literally."

Marianne tried to conjure Addison in her mind's eye. Addison S. was one of three Etheridge Addisons, and she was the one who was friendly with all sorts of kids. Marianne wouldn't know how to put her in a group in any way. They'd had math and science together in sixth grade, and all Marianne remembered was that Addison was given her own more advanced work to do and she set up shop in the back corner by herself.

"She can't be your only friend," Marianne said. "What about Nina and Dan!" She tried to sound convincing.

"Oh yeah right," Vi grumbled. A light drizzle came down and Vi lifted up her black hood. "All they could say is that I'm 'organized.'"

"But, like . . ." Marianne said. "*You* didn't say anything to *them* at all?" Marianne motioned to her mom and added, "I got to go."

If Vi heard her, she didn't let on. "I know no one likes me," she said.

Marianne found herself looking around for Nina and Dan, but she couldn't say why. Maybe she felt like she shouldn't be the only one hearing this. It was too much. She didn't know Vi Cross well enough to know how to respond in a way that would make anything better. Plus, if she'd ever thought about it, she'd always assumed Vi didn't care if anyone liked her, anyway. How else could she explain being so harsh with everyone all the time?

Should Marianne say that she liked her? Or would that be a lie?

Marianne didn't *not* like her. She didn't really not like anyone. She just thought Vi didn't like *her*. And she didn't. Right?

"I really like the way you teach me," Marianne said, telling the truth. "You make things sound really exciting, and . . . I don't know what the right word is . . . *Big*."

"Ha. Big?" Vi looked down at their shoes, getting wetter by the minute.

"What I mean is you're a great teacher." She shuffled side to side to stay warm.

"I told Addison earlier during practice that you said I had to be nicer," Vi reported.

So *that* was who Vi was always texting with during breaks. Of *course*.

"She said if I want to be a good leader I have to be kind," Vi went on. "So she thinks you're right."

Marianne said, "But hey, you're really honest, so that's good, right?"

"I always thought so," Vi said, her voice a wisp, the rain speeding up.

"I think people just don't always need to hear the worst thing about themselves?" Marianne said, raising her voice above the rain.

It seemed so obvious. But maybe it wasn't to Vi.

Vi stood there for several seconds until Marianne's mom rolled down the window.

"Hey, honey, it's raining," she said. "Everything okay?" she asked.

"Hi, Ms. Blume," Vi greeted her.

"Her last name is Byrne, actually." Marianne grabbed the car door handle. The rain intensified.

"It's alright, Blume'll do," her mom said. "Do you need a ride?" she asked Vi.

"Oh, no, I walk home, Ms. Byrne," Vi said, beginning on her way immediately, head still down.

Vi had one of those different voices for grown-ups—more formal, softer.

"Technically it's *Dr.* Blume," Marianne yelled above the rain, hopping inside the passenger's seat.

"Oh, stop, it's Norah," Marianne's mom said. "And it's raining. Get in."

Vi jumped in the back seat, and they drove off.

"Alright, where am I going?" her mom asked.

"I'm over on Sycamore," Vi answered.

Ooh la la. That was quite the elegant street. Marianne knew her mom was thinking the same thing.

"It must be nice to be so close to the school," her mom said, talking to Vi through the rearview mirror.

"It's definitely convenient." Vi paused. "So you're a doctor?" she asked.

Marianne's mom playfully smacked Marianne's leg for making it sound like she worked in a hospital or something. "No, I have a PhD in linguistics. I'm not saving any lives here!"

"Oh!" Vi perked up. "Are you a professor, or . . . ?"

How did Vi know how to talk to adults about their careers like this?

"That didn't really work out," her mom said, slowing down as they neared Sycamore. "I'm doing translation work at the moment. I like it," she added.

Vi directed them to pull up in front of a large brick house with a gazebo visible in the backyard. They looked like people who had gardeners. Every fall, Marianne and her mom spent hours uprooting their annuals, trimming the perennials, and planting bulbs, and each spring they spread wildflower seeds in new corners of their patch of land in the backyard. Marianne didn't know people actually hired gardeners until her dad made a snide comment about it one day as they drove past the very area they were in right then.

She had thought that only people in mansions or Hollywood did that.

The house had no lights on. Were her parents not home?

"Do you have siblings?" Marianne found herself asking.

"Just me," Vi said. "Thank you so much for the ride, Norah." Then she spoke to Marianne in her normal voice. "Talk to you tonight. And please look over what I send beforehand." She seemed to take note of Marianne's mom's questioning look and added, "If you have time, of course."

Vi hopped out of the car as quickly as she could and ran inside.

"Spill," her mom commanded before driving off. "What's the story?"

"So . . ." Marianne unwrapped a stick of Big Red and explained the complications of the absence of Addison, the tension between teammates, and the strange case of Violet Cross.

"Hmm," her mom said as they pulled into their driveway. "It sounds like they really need a Marianne on the team."

She found herself echoing Vi earlier with a disbelieving "Yeah right." What on earth could she add to Quiz Quest besides wasting their time and cheerleading them against Remington? There was a reason schools didn't have cheer-leaders for trivia teams.

"Just my two cents," her mom said, giving her knee a squeeze, which was her mom's "I love you" code. "As long as you're still able to do your schoolwork," she added because,

Marianne knew, she couldn't help herself. "Ready?" she asked Marianne. "Run!"

They dashed for the door and got soaked.

After Marianne's dinner and nightly homework marathon, Vi texted her that she couldn't do one of their sessions that night.

Maybe Marianne had really hurt her feelings.

To Marianne's utter shock, she sort of *missed* it. She found herself wondering what the next fact would be. They'd been like little surprises each night, things she'd missed along the school path. Maybe if she could start again somehow, if she could learn a fact at a time, one by one, she'd be able to have a fresh start. But, of course, that was impossible.

She was only a handful of facts in. It had been a few days. She was being ridiculous.

Marianne changed into her coziest pajamas and hopped on her bed. She grabbed *A Tree Grows in Brooklyn*.

Chapter two. Francie wanted to read every book in the library in alphabetical order. Francie had never owned a book. She dreamed about having her own one day.

Half of this book was about a girl reading books. Did that count as a story?

When had Marianne last loved a book at school?

She liked graphic novels, but lots of her teachers didn't allow them.

She opened the book again, but her eyes immediately drifted once more, and they fell on the flash cards from Vi.

They sat on her desk, just waiting for her usual Violet Cross class.

She picked up the cards.

She had to win.

She removed the top one.

Win. Win. Win.

Five facts so far. This would be number six.

A group of elephants is called what?

A parade.

What a perfect fact.

A *parade* of elephants?!

Marianne pictured elephants dressed as clowns and holding batons and marching with drums and horns.

She leaned back in her chair, put her feet up, and googled it.

Wow! A group of wildcats was called a *destruction*. Amazing! Cobras—a quiver. Ferrets—a business. Sharks—a shiver. And a pack of crows was called a murder! Creepy!

She texted Vi:

A group of FELIS SILVESTRIS—imagine if we really called animals those names?—is a destruction. So cool. My favorite is crows being a murder lol like wow seems like unfair publicity for crows right

Three dots appeared on her phone, letting her know a response was coming, and then Vi wrote back:

One fact at a time. Okay?

 125

Vi was right. It was too many facts at once. She had to stick with one at a time, so she could remember them. That was the key.

"Elephants—parade, elephants—parade, elephants—parade."

She said the words aloud, circling her room, almost turning it into a song.

Her phone, laying on her bed, lit up. She ignored it and continued her recitation.

Then it lit up again. Over and over.

With a little skip, she went to pick it up.

A couple of missed calls from Skyla. Weird.

A handful of texts that made no sense like Lol you are hystericaaaaal and is this 4 real.

Oh no.

Her thumbs, moving as fast as if she were playing allegro on the piano, opened all her accounts.

And then she saw it.

Dan had posted an announcement of Regionals. Underneath it he wrote, "We made the big time. Come check us out. There's a live feed, too! Link in bio. #QuizQuest #Regionals #EtheridgeErmines," and, fatefully, he had tagged Nina, Vi, and Marianne.

It had been shared a dozen times.

They knew about Quiz Quest. All of them.

And there would be a live feed? A live recording? Oh no no no no no no no . . .

Underneath Ava Hayes's posting of it, Lucas, Ava, Niko, and about thirty others had commented on it already.

OMG LOLOLOL NO WAY
its jeopardy for morons
lol this is so embarrassing i cant even handle it
Baaahahaha
is @itsmariannebb like the water boy or something
is she the mascot i dont get it
Watch party?
omg omg she is so stuuupiiiiid this is amazing
lets do it
the horse strikes again folks

As if it had burned her, Marianne threw her phone on the carpet.

She squeezed her eyes shut and tried to send Skyla a telepathic message: *stop being mad at me and help meeee*.

She wanted her mom. She wanted to jump into her arms like she did when she was little and skinned her knees.

Instead, she couldn't help but pick up the phone once again.

But the page had disappeared. She reloaded it and reloaded it again. It wasn't there.

Navigating back to Dan's page, she saw he'd deleted the post.

But Ava Hayes had posted a screenshot. And so did others.

It would circulate in eternity now.

But where was Skyla commenting "don't say that, she's our friend" or "stop that, she's nice"? Marianne reloaded the pages again and again, over and over, to check and see if anyone came to her defense.

Nope.

She'd always known she was a joke, but she thought it was a joke she was *in* on.

She'd thought she was laughing along with them, but she'd been wrong.

How could she try to win with all of them watching?!

As if she were in a trance, Marianne picked up her phone again.

Underneath all the comments, Marianne wrote: **haha yup haha that's me**.

She didn't know how to be anyone else.

7

ALL DAY, MARIANNE HEARD about nothing but the Quiz Quest livestream.

"You really did it, Blume," Lucas said to her several times in delight. "Thank you for doing this for us."

"We love you, Horse," Niko told her.

"You're so brave," Kylie cooed. "That would be like me joining the varsity football team or something. And I'm barely five feet. But it's for a joke, right?"

Marianne nodded.

She tried to play along. How was she supposed to turn back now?

During math, Mr. Garcia called on her.

She felt the familiar rush of nerves. She put on a confident, upbeat grin. She didn't know what else to do.

All the homework with her mom? It hadn't done much. She could do one piece of a math problem, but never the whole thing.

On the screen he wrote, $-24 = -x + y$.

"Alright, so that's our equation," he announced.

Negatives?! Oh no. The second she saw them it was game over.

"Now, as we've discussed, we just need two points. And those two points will be what?"

She knew he was doing the easy bits with her. Everyone else knew, too.

But she remembered this one because he'd said it over and over again the week before.

She had to get Mr. Garcia to see her differently, even if the rest of them laughed. She had to.

Should she answer for real?

"The intercepts," Marianne mumbled.

If people were surprised she'd actually answered something, she didn't want to know it. She kept her eyes on Mr. Garcia's pen, though she felt her face flush pink.

He went on to yadda-yadda his way through finding the X intercept, letting Y equal 0, and solving for X. But he'd already lost her. She couldn't remember what to do next.

"Now if we divide both sides by negative one . . ." he went on, and then he motioned for her to come up front to write it out.

The classroom's overhead light felt brighter suddenly.

"Could you draw the graph for us then, Ms. Blume?"

She remained seated. What would she draw? She didn't understand where the intercepts should go. She didn't know which quadrants or which numbers or, most of all, why this

 130

mattered. Yes, they'd done the fish tank example. But in real life, couldn't you eyeball the fish tank? Couldn't you find someone else to help you with it?

"I . . ." she said. "I really don't know, Mr. Garcia."

He was unfazed. "Okay. Let's pinpoint where exactly you're losing the thread here, because I bet a lot of your fellow scholars are in the same boat."

He always called the other kids "scholars," and they made so much fun of it, but when he said it that day, she felt bad for ever mocking it.

"I don't . . ." She took a breath. How did you put into words what you didn't understand when you didn't understand it? "The part I don't get is how it goes from an equation to a graph."

Lucas Hayes whispered from the back: "Yeah, that's the whole thing we're doing . . . So the part you don't get is . . . the whole thing . . . Ha."

Someone else added a "Neeeeigh."

Marianne didn't laugh along. She *had* to pass. She couldn't distract or let herself get distracted.

She had the sensation of a hamster running on a wheel in her gut.

"Can you offer any more specificity?" Mr. Garcia asked.

"Um . . ." Her spacey voice took over. "I dunno?"

"Okay." Mr. Garcia thought for a second. "We're taking an equation and transforming it into a graph, right? Like a magician turning a rabbit into a scarf. Except useful."

Was he trying to be funny? His joke didn't really make sense, but she tried to show him she appreciated his effort.

"Ha! Math magic," she chirped.

The hamster in her tummy slowed down a little.

"Exactly!"

And in the back, Lucas and a few other kids made some noise: "Hee hee hee math magic," she heard one of them say. Someone whispered something about Quiz Quest, but she couldn't hear it.

Marianne closed her eyes for a second, forced herself not to turn around, not to give a thumbs-up or a giggle, and she opened them again to see Mr. Garcia as still as stone.

"Excuse me?" He spoke toward the last rows. "What was that?"

"What?" Lucas said.

"You all had some commentary back there. Would you like to share?"

"Oh, sorry. It was nothing!" Jalilah jumped in.

"Did you have something to add about linear equations? Tips for your fellow scholars? Other ways to envision the problem?"

They all stammered various forms of "no" and "sorry."

Mr. Garcia froze again. Then he closed his eyes for a moment and lifted his chin toward the ceiling like he was praying.

"How dare you?" he said.

No one spoke. There was no silence like that of a class that had angered a teacher.

"Truly," he said to them. "How *dare* you mock a fellow student for the pursuit of knowledge?"

Was this the guy who was raising the bar for her and her only? Suddenly so sympathetic? It must have been about disrespecting Quiz Quest. No one should ever mess with Mr. Garcia and his Quiz Quest. What was Lucas thinking?

Teachers had told kids to stop making jokes about Marianne before, but they'd never stopped class entirely to do it. It was kind of miraculous.

Marianne wanted to break out into a little dance, but she held it inside.

"Do you think Luke Skywalker would do that?" Mr. Garcia asked.

Marianne, confused by the reference, took a peek toward the back and saw that Lucas wore a *Star Wars* shirt.

"Do you think Luke Skywalker would be a . . . a *bully*? That he'd mock others in the Rebellion?" He shook his head. "Han Solo, maybe. But Leia would set him straight." Then he turned his attention to the whole class. "I don't *ever* want to hear someone put down for trying to learn *ever* *again*. Not in this classroom. Not in the hallways. Not *ever*. Understood?"

Then he spoke to Marianne but kept his eyes fixed on the math problem. "Nice effort, Ms. Blume. Thank you," he said.

And he went through the rest of the problem without making Marianne say anything else, and she tried to take notes whenever Kylie did. They were largely meaningless to her, but her mom would be happy to see them.

 133

Had Mr. Garcia really stood up for her?

At the ring of the bell, she grabbed for her phone to text Skyla "Guess what Mr. G. did to Lucas today?" but before her thumbs hit the letters she put it down. Skyla probably wouldn't care.

Marianne waited until she was the second to last one left in the classroom. She wanted to say something to Mr. Garcia, but she didn't know what. And Kylie had so many questions for him. And she'd be late for Ms. James.

So she left, but not before she hollered, "Go, Ermines!" on her way out the door.

***

Marianne arrived a few minutes early to Quiz Quest. Dan and Nina were already there, going through flash cards.

"Come do a few with us?" Nina asked. "We have, like, five minutes."

What is . . .

Who is . . .

Where is . . .

After not getting any for a couple of minutes, Marianne checked out. It wasn't even time to start yet. She needed some relief. She looked at the seventh-grade social studies projects up on the wall, posters on figures in Michigan history, like Henry Ford, Francis Ford Coppola, Berry Gordy Jr. . . .

Unfortunately, her thoughts couldn't stay in the beautiful

world of movies and Motown—they kept returning to the comments section:

Lol
Horse
Hilaaaaarious

"Hey!" Nina clapped. "Come back!"

"Huh? What?" Marianne said.

"Pay attention?" Nina requested apologetically.

"That's good," Vi's voice said from behind Marianne. She had just entered the room, stalking toward them with stacks of papers and books in her arms that couldn't fit in her backpack. "I like that. Clap when she's getting too bored."

"Clap three times so I know it's not just a freak accident or something," Dan requested.

"Done!" Nina clapped three times as practice.

"Okay, okay, I'm listening," Marianne said.

"We have to start," Vi said. "Unfortunately, today, something different is happening—"

Before she could explain it, Kylie, Jalilah, and Ava walked into the room.

They sat at the desks, smooshed together opposite where the Ermines sat. Vi began arranging their chairs into a similar row to the Ermines', each on one side of the teacher's desk.

"Um, hi?" Marianne said.

Kylie threw Marianne a friendly wave.

"Hey!" Jalilah mouthed from across their tables, as if speaking out loud wasn't allowed in such a serious place as Quiz Quest practice.

Ava ignored her, instead concentrating on twisting her many rings so they all faced gem-up.

Mr. Garcia entered right behind and sat at the desk in front, with a timer and a stack of papers.

"Thank you to these gracious volunteers for agreeing to our mock scrimmage today!" Mr. Garcia announced with enthusiasm. "Yes," he sighed, "there's credit."

Oh no. Mr. Garcia didn't understand that they weren't there for the credit, they were there for the show, for the story to tell afterward about seeing Horse on Quiz Quest.

Marianne, sitting next to Dan, whispered to him, "I didn't know about this."

Dan ignored her and said right away, "Hey, I'm really sorry about the post last night. I guess I wasn't thinking anyone looked at my page."

"Pssh," she said. "It's okay."

"I deleted it," he told her.

"I know." She gave his shoulder a couple of pats and turned to listen to Mr. Garcia.

"I'm going to confer with our new rival team for a moment or two to make sure they're all set on the rules, and then, scholars, we will begin," Mr. Garcia went on.

Gosh, he loved Quiz Quest. He was practically . . . chipper. As cheerful as his neon tie.

Marianne leaned behind Dan and poked Vi. "What's happening?!" Marianne hoped Vi could see the panic on her. Then maybe she'd call this off.

"I didn't know about it either or I would've told you," Vi spoke quietly. "He does this sometimes. Usually no one agrees, so he gets the sixth or seventh graders, but today . . ." She didn't have to explain.

Today it would be funny.

Someone knocked on the classroom window, and, in horror, Marianne turned to see a group of kids waving to come inside.

Mr. Garcia, jolly mood disrupted, grumbled something to himself, and headed to the door, speaking in inaudible warnings to the students.

Marianne caught sight of Lucas and his big, grinning mouth. Ava signaled to him to come join.

Even though Nina sat two people away from Marianne, she could feel the table shaking slightly from Nina's jittery legs.

From the doorway she heard Mr. Garcia say, "I'm a big believer in a second chance," and "If I catch even the slightest—"

And she knew Lucas would be sitting at that table across from her soon.

She'd never felt more like Horse Girl.

And Mr. Garcia was a big believer in second chances? Since when? Only for kids who aced their math tests?

Lucas came in and joined his sister.

137

"Thanks a lot, Mr. G.," Marianne said under her breath and into her crossed arms.

"Huh?" Dan asked.

Into his ear, Marianne whispered what had happened earlier—how Mr. Garcia had stood up to Lucas, but it was obviously for the sake of Quiz Quest, not her. Either way, she had thought Mr. Garcia was finally getting a little nicer.

"I doubt Mr. Garcia knows about the post, though, to be fair," Dan said. "Or he wouldn't let any of these kids do it. He's probably just happy it seems like they're interested in Quest."

"Maybe," Marianne grumbled.

Vi and Nina sat straight forward, serious, ready, as the kids across from them whispered and giggled.

"So he basically called Lucas Darth Vader, though," Dan added.

"Yeah, kinda. But Lucas jokes around with everybody. He really isn't that bad," she whispered, checking out of her periphery to see if Lucas could hear them. He was deeply involved in telling some kind of entertaining, dramatic tale to the three girls.

"Are you kidding me?" Dan said. "Sounds like he's the *worst*."

"Alright, scholars, prepare your buzzers and your minds!" Mr. Garcia pointed to the tape on their tables to remind them to keep their hands behind it until they were ready to hit the buzzer during a question.

"But my left arm sometimes—" Dan started to remind

him, but Mr. Garcia nodded, to show he knew. He remembered Dan's arm might have to rest beyond the tape line.

Nina's knees jiggled up and down so much that Vi finally hissed, "Will you *stop*?"

And the scrimmage commenced.

"If a cube inscribed in a sphere has one side with a length of two units, what is the circumference of the sphere?" Mr. Garcia began.

"Of course he starts with a math question . . ." Marianne muttered to herself.

To her shock, Dan shushed her.

He'd never done anything like that before. Looking over at her teammates, she saw a ferocity in their eyes. They sat hunched over, as close to the tape as possible, and she could swear they looked like they might growl at the other team.

Vi got the math question right immediately, and they went into an extension round.

The Ermines huddled, scribbling, then showed one another their papers and with a quick nod, Nina buzzed in and gave the correct answer. And then two more times, the same routine. Marianne, not writing a thing, hearing only a swirl of numbers that went much too fast, allowed herself to glance toward Lucas, Ava, Jalilah, and Kylie.

Kylie waved once again, friendly as ever.

Lucas and Ava, their mouths rising in slight smiles, seemed to take note of Marianne's blank notebook. They whispered something to each other.

Next, a history question.

"Oh yeah, my time to shine! Bring on some Founding Fathers!" Lucas announced, rubbing his hands together.

"No commentary, please," Mr. Garcia said, ice cold.

"So sorry, I'm super sorry," Lucas said.

Ava and Jalilah giggled.

"Just like Andy," Dan whispered. "*So* cocky. It's not all Founding Fathers, you know . . ."

Marianne loved Dan. He was going to destroy Lucas.

"Ahem," Mr. Garcia quieted them. She wondered if he'd lose his cool again that day. Twice would be a lot for the typically inscrutable Mr. G. "Who led the Nez Perce tribe as it marched to Canada, fleeing the US Army?"

Lucas buzzed in so hard the buzzer flew off the table.

"Chief Joseph, baby!" Lucas hollered.

He stood up and slammed high fives to each of his teammates. "Team Hayes!" he shouted.

"Um, I object?" Jalilah said.

The four kids laughed. "Okay, okay, fair. Team . . . Einstein?"

"I like it," Kylie said.

At least Kylie wouldn't be able to dominate a subject like the other three. Marianne had a bad grades soul mate on the other side of the tables.

Next to her, Dan deflated.

"Lucky guess," Marianne whispered to him.

"He knows his stuff." Dan seemed to disappear into himself.

Oh no, he couldn't give up that easy! Marianne craned her neck to check on Nina. She had gone all in on her fingernails and her limbs bounced on overdrive.

Marianne felt so bad for her. Was she extra nervous because she'd seen them mocking Quiz Quest on Dan's post? It was all Marianne's fault. Marianne quickly wrote down a note and passed it to Nina. It read: *it's okay! stop worrying!!!*

Nina tilted her head forward and looked sadly at Marianne like there was nothing to be done.

Lucas retrieved the buzzer from the floor and performed a goofy dance with it all the way back to the table, to his twin's delight.

History questions came again, and Dan seemed to have disappeared.

The Stamp Act

Frederick Douglass

"Remember the Alamo!"

The Oregon Treaty

Lucas and Jalilah took turns answering, and Marianne could feel Vi seething from a seat over.

"Now for some cinema!" Mr. Garcia said.

Dan fidgeted in his chair, pulling himself up a bit.

"I'm back," he whispered to Marianne.

"Go, Dan," said Vi.

"I *just* created a memory palace for Best Actress Oscar winners," he went on, stretching his neck, preparing. "I've got every year down. Let's go." He stared right at Lucas.

"*No. Commentary,*" Mr. Garcia reminded them. "This will not be allowed at competition. Do you hear me?" he asked, clearly trying to restrain his annoyance.

They all nodded, Nina particularly vigorously.

"Here we go, here we go . . ." Dan said under his breath.

"Who was the youngest actor/actress to ever win an Academy Award?" Mr. Garcia asked.

As Dan jumped forward to buzz, Kylie hit the buzzer first.

"Tatum O'Neal for *Paper Moon*?" she answered in her sing-songy way.

"Correct," Mr. Garcia said. "Extension round."

"What?!" Dan whisper-screamed.

"I didn't like it," Kylie announced to everybody. "A lot of overacting, in my opinion."

"Go, Kylie! Go, Kylie! Go, Kylie!" Lucas cheered.

The four of them stood up and shook side to side in a victory dance.

"*Extension round!*" Mr. Garcia repeated.

And Kylie knew them all, every single one. She didn't confer with a single teammate, just buzzed right in. And she had loads of "commentary."

Delroy Lindo "was robbed and it's an actual crime." Sofia Coppola "just had a famous dad and that's not fair." And all movies were "better in the old days."

The "Go, Kylie" chants resumed.

Marianne must have looked shocked, because Kylie said,

"What? I want to be a screenwriter. You don't need *school* for that."

"Everyone! Focus!" Mr. Garcia snapped.

And the Ermines continued to lose.

If they couldn't beat a few classmates from Etheridge, how could they beat the mythical Remington?

Not only that, Marianne had to answer 10 percent of the questions. *Ten percent!*

Vi seemed to realize this at the same time as her, because during a victory celebration over Ava acing a few math problems, Vi seethed, "You *have* to answer *some!*"

"Okay, okay." Marianne nodded. "But I've only learned a few facts!" she added. "But okay!"

Marianne used her hands to physically push her ears out and forward to force herself to take in every word Mr. Garcia said.

She tried to ignore the muffled laughter a few feet across from her.

"The Grand Canyon National Park is in which state?"

Nina buzzed in immediately, but she was so nervous that she had to hit the buzzer several times to make an actual buzz sound, and then she said, "Oops, oops, oops," over and over again, to whispers and hidden giggles from the other side.

"Arizona?" she answered, her voice a peep.

"Correct."

"Finally," she heard Vi grumble.

If Vi kept talking to Nina like that, it would make Nina's stress so much worse.

As the Ermines worked through the extension round, Marianne wondered if she'd even know a *single* answer. Out of thousands of trivia answers, how could she think the few she knew would come up?

"What is the largest organ in the bod—"

"The skin," Jalilah said, waving her arms in the air to emphasize her win. Kylie clapped. They got every anatomy question, working as a team and cheering after each "correct." They laughed and high-fived and made up funny Team Einstein victory rituals, and when Marianne looked over at the Ermines, all she saw was . . . well, misery.

Vi glowered. Nina whispered something to herself, her eyes closed. Dan drank some Gatorade and smacked his lips, angry.

The three of them had been doing fine at first. But they were thrown off so easily. They just didn't seem like a *team*.

And Marianne knew . . . they were going to lose.

"This is, like, actually not that bad!" Jalilah sang to Mr. Garcia and the rest of them as they achieved more correct answers.

And then, just like that, out of the waterfall of questions, Marianne heard Mr. Garcia ask:

What is the proper term for a group of the mammal felis silvestris, *commonly referred to as wildcats?*

Oh my God. She knew it! She actually knew it! Zoology! The flash cards!

Marianne smacked the buzzer.

Nina, Dan, and Vi snapped their heads her way.

"It's—" she said.

And she saw Jalilah watching her. Kylie, watching her. Ava, watching her, ready to laugh, her mouth already breaking out into a grin. Lucas, snickering silently.

The comments. *The comments.*

omg omg she is so stuuupiiiiid this is amazing
lol this is so embarrassing i cant even handle it

And then her mouth wouldn't move.

"You have to answer now," Nina told her, gesturing to go faster.

"I know it, I know it . . ." She'd just read this. It was on the card, but it wasn't the parade of elephants. What was it?

"Time is up. You have to answer," Vi said.

She could feel all their eyes on her.

"No, I know it. It's . . . It's right there—" She pointed to her forehead.

"Time—"

"Come on, Marianne," Vi said. "You know this one."

Vi had seen her text. She knew she knew it.

And she did. She remembered it. She knew the right answer. *A destruction.*

Lucas let out a snort, but at Mr. Garcia's immediate glare, he coughed, covering it up.

"Uuuum . . ." Marianne said, spacey, bubbly, cute, stupid. "Aw, a bunch of wildcats sounds so cute. Maybe . . . a cuddle?" And she giggled.

"Baaahaha," Lucas laughed.

Mr. Garcia stood up, opened the door, and said "Out. Mr. Hayes?" He pointed to the hallway. "Out."

Lucas and Ava left, laughing.

Kylie and Jalilah got up, but Mr. Garcia told them they could stay and do another few minutes of practice.

He sighed. "What a day today, hmm?" he said to the facts on his page. He rubbed his temples. After a beat, he added, "My apologies to everyone for the commotion." Another beat. And then, "The correct answer is 'a destruction.'"

"Ooh cool!" Kylie exclaimed. "That was a hard one," she said to Marianne, her lipstick shimmery, her eyes kind.

Marianne looked up at the ceiling. It had so many brown lines, like cracks, in it. Would the whole building come tumbling down one day?

"Excellent effort, Ms. Blume," Mr. Garcia said. "Keep going for that buzzer."

When the scrimmage of horrors finally ended, and Kylie and Jalilah skipped off to their next activities or to home, and Mr. Garcia went to refill his water glass, Vi turned to the team.

What would she put them down about?

First she laid into Dan. "You knew Plymouth Rock. Why didn't you answer?"

He shrugged.

"You just gave up again!" And to Nina, Vi said, "What is even going on with you? Do we have to worry about you getting to ten percent answered, too? I don't get it, you have some of the best grades in the school!"

"I know, I know." Nina shook her head.

Vi turned to Marianne.

She looked like she was about to say something but decided against it.

Then Nina spoke. "Can you believe that awful Lucas? He was making fun of us! Honestly, it was, like, *freaking me out*!"

"Yeah, well, he was here for the purpose of mocking us," Dan said. "And beating us was just icing on the cake."

"Did you see the comments he wrote? I can't handle this," Nina nearly cried. "It's not worth it!" Nina dug into a fingernail. "Marianne, you shouldn't have to deal with that."

Marianne, thinking of Nina's shaking during scrimmage, rummaged inside her backpack.

"Here." Marianne handed Nina a fidget toy. She had a couple in her backpack. "Take this. My mom thought they'd help me. They're kind of fun."

"Thanks," Nina said, taking the toy and immediately popping the three bubbles on it over and over. "But am I right? That was super mean what he did, wasn't it?"

"Yeah, not my favorite person," Dan added, more

depressed than Marianne had ever seen him. "I really thought my memory palace would help me." He shook his head. "It just disintegrated in the face of Lucas Vader."

"What's a memory palace?" Marianne asked.

And Dan, still sullen, told her it was "a method for memorization that involves imagining a very specific location and visualizing placing data in said location, usually using some sort of wordplay or association."

"Whoa," Marianne said.

These kids were so smart, how could they have lost so badly against a group with no experience in Quiz Quest at all?

"Trivia culture is a whole world, man," Dan went on. "There are so many strategies. I could teach you some."

"That's what we need," Vi said, pounding a fist on her desk and standing up. "We need more teaching, more practice."

"Not that my strategies worked . . ." Dan added, picking up his pencil and twirling it through each finger on his right hand. "I have failed. Again," he added.

"Ugh, this Greenfield Prep thing. Will you get over Greenfield?" Nina snapped. "What? Is *this* school so bad?"

"It's not great!" Dan snapped back.

"Guys, maybe you just—" Marianne almost said "need to have more *fun*," like Lucas, Jalilah, Ava, and Kylie did, but Mr. Garcia came back in the room.

"I made an error today," Mr. Garcia said. Instead of sitting at the teacher's desk, he pulled up a seat next to all of them. She couldn't believe it. Somehow it made him look much smaller.

"I should've planned that . . . better," he admitted, adjusting his tie at the top. But that was all he said. He looked like he didn't know what else to add, how to fix it. "Ms. Blume," he said.

Oh no. "What?" she answered.

"Are you alright?"

She forced a grin. "Totally!"

He nodded. His eyes stopped for a moment on Nina's Pop-it, but then he returned to the matter at hand. "We need to find cohesion." He interlaced his fingers and clenched them together. "As a team."

Yes, exactly. Finally, he was giving them useful information.

"We discussed this weeks ago, but, Vi, as team captain, I'd like you to start incorporating those goals into the practice. And Thursday we scrimmage again—just us. Yes?" he asked all of them.

They all nodded, and he gathered his things as they sat in silence.

Dan began getting ready to go. Nina sat there, using the fidget toy. Vi texted someone.

As Mr. Garcia left and the door closed on him, he added, "Keep your spirits up, scholars."

And practice ended.

"When someone says, 'Keep your spirits up,' you know things are really bad," Nina moaned.

"Yes," Vi said, drained. "That was very, very bad."

They all started to get ready to go, moving slowly, as if they were sore after a brutal beating in a sports game.

"We have to add another practice each week," Vi said as she organized and reorganized the things in her backpack to make them all fit perfectly.

Dan started to protest, but Vi went on. "No, no, listen— I'm being . . . I'm being nice. I'm being *positive* here, okay?"

"No one has ever sounded less positive while saying 'positive' . . ." Dan observed, and Nina and Marianne giggled.

"We have to work harder." Vi looked to each of them, checking in. "In a *positive* way," she assured them. "We have a teammate who is new to this, and we've gotten a little thrown off course. It's okay . . . It's okay." She was clearly trying to convince herself. "Besides adding a practice, we should help her with her schoolwork in order to maximize her time."

"I can't do Wednesdays," Dan said. "I have PT."

"Done, no problem," Vi said. "But if we're going to win Regionals, we need Marianne to be on the top of her game. And"—she looked to Dan and Nina—"we need to be on top of ours. We're not cutting it."

True, they definitely were not cutting it. They hardly stood a chance. After viewing that catastrophe, Marianne couldn't believe she'd ever thought they could win. Even Kylie beat them!

But still. These kids were her only chance.

Vi pulled her ponytail tighter and slicked back the front of her hair.

"Tonight, I'll continue my sessions with Marianne, but we have to begin group sessions off the clock, too," she said.

"Maybe we can, like, have a group hang, also?" Marianne offered, thinking of the fun she saw the kids across from them having that day, the ease of friendship and no pressure. "For 'cohesion,' right?"

"No time for that," Vi answered. She checked the clock above their heads and said, "See you all on the phone."

"Okay," Marianne said without thinking.

They walked to the door and Vi opened it for them, motioning for Dan and Nina to go ahead. When Marianne walked out, Vi grabbed her by the arm.

"It doesn't matter what Lucas Hayes thinks," Vi said.

"Aw, he's just joking around," Marianne said, stepping forward to go.

But Vi held on.

"You are *not a joke*," Vi said.

And with that, she let go of Marianne.

"Losing's not an option!" Vi hollered as she sped off, past Nina and Dan, the first one out the door and out of their sight by the time they exited the school.

8

ONE WEEK INTO HER tutoring sessions with Nina, Dan, and Vi, and her family dinners had morphed into review sessions.

"Did you know there's an island called Brain Island?" she asked them. "It's in Georgia. Not the state, though! Georgia is also the name of a country. And did you know that the rain that falls today is the exact same water that *dinosaurs drank*?"

"That one I knew," her dad said, scooping the mujadara he'd made onto their plates.

"I wonder if a triceratops drank this black cherry seltzer," Marianne examined, as if the can would have the answer.

"I don't think it works *quite* like that, bud." Lillian's seltzer was gone, so she grabbed Marianne's and took a swig.

"Oh, and did you know that one time, Napoleon was attacked by *bunnies*? Like . . . that's a thing that *happened*. In *history*!" Marianne squealed with delight. "Why didn't they teach me that in school before?"

"*That's* a fact for Quiz Quest?" her mom asked. "C'est bizarre."

"Well, no, it's not, it's just something my friend Dan told me to help me memorize some dates about Napoleon," she explained.

"Which dates?" Her mom lit up. She loved French history. French had been the first language she'd "fallen in love with."

Marianne paused. "I can't remember. But I'll review," she promised.

"If I were you, I'd remember bunnies over dates, too," her dad admitted. "You know, I wasn't such a great student myself. Not naturally, anyway," he said, starting on the speech he'd given them a billion times.

"We know," Lillian and Marianne said at the same time.

That didn't stop him.

"But I got by. Because I knew, to achieve what I wanted, I had to. I didn't have to like it, but if I wanted to make a career in a symphony in New York or elsewhere, I'd have to learn how to work the system to get there. I'd have to earn a certain GPA to get into certain music programs, right? That didn't mean I *liked* it. But I did it. So, for example, learning the dates may not be interesting, but school is a *system*, just like everything else in life, and—"

"You have to 'master the system,'" Marianne and Lillian recited together once again, before falling into giggles at how well they knew their dad.

"Okay, okay, so I've said it a few times, but it's *true*." He took a sip of wine and patted his lips with a napkin.

"Dan and Vi say it's easier to memorize something if you really make it 'come to life' for yourself first," she told her dad, ignoring his lecture.

"Hence, the bunnies," her mom said.

"Oh yeah, I remember!" Marianne perked up. "The date was 1812! Napoleon marched to Russia in 1812." She grabbed some more cucumbers and piled them atop her lentils. "System mastered!" she added toward her dad, who grinned at her.

"Nice!" Lillian said. "I told you that you got this."

"Also," Marianne giggled, "he was really, really short, so there's this thing named after him where short guys want to be tougher to make up for being short and it's called—"

"The Napoleon complex," Lillian finished for her. "Yeah, we know, Mar. Dad has it."

"Hey now!" her mom said, choking on some food as she laughed.

"It's true," her dad agreed.

She loved when her family wasn't stressed out, when they could joke and tease one another and relax. Plus, she had more to tell them.

"Wait, I haven't told you guys my favorite thing from yesterday. Dan is full of these fun facts. It's wild. Did you know that a minnow has teeth *in its throat*?"

"A lot of these don't sound so . . . scholarly to me," her dad said, skeptical.

"Zoology is science, Dad," Marianne said. She stood up to go grab another drink. "In fact, I think I'd like to be a zoologist one day."

"Awesome!" Lillian gave Marianne a high five on her way past her to the fridge.

"How is the math going?" her dad asked.

"You really know how to bring down a party." Marianne grabbed the seltzer and returned to her seat, pulling her feet up onto the chair.

"I'm just asking!" he said. "Do they do the math you're working on with Mom in the competitions or no?"

This was another way to ask if she was doing too much Quiz Quest and not enough homework. Anyone could see that.

"Vi works with me on it, too, right, Mom?"

Her mom lifted a water glass. "To Vi! She's quite something. Did I tell you this thirteen-year-old girl called me up on the phone?" she added to Marianne's dad. "She wanted to assure me she'd help Marianne with her work."

"Yeah, she's something, that's for sure," Marianne grumbled.

"What's her deal?" Lillian asked, swigging from Marianne's new drink.

"Hey! Back off! I don't know, she's kind of mysterious,"

Marianne said. "She's obsessed with grades and all that."
Marianne gave Lillian a pointed stare.

"*You* back off," Lillian warned her.

"And she usually seems sad," Marianne went on. "And she wears black pants and a collared shirt every single day in different colors. Like she's in a uniform."

"That's a 'successful people' thing," Lillian told her. "Like Steve Jobs wore the same outfit every day."

"It's so you don't waste a moment of your genius worrying about what to wear," their dad explained. "Although," he added to himself, as he passed around the salad. "I guess Steve Jobs's genius ended up with thousands of people working in sweatshops, so maybe we all would've been a little better off if he'd struggled between the blue button-up or wool sweater . . ."

"More, please?" Her mom held out a plate toward the serving bowl. "Girls, listen to me. If you take any advice I've ever given you to heart, make it this: Marry a man who knows how to cook."

Her dad blew a kiss at her mom.

"Or a woman," Lillian said, holding out her bowl as well.

"Of course," her mom and dad said at the same time.

"I want to get married in Costa Rica." Marianne pulled her hair to the side and started a braid. "Did you know that Costa Rica doesn't have a military? They use their money for schools!"

"Absolutely not," her dad said, pouring himself a

second glass of wine. "I'm against destination weddings. You shouldn't make your guests travel that far. It's insensitive and classist."

Her dad loved to argue.

"Dad, you'd miss your own daughter's wedding to make a point?" Lillian challenged him.

Lillian and her dad were a lot alike.

They debated Marianne's imaginary wedding until dessert ended.

As they cleared the table, Marianne told her mom that Vi was going to come by that weekend for some studying sessions.

"So *she* can do my math homework with me," Marianne explained.

"I think we need to stick to our schedule," her mom insisted.

Marianne didn't fight back. She wasn't like Lillian. She didn't always have the words to explain why she disagreed. But for some reason, work with Vi was so much better than work with her mom, which was funny because her mom loved her and Vi didn't even *like* her.

That Sunday, Vi came to her house on foot.

She not only had on her heavy backpack, she carried a large stack of books as well.

Marianne looked up and down the street for a parent's car.

"I walk everywhere," Vi explained.

"Spring finally feels real, huh?" Marianne said, taking in

a long breath of the warming air. In front of her porch, the daffodils were in full bloom. It made everything better.

Vi looked like she had no idea what Marianne was talking about, and she also seemed to be waiting for permission to even come up the steps.

"We can't be inside," Marianne said. "Not on the first truly warm day. Park? I'll bring some snacks. One sec."

She ran inside to find Lillian sizing up Vi through the window.

"I see what you mean about 'sad,'" Lillian said.

Marianne grabbed her backpack and a towel in case the park was wet, and she led Vi the five blocks to Roseway Park. She lay the towel on a bench and they pulled out some folders.

"Flash cards first?" Marianne asked. "Then homework?"

"Which is more fun for you?" Vi took off her sweater and tied it around her waist.

"Definitely the Vi lectures. Flash cards," she said, reaching in her bag for them.

"Then we start with homework." Vi grabbed Marianne's papers and searched through them.

"Oh man," Marianne groused.

"This is great," Vi said, looking over Marianne's English work. "This will really help you," she said. "It's largely a review of concepts you should know by now, anyway. Symbolism. Imagery. This won't take long."

They went through the comprehension questions and

definitions together until a suspicious Vi asked Marianne, "Have you read the book?"

Marianne looked toward the toddlers splashing in a big puddle by the soccer field.

"Some of it," she said. "I've tried."

"You have to read the book," Vi said in a clipped tone. She shook her head and muttered something. Probably a curse word. Marianne noticed that Vi cursed a lot. It was the only not-proper thing about her. "Read it now." She held out her own copy to Marianne.

"Are you serious? We're supposed to study."

"Reading *is* studying. We have all day. Read it now." The book remained pointed at Marianne until she finally took it and turned to chapter five.

Inside its pages were highlighted sections and notes written in pencil.

For over an hour, Marianne sat with her legs pulled up on the bench, forcing herself to ignore the yells of the kids playing and the twittering of the spring birds. She blew gum bubbles and let them pop. Vi hunkered down on her own work. Eventually, Vi told her she could stop.

"Nothing is ever going to happen if you always put it off for later," Vi said. "So that was one step."

"One fact, one step. You should write a how-to book on school one day," Marianne told her.

"I have bigger plans." And Vi dove into algebra.

After another hour, Marianne begged for a break.

"It's only been a couple hours," Vi protested.

Marianne slapped her own cheeks and pulled down on the bags under her eyes. "Please, please, please."

Vi sighed. "Fine. But we have a lot to do."

Marianne put their things away. "Let's go for a walk. A short one."

Vi rolled her eyes but followed.

Marianne pulled out some more gum and handed one to Vi.

Vi shook her head no. She whipped out her phone and texted, falling a step or two behind Marianne every half a block and hustling to catch up.

"Ooh, the lilacs will be here in a couple weeks!" Marianne squealed.

Vi continued to text.

"Someone made a chalk mandala!" Marianne pointed it out to Vi, who looked up, said, "Cool," and returned to her phone.

They went the perimeter of the park and returned to their bench.

"Is that Addison on there?"

"How'd you know?" Vi asked her.

"You said she was your only friend." Marianne shrugged, worried she'd embarrass Vi by bringing up Vi's admission that rainy day.

Vi put down her phone. "Yeah. She was. She's gone now." Vi waved away a fly in front of her face.

"Looks like you two are still in touch?" Marianne eyed the phone.

"For now," Vi said. "Addison already has new friends in her new school. That's kind of how it goes with someone like her."

"Trust me—I know how bad it feels when a friend is moving on," Marianne said.

"I'm not possessive or something," Vi snapped. "She should enjoy her life."

"Sorry!" Marianne shook her head. Vi was impossible.

"I just miss her," Vi murmured.

"I bet," Marianne said.

"What are they doing?" Vi gestured toward a couple of skateboarders in the parking lot across the way. "They're trying to do a caveman but they're not holding the nose of the board. See? That one kid has his hand halfway down."

Marianne watched the kids—probably around ten years old—topple off their skateboards again and again.

"Oh no." Vi smacked her forehead. "Ha. Now this is just funny. They're attempting a bomb drop before they've mastered the caveman. Hilarious. Anyway"—she turned back to Marianne—"who's the friend who's ditching you?"

"Huh?" Marianne was still trying to figure out what a "bomb drop" was.

"You said you knew what it was like." Vi pulled the end of her ponytail in front of her chest and fiddled with the ends of her hair.

161

"Yeah. It's probably nothing. It's just . . ." And Marianne found herself telling Vi all about how Skyla was in different classes this year, and how at first it hadn't seemed like there was any distance between them, but these days she was always with Julie or Zara, whether in person or texting them, and if Marianne didn't make it to high school, it just felt like she would lose Skyla to those girls forever.

"Hmmm," Vi said, relaxing against the back of the bench. Normally she sat with perfect posture, Marianne had noticed, even outside of school. "At least you can make *new* friends, though. I mean, you've known Nina and Dan for two seconds and they'd already die for you. Everybody likes you."

Marianne did her best attempt at raising one eyebrow. "They're not just laughing at me? I'm not a joke to them?"

"That, too," Vi admitted, and Marianne couldn't help but feel a sting, "But they also like you. Both things can be true."

"Maybe," Marianne said.

"I can't take this anymore," Vi said, and she hopped up and went toward the parking lot.

Marianne scrambled to get all their things together and follow, but Vi hollered out, "Stay there! I'll be right back!"

From across the soccer field, Marianne watched Vi walk up to the two boys. She pointed to the skateboard. One of them, cowering before her, handed it over. To Marianne's utter astonishment, Vi jogged, threw the board down to the ground, and, without missing a beat, landed smoothly upon

162

it. Then she did the move in slow motion and put the boys' hands onto the front of the board, showing them how. After a few unsuccessful attempts, one of the boys seemed to get it right.

"I did it!" Marianne heard him yell.

The boys bumped fists and one of them gave Vi a hug. She saw Vi harden, and then relax into giving him a pat on the back.

She returned to their bench.

"They had to master the caveman first," Vi said as she caught her breath a bit. "Everything is about building on the next thing, building upon one skill from the last skill. It's like using training wheels before riding a bike." She sat back down and adjusted her shirt. "Anyway, where were we?"

"How do you know how to do that?" Marianne asked.

Vi shrugged. "My granddad bought me a skateboard once. I like to learn things."

Marianne watched the kids in the parking lot figure out the trick and proceed to do it over and over again.

"You're good at everything," Marianne said, impressed.

"Not everything," Vi sighed.

And Marianne thought she knew what Vi meant. Vi wasn't great at making friends.

"Hey, why did you pretend you didn't know the answer in scrimmage?" Vi spoke loudly all of a sudden, as if she'd been holding this in and finally had to say something. "Why'd you say 'a cuddle'?"

"Ha. Because I forgot the word and I thought 'cuddle' was kind of funny, so I—"

"No you didn't forget it," Vi said, dead serious. "You knew it."

Marianne watched two kids on the swings, each yelling that they were higher in the air than the other one. Both at exactly the same height.

"You're not as spacey as you act in class," Vi accused her. "Why?"

Vi saw it. Vi saw through her.

"Lorelai Wheeler," Marianne reported. She'd never told this to a soul before. But she'd also never confessed to anyone that she couldn't learn.

Marianne picked off the last bit of polish on her left thumb and added, "I never really thought about it before. But that's what it was."

"Who?" Vi leaned in an inch closer.

"In sixth grade there was this girl named Lorelai Wheeler. She was a little like me, ya know? Bad at school. But, like . . . prettier. And she had great clothes and nothing seemed to bug her. And she was *not* smart. I mean, no way was she getting good grades. Like, she didn't know a *thing*. If she did one sheet of homework in her life, I'd honestly be shocked."

"I cannot imagine," Vi said almost inaudibly.

Marianne kept going. She watched the breeze twist the ends of the tree branches this way and that. "I used to, like, stress out when I got stuff wrong. Which was always. Like . . .

I would feel kind of sick. I knew what people thought of me. I guess I hoped sixth grade would be different? Middle school? But, like, Lorelai blanked out on her entire times tables—even the twos, the threes—and the whole class raised their eyebrows like 'Wow,' but Lorelai? She just giggled and shrugged. Or, like, blew a bubble of the gum she was always chewing."

Marianne could feel Vi giving her a look, but she kept her sights set on the leaves swaying on the trees.

"Sometimes she'd answer so wrong, and she'd just pop up and curtsy real quick or scrunch up her face like 'Whoops!'" Marianne laughed at the thought. "It was funny. And everybody laughed. People just loved her."

"So you did it, too," Vi stated.

"Yeah," Marianne said, her voice airy, like she couldn't quite admit it even though she already had. "Yeah, after a couple really bad days, I started to do it, too."

Marianne didn't know how to explain it.

Lorelai had moved by the end of the year. Her mom was in the army, and Lorelai told them she was always moving. Texas that time. She hoped Lorelai was okay.

In Marianne's silence, Vi moved on. "Well, that's how I know we still have a chance at winning. Because all the 'I couldn't listen because my mind was on lip gloss'? I figured it was mostly for show."

So she'd said it. What they both knew. What was left for Marianne to say?

 165

Vi returned to their papers, to the cards. She lifted up a math folder and waved it back and forth. "It's time. And it's getting cold again."

"I know! Why are there only pockets of wonderful each day?" Marianne shivered and looked to the skies. The once cloudless blue had turned smoke gray.

They headed back to Marianne's house and hunkered down in her room.

It was always strange to have a new kid in your space. You wanted to explain stuff that might seem odd or point out things they might like.

"That's my crafts supply collection," she told Vi as Vi placed her things on top of Marianne's plastic cabinet.

"Fun," Vi said, though she looked like she found it anything but that.

"My mom is going to teach me macramé when this school year is over," she said. "I also want to learn to knit a sweater. Check out my shirt rug!" Marianne lifted up her tangerine masterpiece.

"Very domestic," Vi said. "It's flash-card time."

Marianne sat on the opposite end of her bed and prepared herself. She liked that for this she didn't need notes and she didn't need to answer a bunch of questions. She just listened and repeated and listened and repeated and eventually her brain absorbed it. Well, some of it. She had a couple of dozen facts down as second nature as her home address at that point, and a few she knew only as well as her cousins' birthdays—hit or miss.

But as they rounded the twenty-minute study mark, the mystery of Vi distracted her.

"Hey. Will you be okay if we don't win?" Marianne asked. The closer they were getting, and the harder they tried, the more Marianne worried what would happen when she inevitably let down the team on the big day.

"Will *you*?" Vi asked.

Marianne didn't know.

Vi pulled up a flash card and said, "One more thing."

And Marianne learned it.

And in the three more weeks that went by before Regionals, those "things" grew and grew. She picked up more "things" from homework, too. The math was hard. So hard. But she felt like she could manage *some* of it. At least in Mr. Garcia's class, if not in Quiz Quest, where math questions hit her like a slingshot and Dan and Vi and Nina scribbled away, answering them before Marianne could figure out which step to start with and how to write it down. It just went too fast.

Sometimes, on their Google Meets, Dan grabbed his old puppets and performed the history for her, putting the character on his stronger arm and bouncing it around in long monologues. He had a lot of fun using a king puppet as George Washington. "It's exactly what he didn't want. Get it?" Dan joked.

Nina made Marianne memorize geography songs on YouTube, and they cracked up together at the goofy cartoons that went along with them. Knowing the name of each little spot in the world somehow made the globe feel much larger and smaller at the exact same time. But learning the names of countries was different from *memorizing* them, and she could only get through one-third of most of the songs until she got lost. Still, Nina assured her she was doing great. "Why didn't you learn this before?" she asked her once.

Marianne didn't quite know.

Marianne jokingly called herself Nina's "blow-off-steam advisor." Obviously, Nina couldn't compete at her best if she was stressing so much. So in order to relax between study sessions, they started FaceTiming while watching *Infinity Galaxy* together, a show about a group of the last survivors of an intergalactic war forced to live together on a single spaceship that was destined to self-destruct in five years. When Dan found out they'd watched it without him, he joked that he was "deeply hurt" and insisted on joining in the binge.

"I'm the sci-fi guy!" he said, and he caught up in one night, joining them for episode five.

But Marianne knew that in order to have even a *chance* at winning, they couldn't just include three members in the blowing-off-steam club. They had to have all four. So soon enough, Vi was calling in with them to finish up the season.

"This is *highly* unrealistic," was Vi's first commentary, which elicited hoots of laughter from the rest of the Ermines.

In almost every tutoring session, Dan liked to show off his knowledge to them.

"I just finished my Best Actor Oscar memory palace," he told them. "Test me."

"Nineteen twenty-two," Nina spat out as fast as she could.

"Whoops, sorry, no Oscars back then," he said. "Try again."

"Nineteen seventy-eight," Marianne joined in.

"Richard Dreyfuss, *The Goodbye Girl*," he answered immediately. "I prefer him in *Jaws*," he added.

"When you talk about 'memory palaces,'" Marianne told him, "I think of, like . . . a castle filled with all my old memories. Sounds kind of nice . . . But also awful?"

She imagined walking into a glimmering, Disney World–like palace, where when she entered the dining room, she could relive the first day of sixth grade—Skyla grasping her hand on the way in, convinced Marianne would ditch her for all the kids she'd chatted with at orientation. Skyla whispering to her, "You can't leave me," and Skyla beaming every time Marianne said to the other kids, "Oh, hey, you have to meet my best friend, Skyla. She's the best person in the world." Eventually Skyla had loosened her grip on Marianne's palm.

Dan told her all about the history of memory palaces.

"A whole bunch of smart people figuring out ways to be smarter," she said to him. "My mom would love it."

"I think you're confusing 'smart' with 'enjoys sitting

169

around and memorizing lists.'" Dan brushed his floppy ginger hair out of his eyes.

From behind him on the screen, out of sight, Marianne heard someone copy what Dan said in a mocking voice and then add, "Is this your girlfriend or something?"

"*Get out, Andy!*" Dan growled.

Most of her sessions with Dan ended that way.

And the majority of her sessions with Nina ended with Marianne convincing Nina to show off some ballet moves. She was really good! Marianne cheered her on through the screen as Nina attempted trickier and trickier spins.

Vi was the only one she studied with in person.

She came over on weekends, and Marianne's family took the opportunity to chat with her. When Vi found out her dad was a musician, she almost leapt out of her chair.

"Are you using him to prepare for Quest?" Her head snapped to Marianne.

"Yeah, Mar, why aren't you using my wide berth of knowledge?" her dad had said, and although Marianne had rolled her eyes, she did let him play her some of the songs Vi determined "most commonly showed up in competition."

She hated to admit it after all her years of asking him to change whatever song he had on in the car, but she really liked some of them, especially a song called "La donna è mobile." She added it to a new playlist, until one morning her mom walked by her room, popped her head in, and said, "Just don't Google the words. Yikes."

It turned out the song translated to "Woman Is Unstable."

"Dan, Nina," Marianne told them on video chat that night. "The lyrics are," and she read to them from her phone, "'like the feather in the wind she changes tone and thought. Always a lovable, cute face, in tears or smiling, it tells lies.'" She looked to them for a reaction. "Can you believe my dad listens to that stuff?"

"Unfortunately, when you delve into the classics, you find some mighty troublesome content," Dan said drily.

"Yeah, *tell me about it*," Nina added.

"It's so cool that your dad is into classical music," Nina gushed to Marianne's shock.

After one of those chats, Marianne had gone into her mom's room and announced, "Hi. Ya know what just hit me? If school were only for sharing cool and interesting things all day, maybe more kids would love it."

Her mom put down the book she was reading and pushed up her glasses onto her hair.

"But, honey," her mom said, patting the bed for her to come and sit, "that *is* what school is."

Marianne sat. Her mom's decades-old purple-and-blue quilt felt softer than any material in the world. "It *can't* be that way when it's on a rushed schedule, where you have to 'get' everything by a certain time of the day, or when you have to be on the spot all the time, or when—"

Her mom cuddled her up in her arms. "I'm so sorry it's felt that way to you." She ran her fingers through Marianne's tangled, post-bun hair. "Hey. Listen. High school will be different."

And for the first time since that fateful day a few weeks back when Ms. Clarke had told her she may not make it to ninth grade, Marianne truly believed that maybe—just maybe—she could.

***

Days before Regionals, Marianne came home from practice to hear a smooth, cooing harmony coming from Lillian's room.

As always, she threw open Lillian's bedroom door without knocking. Even though she hated it when Lillian did it to her, it was almost like tradition. If Lillian ever did knock, Marianne would worry she'd been replaced by a cyborg.

Lillian sat in her desk chair across from a girl with half her head shaved. Both girls held guitars.

Lillian contorted her fingers around the strings, cursed, then said to the girl, "It's taking me forever to get this. Argh! Let me try again."

"Hey," Marianne said, making her presence known.

"Oh hey," Lillian greeted her. "This is Harper. Harper—my little sister."

"Marianne." Marianne waved. "You doing book club

here? Where's everyone else?" Marianne asked Lillian. They usually gathered at school.

"Huh?" Harper said. She continued messing around with the strings, plucking and playing even as they spoke, like she was writing a song while having a conversation.

Why hadn't she invited Harper to Literary Lionesses? What was going on?

"I'm actually going to be singing with her band for their next show," Lillian told her.

"Oh!" Marianne couldn't believe it. "You didn't tell me!"

"Yeah, Lil and I are working on a *Jane Eyre* concept," Harper reported.

Lil?

Harper reminded Marianne of what you'd draw if someone asked you what it meant to be "cool." She looked like an asteroid could hit their block and she wouldn't flinch, she'd just keep strumming along, probably inspired to write an asteroid song. She had a flawless sienna complexion and the kind of eyelashes that just *couldn't* be real, but you knew they *were*. She wore a silver crescent moon necklace.

"So you're practicing?" Marianne asked Lillian.

Lillian nodded. She wanted Marianne to leave. Marianne could see it.

Marianne said bye.

The songbirds continued. Marianne stood outside the door and listened:

Creeping from the red room/I see too many ghosts/Oh, Mr. Rochester/Why do I love you the most/Why do I love you the most

Marianne didn't know if the music was good or bad or neither.

She went to her room and blasted Pink Floyd.

And she wondered what Skyla was doing.

It had been months since Skyla sent her a pic of her clothes laid out on the bed with the text **Good?** Usually her choices were okay, but Marianne gave her tips. Nothing major, just no patterns-on-patterns or Sunday school–like dresses.

She peeked out her bedroom window at the redbrick wall that made up the side of Skyla's house. Should she wait until dark and flash the flashlight into Skyla's bathroom window to get her attention, like they did in the old days? They thought using lights would be like the movies, where neighbor kids use Morse code and stuff, but the two of them just ended up annoying Skyla's dads by waving huge flashlights in their rooms in what must have been Morse code gibberish.

Marianne took her cell phone light and pointed it at Skyla's house.

No response, of course. The shades were shut, anyway.

Oh, Mr. Rochester . . . competed with Pink Floyd's "Wish You Were Here."

"Could you quiet down? I'm trying to study!" she hollered toward Lillian's room.

They must not have heard her.

Marianne turned off her music and picked up her flash cards.

Thomas Jefferson, John Adams, and James Monroe, all died on July 4, the card read. For some reason, that made her feel sad.

She texted Vi.

study?

Her phone lit up right away.

always

***

On their last practice before Regionals, Vi told the group that they had one more area they had to address.

"Mr. Garcia said we need 'cohesion as a team,' if I'm remembering right," she said.

"Yeah, that was it," Nina confirmed.

"Yes!" Marianne cheered. She'd been waiting for this.

"So we all have to work better together." She looked at each one of them before saying, "Okay? Like, no fighting. Not on game day. Got it?"

"Um . . . That's it?" Dan said quietly.

A clipped "no fighting" was not going to be enough to fix what she'd seen in practices and in the unforgettable Einsteins scrimmage.

"I mean, we get along fine when we watch *Infinity Galaxy*," Marianne said. "Just . . . maybe we should think of competition time as an *Infinity Galaxy* binge watch, yeah?"

They didn't stand a chance if they bickered on the day of Regionals. Nina would freak out and Vi would be too sour to band them all together and Dan would zone out in defiance. They *had* to get along. They had to work as one.

Outside the class door they heard some wild laughter and the skid of sneakers, then nothing but the awkward silence of their group.

Vi just nodded, with a closed-mouth attempt at an encouraging smile.

"But I do think that TV fundamentally wastes time," Vi couldn't stop herself from saying. "I'm just reiterating that, but it's fine."

"Oh my lord," Dan groaned, throwing his head back in frustration.

"It's all said and done now, though, anyway!" Vi tried to smooth over her misstep and move on. "So let's begin!" She pulled out her folder with scrimmage questions for the day.

But Nina wouldn't drop it. "Would you just *stop*?" she said.

"What?" Vi asked askance.

"You put so much pressure on us, geez," Nina squeaked. She fiddled with the edges of her long sleeves. "Guilting us for watching TV? I thought you said you were going to be positive now!"

"I'm not just working us hard for *me*, you know!" Vi insisted. "Marianne has to win. And I thought *you guys* wanted to win!"

176

"Seems like we're setting ourselves up for a real Simone Biles situation here," Dan added calmly. "Trying to be the best and then the stress kills us on the big jump."

"I don't think you understand the mechanics of gymnastics *or* mental health," Vi hissed.

"Simone Biles is the greatest athlete of all time, Dan, can you not use her as an example here? Agh!" Nina did one of her near-daily facepalms.

"Okay, guys?" Marianne raised her hand.

Vi paused. "Marianne?"

"Um, I really appreciate all you guys have taught me the past couple weeks. But . . . maybe I can teach you something that could help with—ya know—'cohesion'?" Marianne bit her lip. Would Vi accept?

"Like that compliments ritual you did the other week?" Vi asked. "I'm not sure, I— Hmm. What would you teach us?" Vi asked, checking the clock.

"Team spirit." Marianne grinned. She took out her lip gloss and reupped. Then she held out her hands to bring everyone closer together. She pulled her jeans up a bit, shaking her tush to get comfy in them. "Every team needs one thing. Do you guys know what that is?"

They stared at her blankly. And to be fair, she hadn't been on a team since Rec & Ed softball in fourth and fifth grade, so she didn't know, either. But she could improvise.

"A secret handshake, of course," she found herself saying.

"Oh, I don't know . . ." Vi stammered to come up with a

reason not to do it, but Marianne let the protestations slide right off of her.

Marianne created the first move, a hand slap followed by a "psssh" noise as she twirled around.

Nina giggled.

Marianne tried the step with Dan first.

He did it in his own way, his arm crutches spinning around him as he turned on his more stable foot.

"Nailed it!" she cheered. "Now you make up the next one."

Dan rolled his head in a circle.

"Perfect," she said. They put their moves together.

Nina, usually so tightly wound, morphed entirely as she added a graceful, ballet-esque arm in/arm out element.

Vi was resistant. "This is for little kids."

"Who cares? It's fun," Nina chirped.

"Aw, come on," Dan joined in.

Marianne started to chant, pounding both fists into the air in front of her. "Vi. Vi. Vi. Vi."

They all joined in: "Vi! Vi! Vi! Vi!"

"Fine." Vi gave in. "Standing worm. Go," she said.

She performed a standing-up version of a break-dance move where your whole body rolls on the floor. Standing in place, her spine wiggled.

Had Vi mastered break dancing, too?

All three of them whooped and hollered for Vi.

"Learned it from YouTube," she said, only a little out of breath.

Every time they practiced it, a different person got a different part wrong. By the time Mr. Garcia walked in, they were in hysterics.

"Now this is the kind of positive zeal I want to see for Regionals!" Mr. Garcia raised a fist in the air in emphasis, a really peppy move for a guy like him.

"And now"—he strode to the head table and put a timer on his desk—"we focus. Shall we dive right in?"

Scrimmage time.

Vi and Marianne versus Nina and Dan.

Marianne leaned forward, ready.

Albany is the capital of which state?

A negatively charged ion is referred to as what?

Who is the author of the fantasy epic Lord of the Rings?

Ten more questions. Extension rounds. The buzzing of the buzzer on a loop.

Listen for key words, pay attention, don't drift, Marianne told herself.

In 1815, this battle ended over two decades of warfare between France and—

She didn't need to hear the rest. She could picture the bunnies hopping on him. She could see the numbers of the dates of his wars floating in her mind. She could imagine him hollering, "I may be tiny, but I'm tough!"

"The Battle of Waterloo!" she yelled out. She couldn't help but notice that all her teammates answered questions softly, while she really took the volume up a notch.

"*Yes!*" Dan shouted.

"Go, Marianne!" Nina said.

Vi lifted a finger to her lips to quiet them down, but she couldn't suppress her pleased smile.

Marianne didn't respond to anything for another fifteen or twenty questions, not including the multiple extension rounds on which Vi always dominated.

Until!

"In which country would you be able to find the Taj Mahal?"

Marianne banged the buzzer so hard it dislodged and teetered on the edge of the table. Vi pulled it back.

"India!" Marianne nearly screamed. She could envision the illustrated picture of the beautiful palace on the globe Nina let her borrow.

Now it was Nina's turn to put a finger to her lips to remind Marianne to quiet it down a bit. But then she mouthed, "Great job!" before zoning back in, clutching her fidget device, her leg jiggling on hyper speed.

Marianne performed better than she ever had.

William Shakespeare

The Iraq War

Ultraviolet radiation

Electricity crackled in the room.

"Scholars," Mr. Garcia began, standing up and leaning forward with both hands resting on the table. "You have worked hard. And no matter what happens on Sunday, you should be proud of yourselves for that. Maximum effort beats natural talent nearly every time."

"Okay, that's not always true," Nina interrupted.

Taking a beat, Mr. Garcia ran a hand through his hair and then stepped out from behind the table to lean against it.

"You're right," he acknowledged. "It's not always true. But if you're able to put your work on the table and say, 'I gave it my all'? Walk away and say, 'I tried my best and I couldn't do any more'? Then winning doesn't even matter. Now. I'll see some of you in classes and some of you on Sunday. Bright and early."

Wait, how could he say that? When, for her, he'd made it clear that winning was the key to proof of effort! Was this a speech for everyone but her?

Mr. Garcia tipped an imaginary hat and then left.

Once the door closed, Vi swiveled her head in their direction. "Obviously, winning does matter."

"Thank you for that Vi honesty," Marianne said, meaning it.

"Is this the anti-pep talk?" Dan got out of his chair and stretched. "Let's do that handshake again," he added.

"Marianne, you need to answer a couple more," Vi went on. "Even if they're incorrect. Try to worry less about that. Take a guess once in a while."

"Oh, now you tell me," she said.

"Yes, I'm telling you." Vi gave so many instructions Marianne assumed even Dan and Nina tuned out.

Finally, Vi pled with them. "Think of Lansing. Think of it! Picture beyond Ann Arbor. Think of leaving Etheridge Middle School with *this* team being the one everyone wants to join."

In the last minute of practice, Nina raised a hand and requested they do "that handshake bit again, like Dan said."

Vi relented.

"Hands in!" Marianne cheered.

They gathered in a circle, hands atop one another's.

"Gooooooo, Ermines!" she hollered as they echoed her.

"Vi's freaking out," Nina whispered to her as they left for the door.

"Can I give you a ride?" Marianne yelled out to Vi as she hustled toward the school exit.

"Gonna walk, thanks," she said with her face forward as she practically ran out.

"Dan doesn't think we have a chance," Nina confessed to her as they passed by other groups and clubs ending their days and moseying out of the building. It was such a different energy than the wild fleeing that occurred at the end of the last class. Marianne found she liked this quieter, slower version of the school hallways.

"Ugh, please don't tell me that," Marianne begged her.

"Sorry, he's totally wrong," Nina amended.

Nina waved goodbye to so many people from her other activities—kids from German club, Black Student Union, and the Town Cleanup Project.

That whole idea that Marianne and Jalilah had that kids in Quiz Quest didn't have friends? They were clearly way off base.

"How do you do it all?" Marianne asked Nina, who was once again wearing that sunray yellow, this time complemented by bumblebee earrings.

Instinctively, Marianne reached for her own ears to remind herself what earrings she'd put on that day. They were her dangly moonstones she'd bought in Traverse City. Skyla had chosen the moonstone bracelet instead. They sort of matched but sort of didn't, and that had felt perfect. She could still hear the waves of the lake and see the glow of the creamy stones under the bright sky and feel Skyla seated next to her on the sand. If any cliché in life was true, it was that with best friends you could have fun in silence.

"I don't do all the groups at once," Nina explained to Marianne. "Depends on the semester."

"Are you always in ballet, though?" Marianne asked.

They reached the outdoors and saw their respective dads waiting for them in cars parked one right in front of the other.

"What? Oh, yes, for now, but—I'm not good enough to do it professionally. I may not keep it up," Nina told her as she waved at her dad.

"Yeah, but what about just for fun?" Marianne suggested.

"Ha," Nina laughed, but Marianne didn't see why that was funny.

183

They stood together outside the school, not yet ready to drive home.

"So is Dan's fear all about Remington?" Marianne pictured Remington as broad-shouldered, tough football players.

"I guess," Nina said. "And he's so competitive with his twin. It, like, consumes him. I could see them, like, duel to the death. But yeah, Remington is a big concern."

Nina was too sweet to say that the real concern was Remington + Marianne. That was a math problem even Marianne could solve.

"I don't know, I think we have a shot," Marianne said.

"Me too."

They reached their dads' cars and stood in front of the passenger doors.

"Why is Vi like that?" Marianne asked finally.

"I don't really know." Nina tilted her head, thoughtful. "She was definitely happier when Addison was around? But still kind of harsh. She just wants to prove something, I think. Did you see that presidential campaign of hers . . ." Nina made a "yikes" face. "See you tomorrow maybe," she said.

They had one school day left before the big weekend.

Nina surprised her by squeezing her hand before she said goodbye.

Marianne squeezed back.

Unbelievably, it had been a good day. An *easy* day.

And Marianne wore that goodness on her the next day

as she strolled into Mr. Garcia's class, expecting another one just like it.

Instead, a sore sight greeted her.

Graded tests sat on their tables. He'd returned them early.

Marianne needed a C plus, minimum. Otherwise, she'd need to get As or Bs on the next quiz and final exam, and that might be close to impossible to manage.

But there, in bright red, screeching at her, she saw a large, circled D.

She looked to Mr. Garcia, who she couldn't help but feel had betrayed her somehow, but he remained absorbed with his preparations for the lesson that day, paying her no mind.

And he'd said that effort led to a win nearly every time.

What a liar.

9

IN THE CAR ON the way to Ann Arbor, her mom and dad tried to cheer her up.

"Honey, you can still pass," her mom insisted. "You get a B plus on the next quiz and the final and with the extra credit to go along with it, you're set."

She wanted to respond, "Yeah right, like a B plus is possible," but her mom didn't deserve any talking back. Plus, her mom didn't know that she had to *win* this impossible competition to even *get* the credit, and if she was still getting extremely bad grades on tests, ninth grade was just a pipe dream.

So Marianne just stared out the window at the farms and exit signs leading to small towns and said, "Horses," whenever they passed some.

And then, every time, she thought of her nickname and shuddered. Should she "neigh" to the camera for the livestream?

Did people even recall why they called her that, or did they just know that "horse" had become a stand-in for "you're stupid"? No, they probably didn't even remember. But Marianne did.

The name came from the first month of a sixth-grade social studies class.

The very beginning of middle school, when she'd thought maybe there'd be a fresh start. Maybe she'd magically understand every math problem. Maybe she'd have an easy time sitting down to do her homework, like Skyla did, like Lillian did. She'd scribble down the right answers and run off to do whatever she wanted; no nagging necessary.

None of that happened. Except in social studies. She'd really liked social studies. In the first week, at the start of the "World Cultures" unit, Marianne had raised her hand and asked, "I don't get it. Like, there's no way we can learn about *every* world culture, so, like . . . how do you, like, decide which ones?"

Behind her, someone she didn't know mimicked, "Um, like, um, like . . ." to a couple of giggles.

But Ms. Kumar had responded, "Wow, what an excellent question, Marianne! Keep up that sort of thinking and we'll have a great year," and Marianne could still feel that feeling of . . . specialness. She even started to ask more questions.

In the third week, they were placed with groups to study the culture of a country. Lucky her, she got France. Her mom's favorite place! Marianne chose to present on food. She read recipes, learned about how French people ate multiple courses (yum) and how their desserts were world-famous. She created a well-labeled poster. She practiced the presentation with her group in the library.

And the big day arrived.

Marianne couldn't remember much of what she said at first. But eventually, she explained meal starters.

"You see, you've experienced horse divorce even if you don't know it," she said. "And the actual words really just mean 'out of the ordinary,' so all horse divorce is . . . is something out of the ordinary!" She pointed to some of the pictures of food on her posterboard.

A couple of stifled laughs rippled through the classroom. Marianne thought nothing of it. Kids joked around all the time.

"Have you ever been to a wedding? If you have, you've probably had horse divorce."

The entire room started chortling, and Marianne wavered.

"In my opinion, horse divorce are, like, um. They're delicious. Like . . ."

And Ms. Kumar probably didn't mean to laugh on the fourth "horse divorce," but she did. She covered her mouth and let out a smothered snicker. And then she couldn't stop. So the rest of the class couldn't stop, either.

Once Ms. Kumar gathered herself, she said, "Oh, honey, it's pronounced *hors d'oeuvres*."

Marianne turned red, but to fight off the crying she knew

might come, she laughed harder than anyone. She gripped her belly to show how hard she was laughing. She threw her head back.

She cried at home instead.

"What happened, love?" her mom asked.

And for the first time, Marianne answered that question from her mom with "Nothing."

They called her "horse divorce" for a while. Then "horse." In her yearbook her sixth-grade classmates wrote, "Hey Horse—keep that great smile" or "Horse—good year stay sweet xoxoxo." But by fall, they'd probably forgotten the origin story.

Why hadn't the other kids in the group corrected her beforehand? Was it because they thought it was funny? Or were they just trying to be nice each time she said it and didn't think about what would happen?

Group projects were tough.

Quiz Quest was kind of like a group project, except these kids would *definitely* correct someone on their pronunciation *right* away.

In the car, Marianne spotted a group of ponies. "Ponies this time!" she said to her parents. "Do you think they feel bad about themselves when they see horses?"

Her dad, in the passenger's seat, grinned and suggested they go over flash cards together.

She wanted to say, "What's the point?" but she just shook her head. "Too nervous."

He turned on some opera they'd listened to. It was sort of sweet how excited he was that she liked it.

At the same time, why couldn't her parents speak fewer languages and enjoy whatever was on the radio?

She was born into the wrong family. A fun, good, wrong family.

"Dad," she said finally, "this is a little sad for today. Something cheery?"

Her mom fiddled with the controls in the front and, with a big grin, turned to the funk station.

"Alright, be there in a little less than an hour," her dad announced. "Just passed Hell," he said, which he said every time they passed the sign to Hell, Michigan, which famously read: Welcome to Hell.

Two hours until her own hell would begin.

The texts streamed in.

Several kids had reupped the post about the livestream, and it had been shared double the amount it had before.

Hey horse at least you'll be the cutest girl there lol, one said, as if "dorky" kids couldn't be cute. So annoying.

Thank you so much for sacrificing yourself for our enjoyment haha jk we love u xoxo. That one was from Julie.

Was Skyla watching with Julie? If she was, she wouldn't let Julie text that. Right? Or were Marianne and Skyla on such bad terms lately that she didn't care?

They'd hardly even talked since she joined the team.

Skyla had waved Marianne off that morning with a loud "You can do it!" and her dads came out outside, too, gripping their coffee mugs tightly and cheering Marianne on. That meant she and Skyla were okay, right?

Skyla would hate what she was bound to see: Marianne, being her true self again. Since she got the D on that crucial math test, what was the point of any of this, anyway? She could zone out, answer something ridiculous, brush everything off. That would give the kids watching from home the kind of show they wanted, right?

But when she walked into the school building where the competition took place and saw Mr. Garcia, Vi, and Dan looking around for the rest of them, waving her over once they spotted her, and happy to see her, she knew she couldn't do any of that. And she even almost forgot she was angry at Mr. Garcia.

Almost.

"Welcome to Ann Arbor!" he said.

"Hey," she greeted them. "Test me?" she asked Dan immediately, and he whipped some flash cards out of his jacket pocket.

Small groups of kids milled about the hallways, stopping at different check-in points to figure out who they had to play first and where.

A couple of kids walking by scowled their way, and she wondered if they were from Remington.

When Nina arrived, Marianne tried to initiate their group

handshake, but Vi said she needed a minute and rushed to the restroom.

"Her nerves are making me nervous," Nina confessed.

"Ah, just enjoy it," Dan told her.

"That's the spirit," Mr. Garcia told him, patting his back.

But Marianne knew that was just Dan's way of not caring, of giving up.

"Is your brother coming?" Nina asked Dan.

"No, he's at home watching our baby sister. But he told me this morning he'll be sure to catch the livestream so he can watch me, but he just wants to see what I get wrong so that he can mock me for it later," Dan said.

"I told you. Evil twin," Nina whispered to Marianne. "I love being an only child," she added more audibly.

When she peeked into the auditorium, her fantasies of Quiz Quest Regionals struck her as so funny. It was just a school—a plain old school—with normal overhead lighting and a few tables and some chairs spread out for parents to watch. Why had she pictured something like one of those glossy, glam singing competitions?

Marianne spotted a couple of cameras. Oh no. That was how people would watch her. Could she throw her sweater on one of them?

Before they entered the first classroom to compete against Lewis Middle School, their parents scurried in to grab seats.

Dan pointed out his mom and stepdad to the rest of the team and they all waved. Incredible. His mom, who looked *way* younger than Marianne's parents, had tattoos up and down her arms and a large piercing that took up the whole earlobe.

Nina's parents were the exact opposite. Their shirts appeared well-ironed and made of materials that Marianne's mom would never let her buy because they couldn't go in the dryer. Nina's mom kept her hands in her lap with her ankles crossed.

Vi's parents weren't there.

Three tables made a triangle, one for the administrators and one for each team. However, the other team had about nine members, five of whom sat back in the designated parent seats that lined the walls of the classroom.

All those eyes on Marianne really made her squirm. It had only been a few weeks of studying, after all. She knew almost *nothing*.

But, as hard a time as she was having, Marianne saw that Nina was struggling *much* more.

Marianne leaned in toward her. "Where's your fidget thing?"

"I don't think it's allowed here?" she whispered back.

Marianne couldn't keep her eyes off the camera that stood on a tripod facing the tables. Kids at home couldn't be tuning in to every team at once in each classroom. Which room did they air and when? When would everyone be watching her?

The moderator, who said to "just call me Amir," began the

event with a speech about how they all represented academic excellence and passion.

She could just *imagine* the giggles reverberating through the homes of her classmates.

For a moment, she wished she could remember what it felt like before she'd ever noticed anyone laughing at her or frowning at her as she took too long to figure out a problem or feeling sorry for her when they all aced something she had to redo. If none of that had ever happened, would she feel perfectly fine?

The questions began.

The team across from them slammed the buzzer just as fast as Vi, and Marianne flinched a little every time.

Question after question after question and it was as if the Ermines were a team of one. Vi answered almost everything, losing momentum slightly when the other team hit the buzzer a split second before her once or twice.

Out of the corner of her eye she saw Dan lean toward the buzzer, only to be too late at every turn. And Nina, seated next to her, kept glancing over at her parents, like she had to check their reaction to every moment. In between those glances, she breathed so loudly and rapidly that Marianne wouldn't have been surprised if the cameras picked up the noise.

The camera's lens pointed right at Marianne. And she could've sworn that all the parents stared at her.

Marianne found herself surveying the row of family

194

members. Could they tell she was a D student? Could they sense it or deduce it from her blank face?

In so many ways, she'd tried for years to "look" stupid. Like a uniform. Not because she wanted to, but because she had decided to embrace what she *was*. She knew "dolled up," as her mom would say, and "not smart" sometimes went together in people's eyes. Like Lorelai Wheeler, who had been just the right amount of cute.

That day she had on tinted lip gloss and a couple of shades of eyeshadow. Did that make them see the stupid?

When her eyes hit Mr. Garcia, she flipped her attention back to the moderator.

She couldn't look at Mr. Garcia. He was why she was there. He'd forced her hand. He'd made it impossible to pass. Because winning this? Not. Possible.

"Belize!" she heard Nina squeak out, before immediately slapping a hand to her forehead and crying, "Oh, no, wait!" at the same time Amir the Moderator responded, "Incorrect."

Mr. Garcia was like a Quiz Quest traitor! He had tricked her into thinking that he supported her by standing up to Lucas and made her think he liked her after all the Quiz Quest practices and then gave her that D on the test.

No, no. It wasn't his fault. She knew that.

She was the one who got the bad grade. It was all her and her bad brain. Mr. Garcia always said: You get the grade you earn. She was a D student.

And in the eyes of the world that made her a D *person*.

"Charles Dickens," she heard Vi say, her syllables clipped, her gaze zeroed in on Amir.

Onto the extension round. Vi didn't even confer with them.

"Jane Austen."

"*The House on Mango Street.*"

"Langston Hughes."

A couple of questions later, Dan figured out a math problem, but he was too late. The other team buzzed in first.

Nina kept mouthing things to herself.

Marianne, who knew she wasn't one to talk, nudged Nina with her knee. Someone had to remind the smart ones to stay sharp!

And Marianne had to answer *something*. As the clock ticked on and time felt like it would run out soon, she tried to recall the sound of Nina clapping three times. *Smack smack smack.* Concentrate. And she listened, giving every ounce of her attention to every word Amir spoke.

"Who was the first female candidate on a presidential ticket in the United States of—"

Marianne knew this one! From the first practice! She smacked the buzzer before Amir finished speaking.

And then, as he looked at her, eyebrows raised, expectant, the horrible truth hit her: She couldn't remember the name.

"It's—" Marianne held up a finger to say "one second."

Alberta? Ernestine? Ernestine DeCarlo?

"Time. I need your answer," he said.

"Gah!" she grunted, throwing her hands in the air.

"Geraldine Ferraro," the other team answered.

"I knew it!" she yelled out, and the moderator had to quiet her.

Marianne tried not to notice Vi shaking her head.

Why did her disappointment matter so much?

Not only was there a camera, but several parents held up their phones, recording.

She wondered if the kids from school had seen her on-screen yet.

Thank God she hadn't said "Ernestine DeCarlo" out loud.

She thought of her parents seated behind her.

Was she doing even worse than they'd expected?

Vi's hand went back and forth to the buzzer on repeat.

Dan could've been asleep for all the help he was giving her. Nina was lost to her stress.

Marianne listened in. She didn't know the answer. And she didn't know the next answer. And she didn't know the answer after that. But then . . .

"What is the capital of Washington—" Amir began.

Without thinking, just knowing she had to do something, she buzzed in.

"Washington, DC!" she hollered.

She'd heard "Washington" and she'd heard "capital" and the words just flew out of her mouth.

The sound of stifled laughter in the crowd hit her ears like screams.

Nina's leg shook on warp speed.

"You're fine, you're fine," Nina whispered to her. "We're fine."

Marianne instinctively checked for her parents' reaction.

"It's okay," her mom mouthed. She gave her a big, overly sweet smile and a thumbs-up.

If kids at school had seen it, they'd bring it up on Monday. Would they call her "DC"? What would they say about it? Would she laugh along? Maybe she could wear her dad's T-shirt from the gig he'd played in DC to school. She'd be in on it. She'd get the joke.

Marianne let her brain leave—drift.

She tried to remember a time she'd felt free—jumping into the waters of Lake Michigan with Skyla. The water was freezing. In some spots, you could see little fish swimming around your ankles. What would it be like to be a fish, darting in the water, untroubled by the cold? She envisioned how under the waves, if you looked up, the light would pierce through the water in dozens of strands surrounding you.

"The winner of the match is the *Etheridge Ermines*!" Amir announced.

It was over? They'd *won*?

"Thank you to both teams, and, Ermines—please see your coaches for who you'll be playing next. In half an hour, the next round will commence. To knowledge!"

The room applauded.

Vi had won it for them.

And from the looks of her, she knew it, and she was not pleased.

"Team meeting. *Now*," Vi hissed, as they headed toward Mr. Garcia.

He forced high fives on all of them and tried to perk them up for the next match. "My guess is that Tappan Middle School is going to be some real competition for us. Scholars, let's not leave Vi hanging, alright? Let's embody knowledge!"

As he said it, Marianne saw on his face that maybe he knew he wasn't the best at giving inspirational talks.

"Can we huddle up somewhere around here?" Vi asked him, and he pointed them in the direction of an unused classroom toward the end of the hallway. He went to the administrators out front at the desk to receive their next room assignment.

As their parents came out to greet them, Vi snapped, "Be right back," and cut off any conversation. Nina's parents shoved a bag of almonds upon her as Vi led them off to the classroom.

As they walked down the hallway, Nina nearly cried to Marianne, "I messed up." She repeated it again and again. "I'm messing it all up."

"Shhh, it's okay," Marianne said, rubbing a hand on her back.

Vi ushered them in and shut the door. She kept the lights off.

A model skeleton and biology posters loomed all around them.

"Okay, Vi." Dan leaned against a round table. "Let 'er rip. Let us have it."

Nina sat, her head in her hands. "I know I messed up, Vi, I'm really sorry. Aah! I let everyone down!"

Marianne stood next to Vi, awaiting the brutal takedown she knew was coming. "We *all* messed up," Marianne said, praying Vi wouldn't single out Nina.

"Let's go." Dan motioned for Vi to speak, but Marianne noticed he was looking away.

Vi said something so quietly they couldn't hear.

"Hmm?" Nina said from beneath her hands.

"It won't help." Vi took off her glasses and rubbed her eyes.

"Yeah, I know. We're hopeless, right?" Dan mused.

"No, *I* won't help," she said. Her round cheeks reddened. "I don't think it'll make things better if I talk right now." She took a breath. "I'm supposed to be the *leader*. And you all just think I'm going to *yell* at you. And that *is* what I was going to do!"

For the first time since Marianne had known Vi, she slumped forward, like a melting candle. She seemed to shrink by nearly half. At the table where Nina sat, Vi whipped out a chair, its feet screeching on the tiled floor, and fell into it, mirroring Nina with her head in her hands.

"Can I have an almond?" Dan asked.

Nina, keeping one hand on her face, threw the bag his way and it landed on the floor.

"That felt aggressive." He used the end of his crutch to pull the bag toward him.

Vi groaned a long, low groan. She pulled her hair out of her ponytail and let it fall all around her face and back. It was wavier and longer than Marianne had thought.

"Help us out, Marianne," Vi said from under her mane.

"Who? Huh?" Marianne looked around for another Marianne.

Vi lifted her head. She held back tears. "Your specialization is people stuff. Do you have any ideas for the team?"

Marianne grabbed a tissue from a box on the teacher's desk. She handed it to Vi.

People stuff. Marianne didn't know if she was good at "people stuff," but she did *like* people. Actually, people were the only good part of school. Until Mr. Garcia, she had liked every teacher she'd had, even when they were failing her.

Vi was right that to Marianne, people were more interesting to figure out than intercepts on a graph.

And, if she was being honest, she was pretty sure she had these kids figured out.

"Okay." Marianne spoke carefully, checking in with Vi after every other word. "So, um . . . Vi, I think you have a lot of good ideas about the team. But sometimes it's hard for you to say it?"

"So true," Nina agreed.

"So . . ." Should she just go for it? Was she allowed to take Vi's spot and . . . be the captain for a little bit? "Let's think about what Vi would say, and then do what my mom does—translate. Dan. Vi would say, 'You're delaying on the buzzer, *Dan!*'" She employed her best Vi impression. "'You're better than this! Stop being so lazy!' she'd say. Right?"

Vi nodded sadly, her face still behind her hair.

"So . . . what she really means and what's really going on is this: Dan, you're so nice, and I'm so grateful for that. But . . . you need to care more. And hope more. Like, you just let me on the team. And that was nice, but . . . maybe you *shouldn't* have just let me waltz onto your team? Like . . . Vi and Nina had a point. I didn't know anything. Why wasn't Quiz Quest important enough to you to fight for it? Ya know, you do something I do, in a way, so I get it. You pretend not to care about stuff very much. But it's weird because you're, like, amazing at it. So . . . I don't know, maybe your brother makes you feel bad about yourself sometimes, so you'd rather not try than do super bad and have him feel like he was proved right?"

Dan's jaw dropped. "You're right," he said. "I can't believe I never thought of that."

"But I think you really do care," Marianne continued, her speech speeding up now, her passion kicking in, "or you wouldn't have tried so hard to teach me and to practice. Right? So . . . instead of focusing on facts today, maybe focus on *caring*. Yeah?" As she said it, she knew that was the right advice. And it felt good to be correct. "Don't shrug if you don't hit the buzzer. Instead, decide that you'll go for the buzzer the next time like it's . . . life or death. In fact . . . Oh, I know! I want you to pretend that every kid on that other team is your twin brother. See his face."

"Andy everywhere. Yikes . . ." Dan grumbled.

"Every kid on the other team is Andy, and every time there's a chance to hit the buzzer, you get to prove to him he's not any better than you. That's what gets you competitive. So compete with him! Got it?" Marianne beamed. She knew she'd nailed it.

"Got it." Dan smiled. "I'm in."

"Nina," she began.

Nina had already lifted her head and was staring at Marianne. "Yeah?" she asked. "This is kind of exciting. What are you going to say to me?"

"Vi would say . . ." Marianne thought for a second. "'Snap out of it! Come on! Don't be a baby!'"

"Okay, I wouldn't be *that* mean . . ." Vi jumped in, her old, stronger voice back.

Marianne was in her own world, though, and didn't respond. A buzz had crept into her, an energy that made her want to keep her head in the game. She knew what she wanted to say and now that she was saying it, it was like she had to let out every last bit.

"What she would mean is that Nina, we can tell you're really nervous and really stressed. You keep looking at your parents. Do they make it worse?"

203

"They don't *try* to. But . . ." Nina bit her lip.

"Okay, we need a game plan then. I'm going to get them out of your line of sight as much as I can, okay? And since you can't use your fidget spinner . . . Okay, wait! I know!" Marianne jumped up and down. "Ballet!"

"Pardon?"

"When you talk about ballet, you breathe. When you do whatever that thing is with your arm when you do our handshake—"

"You mean this?" And Nina lifted her arm in three directions with a grace Marianne couldn't even fake a teeny bit. "That's just, like, basic training kicking in, I guess . . ." Nina demurred.

"Okay, whatever, but it *works* for you," Marianne said. "Try this. When you're freaking out during a match, just move your feet like you do in ballet class. Only a little bit—pointing or whatever it is you guys do. And see if that helps. Oh, and also! Try this with me. My mom taught me." And Marianne talked her through "saying hello and goodbye" to the worry thoughts, like she did during math homework. It was worth a shot. "And listen to me. You are brilliant. You soak up information in this incredible way I've never seen. Scientists should study your brain one day. Okay? You can do this!"

Marianne knew that Nina needed to hear that. Plus, it was true.

Nina said, "I'm going to practice now," and sat down, positioned herself like the buzzer was right in front of her, and closed her eyes to breathe. Every other second, her toes pointed.

"And to me." Marianne took a huge inhale and let it out. "Vi would tell me it was all my fault. That I needed to answer like ten times more or you guys wouldn't qualify, and if I don't do that then you'll lose, and it'll be because of me." And Marianne wouldn't pass the year, she didn't add out loud.

Marianne paused. She listened to the chatting outside the door, up and down the hallways.

"But I think for me? Maybe I need to imagine what my friend Skyla would say. She would say to get over this idea that I'm so stupid because thinking I'm so stupid makes me stupid. She'd tell me it was okay to guess. It was okay to try. That my only problem is that I'm . . . afraid."

Marianne felt certain it was true. And she knew that no test from any specialist her parents took her to would pick up on that fear—the terror of truly giving something a real shot, failing, and then having solid evidence that she simply wasn't . . . well, *good enough*.

"What about me?" Vi asked.

Marianne stepped back and took in Violet Cross, the whites of her eyes all pink.

"You're a star student. So, you've got that part down. Maybe just . . . try and have *fun* being you? Instead of, like, hating it? Enjoy being incredible? At least a little bit?" Marianne raised her shoulders.

Vi pulled her hair back up again and tied it into a loop. "Okay," she said. "I'll try."

"Ya know," Marianne said to all three of them, "when I first joined and thought I could answer any question I wanted with the wrong answer and it wouldn't matter? Honestly, I've never felt such relief in my life at the thought. Maybe we can all just try to be okay with, like, being wrong? And remember that another person on the team may help us out?"

Mr. Garcia knocked on the door. "I've got the room." He lifted up his wrist and pointed to his watch. "Five!"

Nina hopped up. "We have to go!" she said. "Hold on." She took a deep breath in, held it, then let it out. "Hello, I-hate-to-be-late thoughts. We will be fine. It's just a short hallway. Goodbye."

Marianne cheered and Nina did a little pirouette.

"You know what time it is!" Marianne hollered. They proceeded to complete their entire secret handshake. "Flawless!" She clapped.

"Goooooo, Ermines!"

As everyone settled into their seats for the next match, Marianne scanned the room for Nina's parents.

"Mr. and Mrs. Anderson?" she greeted them. "I'm so sorry, but my parents didn't really get a great view of things last time and between you and me they're kind of upset they drove all the way to Ann Arbor and aren't really getting to see the show . . ."

Would they buy it? She had to really sell this.

"Do you mind switching with them for this one?"

She hurried them toward where her parents sat, behind the team, and placed her parents directly in front of her, where the Andersons had been.

"I'll explain later," she said.

Nina waved to her parents behind them, and Marianne whispered, "Forget them. It's just you and your genius mind. You got this. Breathe in, breathe out, point those toes, I'm right here."

"Okay, okay." Nina played with her pen, flipping it from finger to finger.

"Dan. Game face on. Every. Kid. Is. Andy," Marianne said. "Vi—*enjoy*."

Their next moderator, Ms. Ruhl, once again explained the game structure, and Marianne sized up the team across from them. Interesting. Two of them squabbled in whispers. One of them, face half-covered in a hoodie, leaned back as if already defeated, and the other had his elbows so far on the table he looked like he might flip forward onto the floor.

They could win this.

"Dan," Marianne whispered before they started, "lean forward as far as you're allowed. And don't move back even if you don't think you know the answer. Like that kid—he's ready the whole time. Try it."

He nodded.

And they were off.

Dan hit the buzzer first, right out of the gate, and Marianne could've hugged him right then and there.

Vi came in next, acing three questions and all extension rounds like a mad genius.

Every time Nina's leg began jiggling next to Marianne, Marianne hummed the Sugar Plum Fairy song from *The Nutcracker*, and Nina let her leg loosen.

"The Canary Islands," Nina answered, her words streaming out so fast they mushed together. "TheSanAndreasFault. Ashgabat,Turkmenistan. TheDeadSea!"

And then, her confidence back in place, Nina went on a correct-answer spree in every subject, losing momentum only when the other team—usually the team member who was leaning forward so far—got to the buzzer first.

Dan answered the history questions after only a few words of them had been read, to the point where some in the audience let out a laugh here or there.

"On July 1, 1863—"

Buzz.

"Battle of Gettysburg."

Question after question he'd cut off the moderator.

Battle of Okinawa. Battles of Lexington and Concord. Operation Overlord. Battle of the Bulge . . .

He began to give more information than was needed. Instead of "1776" as the date of the Battle of Trenton, he slammed the buzzer and said, with a sense of triumph in his voice, "December 26, 1776, Trenton, New Jersey. Eight A.M."

Her team soared.

Marianne had to answer. She had to. Nothing had come up so far that she knew, but she could guess.

But how would she buzz in? She was slow.

On an extension round, when technically they were allowed to communicate if only for a second or two, Marianne whispered to her teammates, "Give me a chance on some. I'll buzz in."

So they let her. The next question was:

"The Brooklyn Bridge crosses what river in New York City?"

Marianne had no idea. Nina certainly knew. Marianne didn't even remember the names of the rivers there. But she buzzed.

Silence.

"We need an answer," Ms. Ruhl said.

"The Erie Canal?" Marianne guessed.

She wouldn't look at the camera. She couldn't.

"Incorrect."

And the other team got it.

Time would run out. She had to keep guessing.

"*The Adventures of Tom Sawyer* was written by which American author?"

The other team buzzed first. Vi and Marianne shared a look. They'd studied this one. A lost point, a chance for participation, gone.

"William Faulkner," the hoodie kid said.

Marianne almost leapt out of her chair. He was wrong. He was wrong, and she knew the right answer.

"Incorrect. Etheridge . . ." Ms. Ruhl repeated the question, and before she finished Marianne shouted, "*Mark Twain!*"

Marianne saw both of her parents quietly celebrate.

She couldn't hide her huge smile.

Moments later, like a miracle, Ms. Ruhl asked, "Which Italian composer wrote the classic operas *La Traviata*, *Aida*, and—"

Buzz.

"Giuseppe Verdi!" Marianne bellowed. "And he was such a *woman hater*," she added under her breath.

She saw her dad laugh and look around like "Isn't my kid so funny?"

She waved at him.

But Ms. Ruhl was not amused and reminded everyone that Quiz Quest involved no commentary.

Marianne answered six more questions, four of them correctly.

Vi, Nina, and Dan split the rest.

They were unstoppable.

And they won.

"Hooray!" Nina hugged each of them.

"Well done, compatriots," Dan said, slowly pulling himself up. "Take that, Andy! Can they do *that* at your fancy school?"

"We can do it," Nina sang. "We can really do it!"

Vi reached across the two other kids and put out a hand for a high five to Marianne.

"Two down," Vi said to her.

"Marianne, you were fantastic!" Her dad enveloped her in a huge embrace, lifting her off her feet. "This is really exciting. Do they show this on ESPN, like with the Spelling Bee? They should show it on ESPN. I mean, only at the highest levels, of course . . ." He went on and on, but Marianne couldn't hear him over all the cheeriness bubbling inside her.

"Gotta go to the next match, Dad!" She skipped off toward her friends, who were following Mr. Garcia to find out their next assignment.

As they walked to their next match, Marianne reminded them of their goals. "Dan, that leaning forward and never going back really helps you. So does whatever you were visualizing . . . Wow. Amazing work. Stay in it. Nina, were you trying the hello-goodbye trick I taught you along with first-position stuff? I could tell."

They talked strategy until the next round, and with that energy in place they won again.

And they took a break and ate some sandwiches, chatting with one another while their parents chatted nearby, and they won once more. Marianne only answered a couple correctly, but still—a couple was more than zero.

As the moderator called "time," Mr. Garcia jumped out of his seat.

"You did it!" he exclaimed. "You did it!"

Whichever team won the next match won Regionals.

"We'll be in the auditorium next," he said, scurrying them out of the room to huddle by the door. "Half an hour. Don't lose momentum now. Take ten, get a snack, I'll find out who we're playing for the final match."

But another kid in the hall told them the news first.

"It's you and Remington, guys," an unusually tall kid said, bending his knees to give out fist bumps. "Good luck. You'll need it."

That buzz that Marianne had felt throughout her limbs while giving the team a pep talk didn't dissipate. In fact, it seemed contagious. Vi was—for the first time in Vi history, Marianne assumed—all smiles. She and Dan even joked around together.

"Addison is going to be so excited," she said. "I have to tell her. Let's check our phones."

All the players' phones had been confiscated and handed over to each team coach before the competition began.

They rushed to Mr. Garcia, and Vi grabbed the large pouch out of his backpack.

As Marianne took her purple-glitter phone from Vi and opened the screen, she understood her mistake right as she made it.

Notifications. Her phone held each and every notification of comments from kids, a group chat that had been formed of kids watching the livestream, texts from other classmates, all of it lighting up her screen in box after box.

 212

As she read comment after comment, joke after joke, she saw something that she could hardly believe: Julie had written, omg this is going to be HILARIOUS . . .

And Skyla had liked the comment.

She'd *liked it*. Skyla_Ray22 had pressed the "heart" button. Was it an accident? Had she hit it by mistake?

Why would she do that?

Marianne just figured that she and Skyla would get back to normal. Once the school year ended, and Skyla didn't see those classmates every day, and they headed into high school as a duo, they'd be on the same wavelength again. But maybe not. Maybe Skyla wished she didn't even live next door to her. Maybe Marianne was a total embarrassment.

Someone ripped the phone from Marianne's hands, and Marianne was left staring into her palms, her heartbeat on overdrive.

Vi stood before her, her face stern. She tossed Marianne's phone back in her bag.

"No," Vi said. "Stop it. Whatever they're saying? It doesn't matter."

"Skyla," Marianne whispered to Vi. "She—"

"You seem to learn a lot just by scoping people out. Go investigate Remington for us?" Vi asked.

"Okay." Marianne took a breath. "Okay," she repeated. "I'm going to take a walk. Be right back." She turned on her heels.

She had to keep herself busy, she had to try to add something to the team. "Research," she whispered to herself.

And she stalked the halls for Remington.

A few people gave her a "congrats" here and there, and it hit her as strange after the onslaught of mockery on her phone. Then, by the doors of the auditorium, she thought she saw them.

It was a group of six. They were dressed professionally, like children in grown-up dress-up clothes. They spoke to one another quietly but forcefully, in what might have been a fight.

Then their coach arrived, and they went silent, some of them standing up straighter, arms to their sides, like she was their sergeant.

Their coach wore her hair back in a high twisted braid and shook her head at all of them as if she were disappointed.

When she stalked off, one of the team members leaned a head against the wall, devastated. The others continued to squabble.

Marianne hurried back to her group as they were about to make their way to the auditorium.

"Remington may be the best," Marianne said breathlessly, "but they don't get along. There's trouble between them, or with their coach, I think. Maybe if we seem like we're having a great time, like we're getting along together really well, it could . . . I don't know. What's the word? It could psych them out. At least a little. If they're not insecure about being smart, maybe they're insecure about something else, something like their friendships or issues between them. As a team. You think?"

"You diabolical genius," Dan said. "So should we play it up, all buddy-buddy?"

"Interesting." Vi bit the end of her pencil. "If we can't intimidate them in other ways, why not this? Okay."

"Love it!" Nina shook her fists happily.

"Instead of showing we think they're better than us, let's just act like best friends without a care in the world," Marianne reiterated.

She was making this strategy up on the spot, but it sounded good and was worth a shot.

Vi still had her phone, Marianne noticed.

"What's up?" she asked Vi. "Don't you have to put it away?"

Vi texted someone with abandon.

"My parents," Vi said. "They're not watching. They thought they'd make it home in time to catch the livestream, but they're busy." She handed the phone back to Mr. Garcia. "Whatever."

"We'll tell them all about it," Marianne assured her. "For now, just think about how if we win this . . ."

"State Championships," Vi said, her face forward. "*Respect.*"

Marianne could see that Vi knew what she had to do.

They took their seats up on the stage. The fold-up chairs in rows before them were about two-thirds of the way filled, containing most of the contestants who hadn't made the cut.

Marianne gave the Remington kids her brightest smile and a huge wave. Vi, Dan, and Nina followed suit.

Then she said, "Love ya, we got this," to each of her teammates and leaned her head on Nina's shoulder before they started.

The Remington kids looked miserable. She noticed that a couple of them eyed their scary coach in the front row.

Marianne threw Mr. Garcia a thumbs-up and mouthed, "This is for you, Coach!"

Amir was back. He re-welcomed everyone to the event and congratulated all the contestants for their hard work. As he reexplained the rules, Marianne peered out into the audience and saw the cameras on her once again.

And the notifications popped up in her mind. She saw Skyla's handle next to the "heart" button. She pictured Skyla laughing with Julie, anticipating how ridiculously stupid Marianne would look.

She tried to say hello and goodbye to the image and watch it float away.

But it came back.

"Let us begin!" Amir declared.

She could hardly hear the first question, but the Ermines must have answered correctly because within a flash they went into a geography extension round, where the team could confer.

"Nina knows this," Vi announced to the team, but she held up a finger to Amir to indicate they had to wait a second more to answer, and she leaned over Dan and Nina to whisper to Marianne: "Hey. Skyla didn't see how awesome you've been today. The camera's on us now. *Show her.*"

Nina hit the buzzer. "Dublin!"

Vi was right. Goodbye, Skyla. Marianne listened in for the rest of the extension round, forcing her mind to stay centered.

She put nearly all of her mental energy into listening to Amir's questions, but she kept her eyes on her teammates in her periphery. They might need her support.

Remington answered the next three correctly, as well as all the extension round questions but one. They were on a roll, and the Ermines had to end it.

Marianne felt Nina's foot start to tap over and over, and Marianne put her own foot on top of it.

Flex. Point. Nina went into her dance world and settled.

If Nina turned out to look for her parents, Marianne would physically move her head back toward Amir.

Luckily, Vi got the next question, and Nina's body stayed relaxed.

On computer-encyclopedia mode, Vi slew every question for minutes.

"East India Company," she said. "Six-thirtieths" and "Toni Morrison" and "USS *Arizona* Memorial" and "The height is twelve feet."

Dan initiated the high fives after Vi's winning streak, and they cheered one another on.

Marianne answered which volcano was the largest in the world—Mauna Loa. She could swear she heard her parents clap in the audience. Who else could it have been?

And she had to answer more, so she guessed.

She guessed the wrong year for the Montgomery Bus Boycott, the wrong author of *Robinson Crusoe*, and the wrong type of glands in the mouth that assisted in digestion, but she guessed that the hottest region of Earth was the inner core and—hallelujah—she was correct!

"Excellent, yes," Amir responded, and Marianne remembered he had said he was a teacher at the school they were at, and she was sure he could tell she wasn't as good a student as the rest of them.

But despite her several wrong answers, they were winning by a hair.

Unfortunately, Remington had a history buff on par with Dan.

She sat about one whole foot taller than the rest of the kids onstage, with a flaxen blond pixie cut and a stare of steel.

Each time a history question arose, Marianne saw the girl lean forward, check out Dan, and beat him to the buzzer more than half the time.

"Come on, come on, come on," Marianne found herself saying under her breath when any history question or extension round came up.

History Girl had been one of the kids arguing outside the door beforehand. Could Marianne discombobulate her? She thought of their coach, with her severe air of disappointment. Marianne tried to exhibit the opposite of that toward Dan: complete and unconditional encouragement. When he got a question wrong, she leaned past Nina and patted his back, mouthing, "It's okay, you're great, you're the best," a whole shower of positivity. It may have been her imagination, but she thought she saw History Girl watching. Maybe it would throw her off a bit.

But whether it did that or not, the reinforcement did seem to help Dan. He went wild on the World War II questions, slamming the buzzer at every turn.

When they neared the twenty-minute mark, Amir announced where the point totals stood.

Next to her, Nina made a note of it, and as they kept answering she made little tally marks to keep track.

The game would be over soon. A winner would be determined.

"What is the name of the circle at zero degrees latitude on planet Earth?"

"The equator," Nina answered.

Extension round.

"What is the name of the far-right party in France once represented by Marine Le Pen?"

"Front National," History Girl across the way answered.

Extension round.

"What is the name of the most powerful god in Norse mythology, the father of Thor?"

"Odin," Vi answered.

Extension round. All mythology. Marianne remembered a couple from reading the *Percy Jackson* series in fourth grade, but she hadn't gotten any further than that.

They only answered one correctly.

Looking at Nina's tallies, the two teams were nearly tied, with the Ermines two points down. The game would end when the timer ran out. If they tied, then they'd go into overtime. If they got an answer correct now, they'd get their chance in an extension round, where the timer was paused. They needed an extension round to catch up.

And glancing at the clock, Marianne saw there was only one minute left.

"Come on, come on, come on," Marianne murmured again.

Next, Amir asked, "What is the name of the largest asteroid?"

They had to get this. Marianne sensed Nina going for the buzzer and heard her take a breath.

"Um, Ceres?" Nina asked, biting a lip.

"Correct."

"Yes," Marianne and Dan whispered.

An audible celebration or two slipped out of the audience. The game was up for grabs.

They were almost caught up. They just needed to get two

extension questions right and they'd be the winners. They were almost there.

"Extension round, with an astronomy focus. Turn the timer off, if you please," Amir announced.

And time really did seem to stand still. Marianne heard nothing but the sound of Amir's voice and the rustle of her teammates picking up their pencils, ready for anything.

"Which moon in our solar system is the only one with its own magnetosphere?"

Buzz. "Ganymede," Vi answered with total confidence.

"The sunspot cycle is how many years?"

Marianne had no clue, but they only needed one more question answered. Certainly, one of the other kids knew it.

But no one said anything.

"What is it?" Nina whispered in a panic.

"Hmmm. I think about a dozen? But I can't remember? I— Argh," Vi growled, slapping a hand to her head. "*What is it?*"

Their time was running out. Someone had to guess.

Buzz. "Twelve," Marianne answered.

"Incorrect," Amir said. "The correct answer is eleven years."

She saw Remington inch forward further in their seats. This was it, the question that would determine who went on to the state championship. If they didn't get it, the questions went back to both teams. If they got it right, they won.

221

"Which groundbreaking theory," Amir spoke slowly and carefully to the dead-silent room, "was directly influenced by the work of Edwin Hubble of telescope fame, who stated that the universe is in a constant state of expans—?"

And Marianne slammed the buzzer.

10

MARIANNE ENTERED HOMEROOM ON Monday morning to applause.

Kylie skipped up to her, pointed to her head, and said, "What have you been hiding in there this whole time?"

Her homeroom teacher, Ms. Robbie, the health teacher at all other hours of the day, stood in front of her creepily detailed poster of the human body and held up a newspaper. "Look who made the *Brookdale Gazette*!"

There they were on page C6. Smiling those smiles that look fake because it's the eighth or ninth time someone's taken your picture. They wore medals around their necks.

Marianne had never won a medal before.

A couple of kids went, "Whoo!"

"We'll post it on the bulletin board outside the main office, mmkay?" Ms. Robbie said. Then she went right on into "goals planning" for high school.

Under the desk, Marianne used one thumb to text Lillian:

ppl r so into the winning thing.

i didnt even get close to as many right answers as

any other person there.

theyre just shocked i didnt totally blow it.

A couple of minutes later, her phone glowed.

three cheers for not blowing it? Lillian responded with a goofy emoji face.

youre into the winning thing too i guess, Marianne wrote back, feeling an anger in her chest coming out through her thumbs. **is it better having a little sister who isnt a loser?**

"Marianne, how's the goal setting?" Ms. Robbie asked, and they both knew she'd been texting, so she practically threw the phone into her backpack and started writing.

Get to high school

Do better in high school than in middle school

Zoology?

In the hallway, Ms. Clarke held Marianne by both of her upper arms and said, "I am so very proud of you," articulating each word with so much intensity and support that Marianne could hardly stand it.

"Thanks!" she twittered, and she wanted so badly to get away that when she noticed Julie and Zara out of the corner of her eye, she practically jumped on them. She needed somewhere to go.

"HORSE! HORSE! HORSE!" a loud boy named Tripp Layson chanted her way as he walked backward through the hall, but he immediately moved on to slamming someone's locker shut and knocking a stack of papers out of another girl's hands, the Horse Girl quickly forgotten.

"Eeek!" Julie hugged her. "Yay! Congrats! It's so weird because Skyla said you were really struggling!"

Why would she say that?

"Ha. Get one answer right and I'm Einstein, I guess," she joked to Julie.

She thought of how Vi had told her she shouldn't be a joke to the Lucases of the world. Julie was a Lucas. How could Skyla like her?!

She found herself searching the hallways for Vi, but she didn't see her. She spotted Dan and scurried to his side.

"Hey, Champ," she said.

"Hey, Champ," he repeated.

Marianne felt a smack on her back. Lucas Hayes strolled up to her side and said, "Making the papers, Blume! Nice!"

He seemed like he didn't know what to say. Like she'd ruined his good time.

"Good job," Niko grunted as he followed Lucas off and away to their next class.

Marianne could see why Vi had wanted to win so badly. Winning *did* earn you some respect, no matter what else anyone thought about you. Was this how Lillian felt after she won at a swim meet or got all As? Maybe all that respect was addictive.

At the moment of their win, Marianne had almost

forgotten that it was just the first step toward *more* attempts to win. As they celebrated afterward, she'd said to her teammates, "Phew! Extra credit, here I come!"

Vi had responded, "What are you talking about? Now things get real. We go to the finals. The state capital. The only win that *matters*."

"So," Marianne said to Dan, who was still standing by her side watching Lucas and Niko walk away with his usual amused, quizzical expression, "Do we get a break in practices or is it, like, straight back in? Any celebrating?"

Dan nodded to the office, where the *Brookdale* article was already up. "That was the celebrating. Now we keep grinding away."

Marianne felt her phone buzz in her pocket and instinctively picked it up. Lillian had responded:

ummm i dont care if my little sister is a winner or a loser but itd be nice if she didnt have little pity parties and take them out on me, followed by a smiley face emoji.

sorry, Marianne wrote back.

Dan stood there, waiting for her to look back up.

"Sorry," she said to him. She was full of sorries. "Sister probs."

"You know I get it." He walked alongside her toward their classrooms.

A group scurried by them, oblivious, knocking both Dan's and Marianne's shoulders as they went by.

"Jerks," they both said.

"So why do you really hate Andy so much?" Marianne asked him, turning off her phone. She didn't want to see any more Lillian texts.

"He's stuck-up! And he doesn't even know he's stuck-up," Dan said. "But you know what really gets me?"

"What?"

"So, like, he stole my air, right?"

"No, sorry, ya lost me," Marianne said.

"Back when I was forced to be around him—when my mom was pregnant with us—he basically hogged all the good stuff from the umbilical cord. So that's part of why I have these bad boys . . ." He lifted a crutch off the ground, and as he did so, he tilted further onto his toes for a moment. "But what's so maddening is he thinks *that's* why I don't like him," Dan seethed in disbelief, "when I actually don't like him because he's a conformist and a social climber who only cares about school because he probably wants to be, like, an oil tycoon one day."

Marianne laughed a loud, full laugh. "Dan, I only understand, like, half of what you say half of the time."

"Who hates someone because of what they did as a baby?" Dan mumbled to himself. "My sister's a baby. And I'm fine with *her*. Please don't make me put *her* face on the other team next time." He smiled. "She's just really cute."

They lingered outside their respective classrooms.

"Ugh, I don't want to go in . . ." she admitted to him.

"It'll be okay," he reassured her. "See ya. *Infinity Galaxy* tonight?"

When Marianne arrived at Ms. James's doorstep, her favorite teacher smiled her grandmotherly smile and said, "I hear congratulations are in order."

Marianne nodded.

"What'd you think of the final chapters?" Ms. James went on, as a stream of kids sauntered in behind her.

"Um, I'm not quite caught up yet," Marianne admitted. "Workin' on it!" she added.

***

Maybe if you just got far enough into a book, it got good. Or at least by halfway through, you started to care about the characters enough to like it. Marianne was in part three of *A Tree Grows in Brooklyn* and found herself tearing up, despite a lurking boredom that refused to go away entirely. The dad in the story died. And even though he was terrible in some ways, she hated that his daughter, Francie, had to go on without him.

Marianne's sorrows were broken up by a knock on her door. It was her mom, reminding her that her cousins would be there in about half an hour for "fake Easter." Her uncle Sean and aunt Kendi always went to Miami for Easter, so they redid Easter with her mom's siblings in early May, but her grammy didn't join for that one because she said it wasn't "really Easter." Lillian and Marianne had been calling it "fake Easter" for as long as she could remember. They'd already had a Seder and real Easter over spring break, so her parents usually seemed pretty over it by the time her mom's brothers came over to celebrate.

Marianne led her little cousins, Suri and Nia, around the backyard in an egg hunt.

Here and there she gave them hints by tilting her head toward the daffodils or the sprouting crocuses where pastel eggs hid.

As Marianne helped the kids find the final egg, she tried to ignore the familiar tumble in her stomach that started up whenever she thought about Lansing. Was winning ever really fun if there was always more winning to do?

As Nia spotted the last blue egg behind the flowerpot, Marianne took note of Skyla on the other side of the chain link fence. She was waiting for her dog, Sully, to finish going to the bathroom.

Skyla raised a hand in a wave. Marianne did, too.

Besides a "Congrats!" text, they hadn't talked much since the competition. Since the "heart" button.

Or since she'd joined Quiz Quest, really.

Even the thought made Marianne mad. Did she really need someone's "blessing" to join Quiz Quest? Or to do it whatever way she wanted to?

At fake-Easter dinner, which weirdly took place around

4:00 P.M. ("It's a tradition," her mom said), there was lots of talk about how her uncle Joseph had a new girlfriend.

"When are we going to meet this elusive creature?" her mom asked.

Uncle Joseph hadn't ever been married, and they were always setting him up on dates.

"In good time, in good time," he said.

"Do you have a boyfriend?" Nia asked Lillian.

"Or girlfriend," Lillian corrected her, before explaining that she didn't have time for all that.

"What about you, Marianne?" Nia asked.

With the whole table looking at her, Marianne wanted to pull the tablecloth so all the food came smashing down and then run away. She had *never* been asked a question like that before in front of her parents. Plus, the answer was a big *no*.

She shook her head, knowing full well her face flushed, and her uncle Sean jumped in.

"Is she going to be allowed to date high schoolers if she's still in eighth grade at Etheridge?" he asked her dad.

"Sean," her mom warned him.

"What? It's an honest question!" He glanced around the table for backup, but luckily Lillian changed the topic.

"I'm starting to get into music stuff lately," Lillian told them. "We're actually performing at the Youth Zone next month."

Marianne mouthed "thank you" to her sister.

She hadn't realized that everyone knew about her situation.

Was she the stupid one to her whole family, too?

After dinner, her dad pulled up a recording of the last round at Regionals and the family crowded around to watch it. The final round had been posted on a private YouTube link.

"You look so pretty," Nia said from her spot on the couch as she cuddled in the crook of Lillian's arm.

"Um, thanks. Dad, we really don't have to watch this," she said to him.

He talked right over her, telling the whole room about when she answered the opera question right.

His smile lit up his face. When her dad was proud of his kids, he shone.

She'd been letting him down for a long time, she saw.

The questions started flying, and she heard Dan go head-to-head with the other team.

"That's incredible," Uncle Sean said.

"Yeah, these kids—they're something else. I didn't know half that stuff," her dad answered, leaning forward in his favorite chair, still grinning, Coke bottle in hand.

Marianne stood up and walked behind the couch to start picking up the dishes from the dining room table.

"Who is the author of the classic novel *Robinson Crusoe*?" Marianne heard from the other room as she placed a stack of plates in the sink.

She heard herself answer, "Langston Hughes." She'd guessed that name, she remembered, because Vi had said it in an earlier round. He was a poet, she remembered. She'd known she was wrong, but she hadn't cared because she knew she had to say *something*, and Vi insisted that once in a blue moon a guess worked out.

"Ha!" She heard someone laugh in the other room. Who had it been?

"Oh, okay, she got one! Nice! Go, Marianne!" She recognized the voice of Aunt Kendi.

"She's rocking it," Marianne heard Lillian say.

She meandered back toward the room to grab the glasses.

Her dad sat beaming. Next to him, her mom watched quietly.

"Marianne kinda has an Elle Woods thing going on," Uncle Sean said.

"Who's that?" Suri asked.

"From a movie. This airhead type—Valley girl, really pretty—who ends up going to Harvard Law School," Uncle Sean explained to his daughter.

"Oh. Ha!" Suri laughed, but Marianne was sure Suri didn't understand what he meant.

"It's an old movie called *Legally Blonde*," Lillian told the girls. "And she's the best lawyer in the law school."

Aunt Kendi started listing all the movies she liked with that actress. Marianne googled the woman. Marianne did look a little bit like her, actually, but *way* less thin and without the platinum hair. Why were movie stars all so skinny?

Anyway, she didn't think Uncle Sean meant that Marianne *looked* like her.

"Shh, shh, the end is great. It's coming," her dad said.

"And then pie?" her mom checked in with the crowd, but no one answered.

Marianne had cleared the whole table and couldn't find another job. She watched the team tie. She could see how the Ermines were working as one, like one mind, while Remington wore their previous arguments all over them. She'd helped the team that day, she saw. She really had.

Her dad didn't know about that part.

And then she hit the buzzer and said with total calm and confidence, "The big bang theory!" and the whole room on the video clapped and the whole room before her clapped, too, and Marianne remembered Vi turning to her and saying, "I *knew* you could do it!," and then Uncle Sean said, "This is great news. Honestly, I was getting kind of worried for a while there that Marianne would go down the MRS-degree route, but things are really looking up." He laughed at whatever joke he'd just made.

"Sean, shut up," her mom said, her body still and her voice ice-cold.

"Hey, hey—" her dad intervened.

And Uncle Joseph interjected, "Guys, come on . . ." while

Aunt Kendi hurried the girls away by telling them she forgot to grab their activity books from the car.

Meanwhile, Marianne googled *MRS degree* on her phone.

An MRS degree was a commonly used term in the mid-twentieth century and for some time after to refer to a woman attending college solely in order to find a potential husband.

That explained why her mom was berating Uncle Sean by saying, "Are you seriously bringing the 1950s into my home? With our daughters around? What are you thinking? Are you really that fatuous?"

"I was making a stupid joke!" he said. "The 1950s thing *was* the joke! Because it's absurd! Get it?"

"My daughter"—her mom stepped forward toward him, finger pointed at his chest, and Marianne wondered for a minute if they'd have a fistfight because she'd never seen her so ferocious—"is sweet and thoughtful and funny and—"

"I know all these things. I love Mar!" Uncle Sean cowered a bit.

". . . And bright and intuitive and original and *wonderful*, and she may have had some difficulty navigating a traditional curriculum, but I don't know . . . Maybe it's my fault. Maybe I should have homeschooled her or found other options or . . ." Her mom started pacing, and it became clear to Marianne that at this point she was talking to herself. They all seemed to have forgotten Marianne was right there, standing behind the dining table, stiff and quiet. "Somewhere along the way she lost faith in herself. And that *breaks my heart*." She turned with a severe glare back to her little brother. "And, Sean? She is going to get enough awfulness from the world outside, so don't you come into my house and reduce and belittle my little girl with your antiquated digs. Not here."

Her dad touched her mom's arm.

"No, no," her mom said, and walked away from all of them. "It's not funny, guys."

Marianne heard her mom stalk upstairs toward the bedroom.

Uncle Sean tried to say he was sorry to her dad, and Marianne slinked out of the room before he could turn his apologies to her.

She made her way to her mom's room, where she found her lying down, reading a novel.

"Did you fight Uncle Sean just so you could escape everyone to read?" Marianne asked. "Nice one."

Her mom sighed and laid the book down, split halfway open, onto the bed. "Reading calms me down," she said.

"Ugh, reading made me almost *cry* today," Marianne admitted, plopping down on the corner of the bed. She told her mom how sad it was when the dad died in the book.

"You have a deeply feeling heart. Always have." After a beat she sighed and said, "Any time you worry about your grades, just remember that Uncle Sean is living proof that going to Cornell or wherever else doesn't make you an intellectual."

"Ouch!" Marianne giggled.

"I'm serious," her mom said. "And it clearly doesn't make you *kind*. Or *good*. Or any of the things that matter."

"I think you've got to be at least pretty smart to get into Cornell. Or *Harvard*," she added, jokingly elbowing her mom. "But yeah, probably they don't look at your 'nice' scores."

Possum jumped onto the bed and made his way to Marianne's lap. She scratched under his furry gray chin.

Marianne's mom shrugged. "To go to a school like that you have to turn in your homework on time, usually. Show up. Do what's asked of you. Plus, a *heap-ton of privilege* in life helps. And sure, plenty of those people are brilliant, but *plenty* of them *aren't*. Trust me on this one." Her mom sat up and leaned against the headboard, gazing out the windows toward the pink setting sun. "I'm sorry your evil uncle said that about you."

Marianne laughed and pulled her mom's hand to inch her off the bed. "He's not Maleficent or something. Come on. Plus, you're talking to a Quiz Quest champion, Mom. Why would it bother me?"

Her mom interlaced her fingers with Marianne's.

"You have to come down or it's going to be so awkward," Marianne pleaded.

"I know, I know." Her mom sighed and groaned as she forced herself off the bed.

Possum hopped down beside their feet.

"Dad's super proud of the Regionals thing, huh?" Marianne watched her mom's reaction closely.

"We both are, love," her mom said with a kiss to her head.

But Marianne didn't want assurance, she didn't think. She wanted them to say, "I don't care one way or another about Regionals."

They made their way back downstairs to set up the table for Lillian's strawberry-rhubarb pie.

She was supposed to feel good about her parents feeling proud of her, right? But she couldn't. What was wrong with her?

✳✳✳

Marianne's new greetings at school post-win and post–spring break included: "Hey, genius!" "What's up, Einstein?" "Girl Genius! How you doing?" and "It's Big Bang!"

For the first time since Marianne could remember, someone asked her to be on their group project within seconds. Usually, she waited around for whoever else didn't have a partner and teamed up with them. For their final group work they had to present on the history behind a federal monument. It sounded manageable. She just had to do what she did with Dan—find some interesting things about it, make sure to force herself to put in the parts that were less interesting like exact dates and timelines, and bring it to life. Totally doable.

And any time she questioned if it really *was* doable, she'd say to herself, "You are a Regionals champion," and it helped a teeny bit.

Her class had moved on from *A Tree Grows in Brooklyn* to choice reading for their final project. The fabulous Ms. James said Marianne could do a graphic novel and she almost kissed her. Putting a picture to words felt like what the Ermines did with facts. They lifted what she was learning out of a place she couldn't reach and helped her to see and feel each topic.

At the end of school that Monday after fake-Easter, Skyla approached Marianne. "No Quiz Quest practice today, right? Dad's picking me up. Need a ride?"

Skyla spoke like everything was normal between them. Like she hadn't chosen the Lucas Hayes side of life.

Marianne took in Julie, who stood a couple of feet away from them, engrossed in her phone.

"Okay, but I have to study after school," Marianne said. She wondered if she sounded as cold as she felt.

"Oh," Skyla seemed surprised.

She started to walk toward the school exit and Marianne followed. Julie stayed a couple of feet behind, texting.

"Would Mr. Garcia still fail you after the big win?" Skyla asked.

Skyla didn't even know the half of it. She didn't know about how every single hope and dream Marianne had hinged on winning, how if she didn't, Mr. Garcia *would* fail her, because he was an unfair person acting in an unfair way.

"He lives and dies by a code, and that code is not messing around with point totals and rules," Marianne explained. "I have to get Bs or better on everything and turn in all homework—*everything*—and make sure I keep up with Quiz Quest and have *no* attendance or behavior issues, and, of course, stay on the team through State Championships . . . But that's not even the thing. It's that . . . Never mind."

Without any warning, Marianne's breaths went high up in her chest again, like her lungs sat behind her collar bone. She hated when this happened. But there was so much to do, and always more of it. These days, there was never a time with no worksheet or no reading or no event coming up. Expectations never ended.

She missed ignoring them.

Skyla laughed. "What's happened to you? You're stressed about studying? Do I even know you anymore?"

"Ha ha," Marianne mock-laughed with a scowl.

"Hey—it can't be that hard to ace attendance and behavior at least, right? And showing up to practice?" Skyla asked as Julie poked at her shoulder to say something. They conferred about something or other on Julie's phone.

Not hard for Skyla, anyway. She slid by in school by being average. The perfect life.

Marianne used her entire body weight to push open the doors, and the fresh air enveloped them.

"Sunshine." Marianne tilted her face to the sky.

Skyla shifted her attention back to Marianne. The sun hit

Skyla's soil brown freckles on the tip of her nose. Marianne had missed her.

"Sounds like a lot," Skyla said. "I can go over it with you?"

"There's your dad." Marianne pointed to his car.

She hopped in without looking back. Skyla still stood outside. She stopped to chat with Julie, Zara, and Ellie.

"Hey, Jason."

"Hey, Marie Curie." He winked at her in the rearview mirror.

"That's a new one," she said.

If Vi were there, she knew, she would say something like, "Can anyone in this country name a female scientist *besides* Marie Curie?" Marianne knew she'd say that because she'd brought it up every time they studied a woman in STEM.

Marianne found herself chuckling at the thought. Vi resembled what Oscar the Grouch would be like if he were an ambitious young girl.

"Should I honk for her?" Jason said, nodding toward Skyla, who was deep in conversation.

"Can I do it instead?" Marianne asked.

"Ha." Jason tapped his fingers on the steering wheel. "So have you chosen your classes for next year yet?"

"Huh?"

Jason took a swig of his huge Starbucks drink and then said, "Skyla met with the guidance counselor last week to pick out her classes—didn't you? It looks like she's going to take some honors courses, but hopefully it won't be too much at first. Sounds like you have some interesting elective choices? And a language?"

Marianne hadn't been called in yet. Maybe it just wasn't her turn. Or maybe they didn't want her signing up for anything unless high school was a done deal. Skyla was going to take honors courses? She wondered what classes Skyla had chosen, if she'd purposefully not told her about them, and if that was what she was discussing with her friends right then.

"Oh, that. Yeah, I chose French, but I might change it to Mandarin later," Marianne lied. "It would be cool to learn a language my mom doesn't know."

When Skyla finally joined them inside, they all sang along to a Motown station on their way home, and Marianne tried to breathe. She was a winner. She should feel good. And apparently, she was on speaking terms with Skyla again. That was something.

After Jason parked, Marianne started to head home, but Skyla stopped her. "Come in for nachos before you study?"

"I really can't . . ." Marianne said.

Breaking up the awkwardness, Jason insisted Marianne join them for a few minutes, and they went into Skyla's house to feast on his famous nachos. Sully barked wildly at their entrance.

"Can I have a seltzer?" Marianne asked.

"Of course!" Jason rustled her hair.

She still tried to ask for stuff in their house, even though it felt like a second home.

When she went to the fridge to grab her favorite flavor, she saw a couple of Skyla's midterms on the fridge.

They both read **A+**.

What had Skyla said about her scores? That she'd done "okay"?

She'd done *very* okay.

As Jason poured all their favorite items onto the chips, Marianne hopped on a stool and took out her study materials.

"Marianne, give me those flash cards." Skyla reached across the kitchen's high-top table. "I wanna see how many I know."

Marianne handed them over.

"Dad, check this out. Marianne has been studying for this. Let's go," she said to Marianne. "Who is the American general in World War I who—"

"No, I really don't know that many," Marianne interrupted.

"Hmmm." Skyla flipped through them, testing herself. "Jefferson Davis, Thomas Jefferson—two huge Jeffersons!"

"I know, right?! I think about that every time. There's an old TV show called *The Jeffersons*, too. We should watch it together." She found herself chatting with Skyla as if nothing had broken between them, even though something had. Hadn't it?

Marianne pulled out her math homework and stared at it. It was the last thing she wanted to do, but the second-to-last test was in a few days. She'd done okay on a practice test for the first time in her life. Vi said there was no doubt she'd improved.

But if she didn't improve *enough*, what was the point?

"How much cheese?" Jason asked.

"All the cheese!" Skyla commanded.

Skyla was never more energetic than when she was at home. At school she had a kind of calm to her that made Marianne wonder sometimes if Skyla, too, had a certain "school version" of herself. Like that nervous first-day-of-middle-school Skyla had been covered up by cool-and-collected Skyla.

"Done," he said, literally pouring out the whole bag.

"Delicioso!" Skyla cheered.

Would Skyla take Spanish in high school? Her papa spoke it because his parents in Puerto Rico did.

"Okay." She returned to the flash cards, looking up after reading each question and then saying what she thought the answer was before checking the back. "I know these!" she chirped. "Panama . . . Dr. Anthony Fauci . . . Robert Frost . . . Joseph Stalin . . . The Battle of Waterloo . . ."

"I know all about that one!" Marianne jumped in.

"Let's do some." Skyla handed her half the stack.

They began to study.

And Skyla knew so many. Almost all of them, in fact, except for a handful of the literature ones. If she were in Quiz Quest her specialties would have been history, science, math, *and* social studies. Skyla had always been a good student, but when had she gotten this amazing? Where had she picked up all this knowledge? Vi would have been overjoyed if Skyla had entered that room instead of her. No wonder Nina had tried to recruit her.

Strange.

When the nachos were ready and they dug in, Skyla told Marianne, "When you joined Quiz Quest I got kind of curious about *Jeopardy!*. I've been watching it a lot, actually."

"Is that how you know so many of the flash cards?" Marianne asked, scooping up some sour cream.

"No, watching a few episodes wouldn't teach me all those flash cards, right?" She laughed, and Marianne couldn't help but feel that Skyla was laughing *at* her, not with her, like she did with Julie. "I dunno. You just pick things up in school and from reading."

"Not me," Marianne said with a full mouth.

"Yeah, well, come on, Mar, we both know you didn't really do much of the reading." Skyla's phone buzzed. "Zara has been driving me a little crazy recently. So much drama," she said, but then she proceeded to text with her nonstop.

Once home, even though Marianne just wanted to take a nap, she began her new habit of pulling out her homework, talking it over with her mom, and then calling Vi to help her through it.

Marianne knocked on her bedroom wall to signal to Lillian to quit it with the singing practice. It was starting to get pretty annoying.

"My sister doesn't just want to win a gold medal, she wants to be Olivia Rodrigo, too," Marianne complained instead of saying "Hi."

"I would kill to have an older sister," Vi groused. "Do you know how boring it is to be alone all the time? I spent my childhood playing dress-up with my nanny Raina, who mostly just took videos of it and posted it on her social media page. Fun, right?"

"Wow, sorry," Marianne mumbled. "But, like, I'm glad you shared that with me?"

Vi rolled her eyes and said, "Okay, let's start."

"Hey, I honestly don't know if I have this in me tonight," Marianne told her.

"Too bad," Vi said, just harsh enough for Marianne to hunker down and complete the page with her. "Think of States. Don't you want that glory again?"

"It's not about glory for me," Marianne muttered.

"Right," Vi said. "Yeah, I know. It's about high school." Vi paused and her gaze lingered somewhere offscreen. "I wouldn't want to have to repeat a year either," she said. "I get it."

"It's not something you have to worry about, Ms. Cross." Marianne said her name in Mr. Garcia's voice.

"Still," Vi said, serious as ever.

Once they'd finished a couple of worksheets, Vi explained to Marianne that States would be *much* harder than Regionals.

"We'd better do some team-building then," Marianne said.

"We'd better study ten times harder," Vi retorted. "I want you to master science history. Got it? To *master* it in the next two weeks."

"Cool," Marianne deadpanned. "No problem. Done and done."

"But yes," Vi relented, her face slightly fuzzy on the screen. "Team-building is good, too. Math now?"

"Hey," Marianne said, trying to change the subject to stop her breath from quickening again, "did your parents get to watch the recording?"

"Um." Vi paused. "I emailed it to them, so I assume so."

"They didn't say anything to you about it?" Marianne asked in shock.

"They congratulated me on the win. Upped my allowance," Vi added.

"Whoa, that's *awesome*. You get *paid* for stuff? No wonder you want good grades," Marianne blurted out.

"That has nothing to do with it," Vi said. "I'll give you the money. Want it?"

"Yeah," Marianne laughed.

"Moving on," Vi said.

"Wait, are you serious about giving me the money or no?" Marianne joked.

"If you don't have math in you tonight, I have other ideas," Vi moved on.

"Anything else, please," Marianne begged her.

"Alright. Then tonight we discuss . . ." Vi took a big, dramatic pause. "*Evolution.*"

"Monkeys!" Marianne belted out. "I know about this one. And I do love monkeys." This was the good stuff.

Vi sighed. "Here we go."

"Aw, come on, Vi, you know you're starting to love me," Marianne cooed into the screen.

Vi paused. "You have more merit than initially meets the eye," she said, and then dove into Darwin.

11

A C MINUS: 73.5 percent.

That was what she earned in Mr. Garcia's second-to-last test.

No tears, no tears, no tears . . .

But for a brief time, she'd gotten used to the idea of something different. And that was her mistake.

Her mom was wrong: Uncle Sean wasn't terrible. He simply saw her for what she was.

An MRS degree. Ha. She should've laughed. It was funny! He was obviously just joking. He probably just meant she was pretty, which was a compliment, right?

Did girls really go to college just to find guys to marry? Did those girls still get their degrees, or no? If they got into college in the first place, they had to be pretty smart.

Marianne pictured herself in one of those 1950s dresses, cinched at the waist, big skirt, going, "Steak's for supper, dear!" Maybe that kind of life wouldn't be so bad. You could probably watch TV all day.

Marianne took her pencil and transformed the red C into a crescent moon and the minus into a star.

It was the best grade she'd received all year in math and yet it wasn't good enough. *She* wasn't good enough.

She kept her eyes on the marked-up wood on her table: *RL WAS HERE*, two gross carvings, a penciled airplane, *SAVE ME* . . .

And someone had drawn a horse—tiny, with big cartoon eyes and a swirly tail—in the bottom corner.

"Now that we've finished our discussion of X and Y intercepts, let's turn to the other component of the equation of a straight line: slope."

There wasn't a point to this anymore. Bad grades on quizzes. How could extra credit save her, even if they could win the championship? Which they couldn't, not with her on the team?

She could never get a B plus, let alone an A on the final.

She turned off her ears and drifted . . .

She tried to imagine traveling inside a black hole, where Vi told her the body would stretch every which way, getting longer and longer like your arms and limbs and neck became spaghetti. Dan said it would be worth it to go through spaghettification in order to see what was inside one. Marianne wasn't so sure.

Mr. Garcia disrupted her space journey.

"Ms. Blume?" She could tell he'd been trying to get her attention for a while.

Hadn't he seen her test score? Didn't he know she simply wasn't getting it? She couldn't do this with him. Not that day.

"Hmm?" she asked. She tried to smile, but it was hard.

"So again, given this graph, which point shall we make point one?"

"Sorry, I kind of zoned out for a sec," she said as cheerfully and dismissively as she could. Bubbly Marianne, not a care or a thought in the world.

Her act had always worked before, in months past, so it probably would again. He'd go elsewhere for learning.

The Lorelai Wheeler imitation came back to her as if it had never left.

Mr. Garcia took a beat, then continued. "I'm happy to go back a bit. Let's review. Review is good for everyone. So. The actual equation is as follows: m equals Y2 minus Y1 divided by X2 minus X1. Now, Ms. Blume, this may be confusing, but it actually doesn't matter which point you designate as point two. So, again, taking this graph into consideration, what will be point one?"

She didn't know.

"You got this, Horse!" someone said in the room, a room that had begun to feel like a bunch of echoes and far-off voices unattached to any particular people.

Horse. Stupid as a horse.

She hadn't chosen to become Lorelai Wheeler out of nowhere.

After the horse divorce day, after Marianne's mom had seen her crying, when Skyla arrived at their house with sugar cookies, her mom had asked Skyla what was wrong with her.

Skyla admitted she'd told Marianne's mom all about "the horse divorce thing," which Skyla had heard from someone else, who said it was hilarious and that "even Marianne thought so."

Marianne had left Skyla to play some games on her laptop. She went downstairs to talk to her mom, to tell her it was no big deal and everyone thought it was funny. Obviously, Marianne was going to tell her mom, she wouldn't be following in her mom's footsteps with the whole French thing. She was planning on saying to her mom, "You did two years abroad in France. Me? I'm going with the UK. Because *English*. Cheerio!"

But right outside the kitchen door she heard her parents talking. Laughing, actually. Those whisper-laughs that sounded like little wheezes.

"Honestly," her mom said, "it's an understandable mistake. If I'd just read the word without hearing it, I would've pronounced it wrong, too."

"But she's never heard it? Of course she has. She couldn't put two and two together?" Her dad's voice a not-quite-whisper. "*That's* the concerning part, if we can be serious for a second. The not-putting-two-and-two-together that *hors d'oeuvres* are *hors d'oeuvres*."

"Oh, come on," her mom said back, her voice gaining a little volume, as Marianne heard her lightly smack Marianne's dad's arm. "It's not *concerning*. It's just the beginning of the year."

"Love, we're talking about *Marianne* here," her dad said. "She's never been the 'star pupil' type."

"I think it's brave she just goes for it even if she doesn't know how to say something," her mom said. "When I was a kid? I had panic attacks at the thought of doing a single thing wrong."

"My little type A perfectionist," her dad said. And there was quiet for a second. Ew, were they kissing?

"Poor kid," her dad said after a minute. "So she's a bit of a *ditz* sometimes. Doesn't make me love her any less!"

"Ethan," her mom laughed, "don't say that."

"It's true! Not every kid is 'gifted.' Who cares?" her dad said, chewing on something.

"It can't be easy watching Lillian just breeze through life, acing it. That must be hard," her mom said.

"They just come out who they are, don't they?" her dad said. "And she came out adorable and sweet and she will *love* state school."

"Ethan!" Her mom must have smacked him again.

"Hey, it's cheaper for us!" he said. "Kidding, kidding," he added.

They both started laughing harder, and Marianne went back upstairs.

So she's a bit of a ditz *sometimes*, her dad had said.

Was that what Lorelai Wheeler was? she had wondered. A "ditz"?

The path had instantly become clear. They'd carved it out for her. Who didn't love someone adorable and sweet and stupid?

Lorelai had given her the perfect example: Don't cry; don't fidget or hide or blush. Be bubbly, without a care in the world.

Shrug and giggle and disappear.

Her parents had seen her that way, anyway. Why not embrace it?

And it had helped her survive.

"Ms. Blume? Are you still with us?" Mr. Garcia asked, dipping his head a little lower to get her attention, like he was searching for contact. "Ms. Blume, what will be point one?"

With no words but only a smile-free face, she tried to implore him to *please* not make her do this, *please*, not then, not when everyone thought she was a winner, not when she knew she was a fraud.

But he waited for her answer.

She checked the clock. Twenty minutes left to go. No escape.

She glanced at her notes. She'd written nothing.

She could picture Lorelei Wheeler perfectly, twisting her

hair and batting her lashes and putting on makeup during class and cheering everyone else on while she giggled every question away. Marianne wished she could talk to her and find out how she'd really felt about being cute and stupid and discover what she'd really been interested in and confused about and good at.

"Ya know, I dunno?" Marianne took some lip gloss out of her pocket and doused her mouth with it. "But, like, we can just pick any point? Any number? Sooo . . . how 'bout seven 'cause it's lucky."

"Yes! Blume is *back*!" Lucas hollered from the back.

"Mr. Hayes . . ." Mr. Garcia warned.

Several different reactions trickled throughout the classroom—some whispers, a handful of cackles, a sigh or two.

Marianne figured the sigh was from Vi, seated behind her, probably just thinking about how all this would affect Quiz Quest.

He had to move on to another kid now. This was a distraction, she didn't know the answer or how to get it, and time was ticking. She decided to act like he'd left her already and check her hair for split ends.

Mr. Garcia cleared his throat. "No, actually, it's not a pick-your-own-number scenario. Marked on the graph are our two intercepts." He waited for a second, maybe hoping she'd respond. She didn't. "So we have (-4, 0) and (0, 8). So . . ." he lectured on and on.

How could he do this? Hadn't he seen she was doing her best in Quiz Quest? Why couldn't he comprehend that this math thing was *over*? That Regionals was a fluke and there was no way she could win States? Why couldn't he give up on her?

Marianne would end it herself. For good.

She took out her gum and tossed a stick into her mouth.

Mr. Garcia halted in his tracks.

"Excuse me, gum is not allowed in class," he scolded her.

Marianne crossed her arms and leaned back in her chair, chewing.

He returned to his Smart Board, writing out some other type of equation she didn't recognize. "Now, Ms. Blume . . ." he went on, still going after her.

And the question she'd been holding inside all year shot out.

"Why do you hate me?" she asked him.

The class hushed.

"Excuse me?" He froze, his writing hand in midair. It was his turn to act like he hadn't heard or understood, she saw.

"Nothing," she groused. "Never mind."

"Now . . ." He wrote some more numbers and ideas and markings onto the screen.

And Marianne unwrapped another stick of gum.

When he looked up again, she blew a bubble. It popped, and she pulled the sticky remnants off her nose.

Mr. Garcia nearly ripped a tissue out of the box on his desk, marched two feet over to her, and held it out. "*Enough.*"

She let her artificial strawberry lip glossed smiling pretense fall away entirely.

 255

"No," she said.

He looked at her. She looked at him.

Then she lurched her head further toward his, so they almost touched, blew another bubble, and let it grow bigger and bigger, until it popped.

She grabbed her bag, walked out the door, and headed home.

***

When she entered the house, she could hear the melody upstairs of her mom speaking Italian to someone on the phone. She sounded happy, so she must have been working on a translation project she really loved.

At the sound of Marianne shutting the front door, her mom appeared at the top of the stairs. Her face dropped and she must have told the person on the call that she had to go.

"What are you doing here?" her mom asked. "What happened?"

"Where's Dad?" Marianne asked nonsensically. She knew her dad didn't work from home all day like her mom did.

"Is everything okay?" Her mom hustled down the stairs.

Marianne hooked her thumbs around the bottom straps of her backpack. She examined the tips of her dirty sneakers—once white, now all scratched up.

"I just . . . left," Marianne told her. And, in light detail, she summarized what had occurred in Mr. Garcia's nightmarish math class.

"Get in the car," her mom commanded, snatching her purse and slipping on her shoes.

At Marianne's frozen stare, her mom repeated, "Get in."

"School's almost over now, anyway," Marianne argued, even as she followed her mom outside to the car.

Her mom's keys jangled as she fumbled with the ignition.

They rode in silence until they were a block away from the school, when her mom snapped, "Do you not care about your future at *all?*"

Marianne tried to count the trees they passed. A couple dozen on each street.

"We don't need you to be an A student, *don't you know that?*" Her mom pleaded with her as they made the final turn toward Etheridge. "We just need you to have even *some faith* in yourself. To do the best for *you*, not for some other kid."

"So cheesy, Mom," Marianne said, joking with her.

But her mom didn't crack a smile this time, not even a little bit.

As they parked, her mom spat out, "You made a deal. No behavior problems, no attendance issues, and you just . . . *leave school?* In the middle of a class? You managed to combine both things?! I just—" Her mom shook her head, grabbed her purse, and together they walked toward Ms. Clarke's office without saying another word.

Marianne kept her eyes down to avoid seeing anyone from Mr. Garcia's class.

Kids exited their last period in excitement. They chatted and hollered and slammed locker doors shut.

Ms. Clarke's expression suggested she knew what had happened. Mr. Garcia must have told her between periods.

She opened her office door and let them in, following behind.

"Come on in," she said with a kindness in her voice that Marianne imagined would not last.

"Even as I did it, I knew it was bad," Marianne said as they all sat down before anyone could get a word in.

Ms. Clarke interlaced her fingers and leaned forward. "We had a deal, my dear."

Immediately, Marianne's mom made excuses for her. "She's been overwhelmed," she said. "Quiz Quest was too much . . . That's an error on my part."

"Mom," Marianne said, stopping her.

"We have bent a lot of the rules for Marianne," Ms. Clarke said.

Her mom surrendered. "I know, I know, you're right."

"Typically," Ms. Clarke continued, "skipping class would result in detention, and as we discussed a couple of months ago, any behavior issues—detention and the like—jeopardize Marianne's already fragile standing in passing the year. And going by our deal, this would mean an end to participation in Quiz Quest. And yes, that results in a math grade too low to pass the year."

"But I—" Marianne jumped in.

"And yet"—Ms. Clarke held up a palm to silence her—
"you are merely two weeks away from the final competition,
and your team is counting on you."

Marianne and her mom waited as Ms. Clarke tapped her
fingers and seemed to think aloud.

"On the other hand," she lectured, "you made a promise. You broke your word, and I can't reward this behavior."
She sighed. "You know, if your recent test scores were better,
I . . ." She reached into her drawer and pulled out some mints,
offering them to Marianne and her mom. "Oh, and—that's
right—" She held up the mint case as if it reminded her. "We
didn't even get to the gum yet!" Softly she added, "This is
certainly tricky."

Her mom, rejecting the mints, turned to Marianne and
mouthed, "The gum?"

Marianne dropped her face into her hands.

"What's this about gum?" her mom asked Ms. Clarke.

Ms. Clarke explained and concluded, "I am at a loss."

So was Marianne.

She didn't know how she'd explain her actions to her parents or to the Quiz Quest kids. She immediately wanted to
apologize to Mr. Garcia, yet simultaneously she never wanted
to face him again. If Ms. Clarke didn't let her compete,
Marianne would be the kid who ruined Quiz Quest for him.
He would hate her even more.

And she would have to repeat the eighth grade. Without
the extra credit, even an A plus plus on the final wouldn't get

her past the points threshold to pass math. Her Ds and Fs added up to make this moment happen.

And it was her fault.

Was it really true that her mom and dad didn't care if she wasn't an A student? Really? Surely, a part of them wanted that.

She lifted her head and her gaze drifted once again, as it had when Ms. Clarke had told her she was failing eighth grade, to the big skull painting on her principal's wall. It was filled with a patchwork of colors, some parts of the face just bone and others with simple features. She hadn't thought much of it at first. Now she wanted to know what it was.

"What's that painting?" she asked her principal.

Ms. Clarke smiled.

"It's called *Untitled*." The grin grew. "By Jean-Michel Basquiat. The original costs over 110 million dollars. Isn't that something?"

Marianne shook her head. "It kind of looks like he wasn't finished with it."

"True," Ms. Clarke said.

They all checked out the skull until Ms. Clarke exhaled and said, "So. Where to go from here?"

***

From Vi: WHY DID YOU DO THAT?????
From Nina: hey r u ok what happened why arent you

at practice did you really curse out mr g omg he must
have flipped
From Dan: please come back vi is going full vi
also i cant watch infinity galaxy without u but if i dont
watch it soon i dont know what ill do

She was suspended for two days, with her mom set to pick up homework packets on her behalf. She couldn't attend practice. And she couldn't bring herself to respond to the Ermines.

The only person she could talk to was the person she'd always talked to about everything.

She texted Skyla:

Hi

porch

cant. im in trouble

so i hear. did u really push over a table and chair

Without warning, Marianne began to cry. she wrote,

lol no, just cant hack it in mr garcias class.
got a c- on the test. couldnt take it anymore.
oh nooo im so sorry

The tiny dots indicating Skyla would type something else pulsed on the screen for too long. She'd probably written something and stopped, thought better of it, and started again. But what?

Marianne wrote,

they probably wont let me do quiz quest anymore. and without the extra credit i need an a+ on the final to pass. an a+. you know thats not possible. i dont know why I even tried.

She wiped away her tears and then rubbed her hands off on her jeans.

She put down the phone, changed into her PJs, and slid under her covers. The sun was still out, but so what?

The next text from Skyla read,

I told you—I will study with you
just let me!
why did you like julies comment during regionals

Marianne felt a sob pour out. She put a hand over her mouth and squeezed her eyes shut. When she opened them, she saw:

What??? I did???
she said omg this is going to be hilarious and you liked it. just seemed really mean i dunno i cant stop thinking about it

omg no

I get it it's because you don't want to be friends with the dumb girl.

wait not dumb i learned that's a really bad word

what?!?!? porch! now! if ethan and norah flip i will personally tell them to relax

k fine

They stood at their railings. Marianne rubbed her forehead. It was like there was something spiky inside there that couldn't get out.

Skyla looked like she'd been crying, too. She spoke first, her words spewing out: "You think I don't want to be friends with the 'dumb' girl? It seems like you don't want to be friends with the loser who studies every night! But that's just what weekdays are *like* for most people, okay?"

Marianne had never felt like she was pressuring Skyla all those times she wasn't studying and Skyla was. She never wanted Skyla to feel like she couldn't go be her own person or be proud of her school stuff or anything like that. But maybe this whole time Skyla *had* felt that pressure.

"I'm not some nag because I want you to study and get better and be with me next year," Skyla went on.

"What? I never said you were—" Marianne whispered across the way.

Skyla could speak as loudly as she wanted, but Marianne didn't want to get caught.

 263

"Look, I'm really sorry," Skyla interrupted her, leaning so far over her railing Marianne thought she might fall. She pressed her lips together and looked up, tears welling. "I shouldn't have liked a comment like that."

Marianne, feeling her own tears return, wiped her cheeks with the edge of her sleeve. "I just don't get it."

"Marianne, not that it's an excuse, but I thought we were in a fight? You were giving me the silent treatment? I was mad."

"Huh?"

"Yeah," Skyla explained, like it was so evident, like she was shocked that Marianne didn't know what she was talking about. "It was after you told me you weren't gonna try! Don't you remember? You basically said you were going to sink the Quiz Quest team to save yourself."

Marianne didn't know what to say. "But—but I did try! I've been showing up! I've been doing it! I mean, haven't you seen it? I-I figured you knew that." She scanned the windows to see if her mom was looking. The coast was clear. "But it's not because I'm a good person, that's for sure," she added.

"What do you mean?" Skyla asked her.

"I only get the extra credit if we win. Vi told me. It's the only way to show Mr. Garcia I'm not faking it. He heard me making fun of Quiz Quest, so he doesn't trust me, which I get, but—it's a lot. It's a lot." She teared up again. "So I had to go for it, to try."

A neighbor walked by with her bulldog and Marianne waved.

"That doesn't seem fair," Skyla acknowledged. "And you're not a bad person. It just bothered me that you'd do that."

"I know! It was bad!" Marianne interrupted, crying again.

"And I didn't know what's been going on!" Skyla continued. "It's not like you said anything to me . . ." Skyla's tears stopped, and she immediately seemed drained of energy. Just . . . sad.

"You still thought I was sabotaging the team? This whole time?" As Marianne asked her, she realized she hadn't exactly explained to Skyla how much had changed between her and her teammates. And a lot had.

"You've hardly spoken to me recently," Skyla said in a sad, low tone.

"Because I've been busy finally *studying* and *working* at—"

But before Marianne could finish, Skyla burst out, "You've been talking nonstop to the kids on Quiz Quest, though. Instead of me." Skyla shook her head. "And I get it!"

"What?!" Marianne couldn't help but raise her voice a little. "I haven't talked to you much because you were spending all your time with Zara and Julie and—"

"*Julie?*" Skyla's dark eyebrows scrunched up in confusion. "Ha. If we'd been talking more maybe you'd know that Julie kind of bothers me."

"What?"

"She's fine, she's just . . . a little nasty sometimes. She's gossipy. She's always texting me bad stuff about people, and I try and think of ways to respond where I'm not making her

265

mad, but I'm also not agreeing, and it actually gives me a bad feeling in my whole body like . . ." Skyla shivered dramatically. "And me liking her comment was exactly the problem. She kind of, like, brings out a side of me I don't love."

"Oh." It was like the distance between them this whole time hadn't been half a front and back yard but rather a whole continent.

"And I mean if she's talking about everybody, she's definitely talking about me, too, right?" Skyla played with her moonstone bracelet. The bracelet, Marianne saw, that they'd both gotten together in Traverse City two summers ago. "You know, once she told me that people used to say I was your sidekick."

"What?! She's so mean!" Marianne held a hand to her heart in shock.

"Yeah. She's probably right. Who knows what else she says about me . . . That I'm her sidekick now, probably," Skyla grunted under her breath.

"No way. And I don't know what anyone could say bad about you, even a jerk like Julie . . ." Marianne said honestly.

"That's because you love me." A tiny smile overtook Skyla's frown.

"I do!" Marianne collapsed her forehead into her forearms, which rested on the railing. "We're just . . . Maybe we're just too different," she said, her words muffled.

Skyla groaned. "No! I just shouldn't have liked Julie's mean comment. I thought you were making fun of yourself, too. That's always been your thing, right? But still, I . . ." She paused. She rested her elbows on the railing and closed her eyes for a moment. "I shouldn't have." She opened them and looked at Marianne. "I got a little jealous of that Vi girl. Even though she's . . . the way she is."

Marianne laughed. "She's not so bad, actually. You'd like her after a while."

Skyla laughed, too.

"So you got a C minus, huh?" Skyla asked.

"Yeah."

"I'm really sorry," Skyla said. "Are you ready to let me help you now? I'd really like to."

Marianne's memory flashed to pushing a terrified Skyla off the dock into the lake at camp. The way Skyla wiped her eyes and laughed and screamed. And reached up to pull Marianne in with her.

Marianne nodded. "Okay."

***

Back at home, her texts read:

Vi: what were you thinking?!?!?!??! are they kicking you off?

Nina: weve practiced so much, they cant do that now!

Dan: The gum pop heard 'round the world. Funnily enough, that phrase "the shot heard round the world" actually refers to the first shot at the battles of Lexing ton and Concord, though for years I thought it was first

 267

associated with the assassination of Franz Ferdinand. (Wikipedia link)

Vi: dan. relevance. come on. i told you months ago that you cant have gum in class!

Marianne: **actually you said in the hallway and that wasnt right but ok.**

Vi: (eye roll emoji)

Marianne: **plus I knew I couldn't have it in class!**

Nina: my mom says "your friend Marianne is a rebel without a clue" lol

Marianne: **you told your mom???? the whole story??? (head slap emoji)**

Dan: Rebel Without a Cause was a movie starring James Dean—three Oscar noms, no wins (Wikipedia link)

Nina: i know its a movie dan. thats the joke.

Marianne: **i didnt know that. but james dean was real cute.**

Nina: true

Dan: true true

Vi: i have to go study. you guys should too.

Marianne: **ms clarke says shell let me know by next week. ill still study ok?**

Vi: let us know the second you hear.

Nina: good luck!!!

***

For all of Marianne's suspension and into the weekend, she and Skyla studied side by side.

On Sunday night, Skyla announced, "I don't mean this to be mean, but I think the word for what's going on with you is 'innumerate.' It's like illiterate, but with numbers. Dad was telling me about it the other day."

Marianne wondered why they'd been talking about it. The most obvious conclusion was that they'd been discussing her. Maybe Skyla's parents were trying to comfort her about Marianne not going into freshman year with her.

"You just left the math party at some point and didn't come back, right?" Skyla went on, her kind eyes earnest. "So it's like you know your ABCs and some words, but you can't read a paragraph."

"So how do I ace a test?" Marianne asked her.

Skyla sighed and fought her endless battle of putting her hair behind her ears as the strands fell out again and again. "We'll give it our best," she said.

Her mom and dad both separately checked in on them multiple times to see if they were actually studying.

And after Skyla listened in on her "learn one thing a night" sessions with Vi, Dan, and Nina, they practiced flash cards, focusing on math.

Skyla already knew many of the answers, like the degrees of the inner angles of a triangle and the myth behind the Orion constellation. And after a couple of rounds on each stack, Skyla remembered even more, like "antipodal points"

and "orthodromes" and "Bernard Montgomery" and "the House of Tudor."

"Which element has a name meaning 'light-bearing'?" Skyla asked, trying to go as fast as they could.

Marianne's mind blanked. Elements swirled in her mind—iron and copper and helium.

"I don't know," Marianne sighed.

"Phosphorus," Skyla said.

"You didn't look down. You just knew it?" Marianne asked her.

"Well, we just did it a couple times. So now I know it." Skyla shrugged, and Marianne could tell she was trying to be casual about it.

"You're really good at this stuff," Marianne told her.

"Think of the word 'phosphorescent,'" Skyla said, ignoring her. "Like a phosphorescent ocean. Bioluminescence. Have you ever seen those pictures? Where the ocean glows blue or green because of the algae?"

Marianne shook her head, and Skyla pulled up a bunch of photos on her phone.

"Whoa, so pretty," Marianne said. "I'll remember now."

But Skyla was able to recall these things with no effort, no tricks.

Marianne laid her papers and flash cards in her lap. "How do you do that?" she asked her. "Really?"

"I've been getting good at school stuff this year, I guess," Skyla mumbled, shuffling through some of the flash cards.

Perking up, she added, "That's why this whole time I've been saying, I can really help you out!"

If that was supposed to make Marianne feel better, it didn't.

Skyla had always been fine at school, so compared to Marianne she was Isaac Newton. But she'd never been intimidating, or the kid in class with all the answers, or so obviously in a whole other league than Marianne, the way she was now.

When had she changed? Had she actually always been this way?

"I don't want to go back to school tomorrow," Marianne told her.

"Should we take a break and check out Lillian's telescope?" Skyla suggested. "Clear night."

"Have you hidden how smart you are from me?" Marianne asked her point-blank.

"Psssh." Skyla stood up from her cross-legged position on the floor, where they sat surrounded by papers in the center of a homework spiral.

Maybe Skyla didn't even know she'd been doing it. Or if she did, she wouldn't admit it.

"No, you just never let me help before! With anything. So you haven't seen this part of me, I guess!" She put out a hand to help pull Marianne up, but Marianne didn't take it.

"I'm stupid," Marianne said. "I am truly, honestly stupid. And my parents and you are too afraid to say it." She paused. "To my face, anyway."

So she's a bit of a ditz . . . they'd said.

"Ridiculous," Skyla scoffed. She went to the window and opened the shades. "Like I've said before, you just don't know how to study. It's a *skill*. And yeah, I'm really good at that. That's what you're learning how to do right now."

"You're wrong. I've tried. This time, I've really tried. And I'll never be able to do *that*"—she gestured to the papers on the floor before her, the papers Skyla had immediately internalized—"like you can."

Skyla walked to the door. "Up to the attic," she said. "We need a break. Stars time."

On their way out of her bedroom and toward the stairs, they heard a noise coming from Lillian's room, but it wasn't music.

"Shhh." Marianne held a finger to her lips and pressed her ear against the door.

Crying.

She turned the doorknob and heard "*Get out!*" before seeing anything.

Shutting the door immediately, she followed Skyla upstairs.

"What do you think is going on?" Skyla asked as they made their way toward the telescope.

"I really don't know."

Making their way past her dad's stacks of sheet music and shelves of records and CDs, and her mom's three filing cabinets filled with who-knew-what, they reached the window that led to the stars.

"I'm so happy you're finally into this." Skyla giggled like a little kid.

They searched for Uranus and Centaurus but had no luck. The patterns in the sky that night seemed random, and as Skyla took out Marianne's dad's handbook to find some constellations, Marianne lay on the cushions instead.

"I give up," she told her friend.

"You just have to keep searching," Skyla insisted.

But Marianne hadn't been talking about the stars.

She didn't belong with the Quiz Quest kids. She didn't even belong with Skyla. Skyla had been afraid she'd move on from Marianne if they weren't together. But she already had. Whatever Marianne had tried hadn't been enough, and she could see then—as clearly as the nearly full moon outside the windowpanes—that it might *never* be. If she got to high school, Skyla would *still* have to move on. Marianne would bring her down.

"Maybe I want to be an astronaut," Skyla said, her eye pressed to the tiny lens. "After we open our shop, of course. Or maybe we'll do the shop in our retirement. Kids always say they want to be an astronaut when they're tiny—"

"Suri does," Marianne jumped in.

"But *someone* has to do it for real." Skyla paused. "I see Venus! Come look!"

Marianne stayed where she was.

If Mr. Garcia or Ms. Clarke decided she couldn't compete due to her behavior, it would probably be for the best.

"If I got you a free pass to the moon, you'd come, right?" Skyla asked her, eyes still searching for a far-off planet.

"Yeah, of course," Marianne said, looking up at the white ceiling. "I'll bring the lemonade."

***

At bedtime, Marianne approached Lillian's door. This time, she knocked.

No one answered, but the light was on, and Marianne sneaked in.

Lillian sat on her bed—no music, no podcasts, no book, no phone—just painting her nails a dark color, thinking. Lillian was not one to sit and think. She was always doing, and going, and doing more.

Marianne wasn't about to beat around the bush.

"What's up and why were you crying?" she asked her, jumping onto the bed and curling up like a cat.

Lillian gave her some side eye and said nothing.

So Marianne held out her fingers. "Do me, too," she said.

Lillian dutifully started to paint them.

"Did Samia break up with Jack yet?" Marianne asked. "He's really the worst, right? I mean, he sounds like he's one of those guys who's nice, but then if you get mad for even the smallest thing, even if it's totally fair to be mad about, he's like, 'I'm so nice, you don't appreciate how nice I am,' you know what I mean? That's like a fake-nice."

Out of nowhere and extremely casually, Lillian changed

the subject to say, "I'm just a little bummed because Harper doesn't think I'm ready for the show at the Youth Zone." She painted Marianne's middle finger and shrugged. "I get it. I was new to it."

"Um, *excuse me*?" Marianne hadn't been over the moon about this Harper girl, and now this?

"She's right," Lillian snapped, like she was annoyed with Marianne, not Harper. "She said I'm a little pitchy. Not the right tone mixed with her voice or something." Lillian raised a hand and shook it as if erasing the whole conversation with her palm. "Doesn't matter. She asked Juliana instead, and that's fine."

"*What?* Well then Harper is, like, a *fool* because you, Lillian Ruth, are good at *everything*. It's like she hasn't even *met* you." Marianne blew on her fingers and put out her other hand.

Lillian shot up, sitting straight as an icicle. "*I am not good at everything.*"

"Okay . . ." Marianne said, deflating. "Geez."

"I just hate when you say that because then it's like . . . It takes away all the work I put into it," Lillian said, softening.

Marianne blew a hair out of her eye. "Huh. I can see that," she said.

Lillian sighed. Her shoulders relaxed. "I *wanted* to be good at it." She started painting Marianne's other hand, shaking her head. "But it's fine."

"You can sing for fun, right? It doesn't have to be with a band, or even be good, right? I love it when you sing,"

Marianne told her gently, worrying she'd get snapped at again.

But Lillian just said, "Totally. You're so smart, *Marianne Bess*."

"Yeah, I'm pretty much Ken Jennings," Marianne said, thinking of a *Jeopardy!* champ Dan had told her about.

"Who?" Lillian asked before adding, "Doesn't matter. Mar, you don't have to be an A student to be smart."

"Ha," Marianne said flatly. "That's a lot like what Mom said. You're her clone."

Lillian groaned dramatically. "You know there's a whole world between acing a test and failing it, right? And you can shoot for whatever *your best* is? Or what's possible *for you*? Like, in the pool"—Lillian leaned toward Marianne, switching to swim team mode with her whole self—"your greatest competitor is really *you*. You want to beat your own time most of all. Do you *really* not get that?"

Marianne shrugged.

"I swear, you're, like, infuriating," Lillian said. Finishing up their nails, she told her, "The topcoat is in the bathroom. Come on."

They headed down the hall and Marianne sat on the sink counter while Lillian knelt on a stool in front of her.

"Honestly, Mar?" Lillian said as she applied the glossy layer.

"Yeah?"

"I don't care that much about the music part." She bit her bottom lip.

"What do you mean? You love music."

"Sort of," Lillian said. "It's fun . . ."

Marianne waited for her to say more, but it took a few fingers.

"What I cared about was being around Harper," Lillian confessed finally.

"Oh." Marianne didn't know what to say. "Like, you're into her?"

Lillian nodded.

"Did you ever get her to join Literary Lionesses?" Marianne blew on her nails.

Lillian shook her head. "You called me a wuss and you were right." She slumped on the stool.

"I do not understand you," Marianne admitted. "You're perfect. Why are you so freaked out by this girl?"

"Mar, *what if she doesn't like me*?" Lillian's open, asking face told Marianne that Lillian really needed an answer.

But Marianne didn't have one.

"It's like . . ." Lillian said, "I can organize a club, I can swim a meet, I can turn in my essay, sure. If I do that, I'll probably do well. But with Harper? I don't know how she feels!" Lillian lifted and dropped her glossy hands. "I don't know what will happen! Do you know what I mean? I can't handle it!" Lillian sighed and added dismissively, "I hate this."

"Just tell her how you feel," Marianne said. Wasn't that always the way?

"She wouldn't disinvite me from her band if she liked me, too," Lillian said, sounding the most insecure Marianne had ever heard her.

"Or maybe she's just as pretentious as she seems and it's truly 'all about the music'?" Marianne offered.

And, to Marianne's delight, Lillian grinned.

"That could be it," Lillian said.

"You *have to tell her*," Marianne said. She motioned taking a big dive and added, "Jump in the pool."

"Yeah . . ." Lillian said, lost in thought.

Marianne tested their fingernails. Not dry yet.

And they sat together for a moment. They could hear their dad's muted practicing from downstairs.

"Your suspension is over tomorrow, yeah?" Lillian asked. "How are *you* doing?"

Marianne nodded. "Well, I ruined Quiz Quest for the team. And I only liked Quiz Quest because of the team. So I'm the worst."

"Wait, you *liked* Quiz Quest?" Lillian asked with a smirk.

Marianne let out a surprised laugh. "I like the *people*. They really deserve to win. I messed it up for them."

"What about for you?" Lillian asked.

Without winning there'd be no high school. No homecoming with Skyla. No new people. No new chances.

"Eh, they probably won't let me compete, anyway, so it's a lost cause," she said. "I feel really bad."

Their nails finished, Lillian turned off the bathroom light and they headed toward their bedrooms.

"Could they get someone else to take your spot?" Lillian asked, leaning against her own doorframe, her foot propped up against it so her knee popped out.

"Hmm," Marianne said. "I dunno."

Their mom walked down the dimly lit hall and kissed each of their heads to say good night.

They stood in silence as she walked off.

"I'm sorry you had a bad day," Marianne said.

"You too." Lillian tried to hide a small sniffle. "Thanks for being there, Mar."

"Right next door!" Marianne made jazz hands, walked backward into her room, and closed the door.

Lying in bed, pulling the covers up to her chin, Marianne felt the expansion of the universe pulling everyone further apart—Skyla and her brilliance, Lillian and her perfectionist pining, Vi and her constant effort now maybe all for nothing—and she wished for one minute that the Earth and all its many parts could just stay still.

12

HER MOM DROPPED HER off super early to apologize to Mr. Garcia before school started. The sun was only just coming up, and Marianne wrapped her wool cardigan tightly around herself.

Before she even reached Ms. Kelley, who manned the doors in the early hours to let in the athletes and breakfast kids, Mr. Garcia strode up to the entrance holding a helmet. He must have biked to school.

Even though she was there to talk to him, she hoped he wouldn't spot her.

But there was no escape. He saw her.

"Mr. Garcia!" she said.

He took out the headphone in his ear, pocketing it.

They stood a few feet from the doorway.

"Watcha listening to?" she stalled. It was so weird talking to him like she hadn't defied him so epically that she'd ruined her year and embarrassed him only a few days before.

He held up his phone as he said, "True crime podcast."

"Oh! Dark!" Marianne heard the surprise come out.

"I like to . . . I don't know. Solve things," he said. He laughed awkwardly, which surprised her. Was he embarrassed?

The world filled with a little more light as the sun slowly rose.

Mr. Garcia leaned the helmet against his hip and waited for her to speak. They both knew she had to say something.

Marianne took a huge breath. "About last week . . ."

"Yes. About that."

She thought maybe he'd say more, but he didn't.

"I'm really sorry," she said, too softly, she knew, and without enough of an explanation. She could hear the words of her mom after a big fight with her sister. "Sorry for *what*, Marianne?" she'd always say. "It helps to specify."

Marianne heard the gum pop over and over again in an awful mental soundtrack to her shame.

"I'm sorry for disrespecting you," she added.

A couple of kids walked toward the doors and waved at Mr. Garcia. He nodded back.

"If it makes you feel any better," Marianne went on, "I'm in a lot of trouble."

Mr. Garcia took off his glasses and cleaned them with the ends of his shirt. "Thank you for the apology."

Was that it?

Maybe he was used to this.

Marianne thought of all the other times kids had acted out in his class. A boy named Liam had cursed at him once. One girl who didn't go there anymore had stolen money from the shared snack bin, breaking the honor system they all shared.

Mr. Garcia nodded toward some other kids leaving the building who yelled a "hello" his way.

"It's . . ." He started to speak and then stopped. "It's not the disrespect that . . ." He seemed to be stumbling to find the right thing to say. "That bothers me." He paused and then said, "I thought we were making . . ." He paused again, sighing. "Some *headway*." He put his glasses back on and shook his head.

And his disappointment overwhelmed her. She saw it all over his face. It reminded her of her dad.

He couldn't seem to look her right in the eye. He swayed back and forth from toe to heel.

A few cars started to pull up by the school. The sun sat in the sky, ready for the day.

Marianne loosened her hold on her cardigan as the sunshine warmed her.

"But what distresses me . . . I—" he said. He looked around at the students starting to gather into little clusters. "Well, let's head into the classroom," he suggested.

Marianne followed him. They walked past Ms. Kelley.

"Hi!" Marianne greeted her. "How's it going, Ms. Kelley?"

"Another day, another day," Ms. Kelley said.

"I hope it's a good one?" Marianne called out behind her

shoulder as Ms. Kelley raised her voice to say back, "You and me both, kiddo!"

Once inside the math room, Mr. Garcia flipped on the overhead lights, and he took a seat at his desk, sliding his helmet and bag beneath it.

Marianne sat at hers.

In those positions, and without other kids around to hear them, he seemed a bit more comfortable.

It was as if outside the world of the math classroom, he was a totally different person: nervous, like Nina, and struggling with how to be friendly, like Vi.

He ran his hand through his hair a couple of times and rearranged a couple of items on his desk. "Ms. Blume, you're at the point in your path, I believe, where you can choose: Am I who others expect me to be, or am I who I want to be?" He tapped both hands on the desks as if he'd perfectly said what he wanted to say. "Yes, that's the crux of it," he added.

"Okay? Sorry?" Marianne rubbed her fingers over the horse drawn on the desk.

Mr. Garcia sighed and leaned forward, his elbows on the table. "Look, I know you hate algebra."

"I like it okay when I get it!" she interrupted before he could go on. "But that's almost never! It takes me, like, *months* to get something other people get in a *minute*. Literally. And you *know* that."

"You know . . . It's true that many adults get through life without finding the slope or solving for X," Mr. Garcia

283

admitted, actually chuckling to himself a bit. "Even if I try to give you real-life examples in class . . . Listen—I know a lot of the stuff we learn won't show up in your life . . ."

"Thank you! That's what I'm saying, Mr. Garcia!" she exclaimed to him, pounding the table. "I've been trying to explain that to my parents!"

"But what *will* show up in *all* your lives," he went on, appearing to concentrate on each and every word he said, "is that sometimes *you have to struggle in order to learn something*. Or achieve something." He displayed a touch of the passion she saw sometimes at Quiz Quest.

Marianne had no response.

"I actually see this attitude from a lot of you Quiz Quest kids . . ." he said, standing up, pacing like Vi did.

He thought of her as a Quiz Quest kid?

"You guys think being smart means understanding something right away," he went on, in lecture mode as always. He sighed and seemed to go into his own world, resting his hands against the teacher's desk. "I just wish for you, Ms. Blume, and so many other kids, that you could *sit in the discomfort of not knowing*, of not getting it at first."

She crossed her legs and interlaced her fingers tightly. "You still don't understand," she muttered.

"Excuse me?" he asked.

A couple of students arrived and he hurried over, opened the door, and told them he needed five.

Marianne went on. "Is that what teachers tell themselves when they call on me and don't drop it even though they

284

know I'm not going to understand it at all? I don't want to be rude, but you're a math teacher. *You* get it already. Do you *always* have to push me *so hard*?"

"Always?" He raised his eyebrows.

True, it wasn't like he called on her every day. In fact, she never knew when it was coming. It was actually the unpredictability of it all that was part of what freaked her out.

"I dunno." She surrendered. "I'm sorry," she added. "I'm wrong."

"No, no." Mr. Garcia returned to his seat and leaned back in the chair. "You're right."

"Oh." Marianne felt like she'd stepped out of reality for a minute.

"I don't always know when to push, when to hold back. I-I don't always read people as well as I do numbers." He tapped a pencil against the desk in a way that reminded her of Nina and added, "Just because I'm a teacher doesn't mean I always have all the answers."

For an instant, Marianne could have sworn she could picture him exactly as he must have been in middle school. Trying to talk to people in the hallways but clamming up. Answering every question in math class. Maybe someone people called weird.

"That must be really tough for you," Marianne said.

"Hmm?" Mr. Garcia said, eyeing the clock. It was almost homeroom time.

She paused and explained, "Not knowing something. Because . . . you like to solve things, right?"

He tilted his head from side to side as if weighing various arguments in his mind. "Right. You're right," he acknowledged, sounding surprised.

As the crowd of kids outside the door grew, waiting to come in and sit for homeroom, Marianne stood up, readying herself to leave.

Mr. Garcia stood up, too.

"I'm pretty mad at myself," she said, twisting a strand of her hair so tightly she made a knot. "About Quiz Quest especially. Ms. Clarke might not let me do it."

Mr. Garcia walked with her to the door and said, "Look, Marianne." He put a hand on the doorknob. "I'll talk to Ms. Clarke. You're certainly welcome to compete. You've become . . ." He paused, considering his words. "The heart of the team."

Marianne didn't know what to say.

"But walking out the other day was careless." His voice was once again strict. The Mr. Garcia she knew. Like he was preparing himself for the class of kids about to come roaring in. "You *have* to choose who to be."

He opened the door and Marianne walked out.

***

you dont have to worry, Marianne texted the Ermines. **i have a plan.**

Ms. Clarke said you could do it?????? Nina wrote.

i have to double check on some stuff but ill let you know later today for sure, Marianne answered.

Marianne did have a plan. A plan to make sure the Ermines had a true chance to win States.

porch

When Skyla arrived on her steps, Marianne led them down the sidewalk. They headed toward Roseway Park, where spring was in full swing. In only a little over a week, school would end, and a whole new era would begin.

"Did you bring the flash cards?" Skyla asked. "I'm kind of loving the history ones. It's absurd what they don't teach you about American history!"

Marianne headed toward the big tree next to the playground, where they used to have pretend picnics when they were little. They each found a seat on a root.

Skyla ran her hands over the grass. "Man, I love this park," she said.

"Me too," Marianne agreed. "Remember when you wouldn't climb this tree because your dads terrorized you with stories of broken bones?"

Skyla cackled and said, "Yeah, and it's like five feet off the ground."

"Thank God you at least made it up there by fourth grade," Marianne recalled.

"Only after you lay on the ground and promised to catch my fall!" Skyla squealed with laughter, and they both cracked up remembering it all.

After taking in the sounds of the park—the kids screaming, the basketballs pounding the concrete, the birds tweeting as they swooped—Marianne said, "So I apologized to Mr. Garcia."

"What'd he say?" Skyla asked her. "Is he so mad? Did he say he'll let you compete still?" Skyla held up two pairs of crossed fingers.

"He said . . . Well, first of all? He is, like, *super* awkward in real life," she said.

Skyla's nose scrunched up as she laughed. "'Real life,'" Skyla repeated. "Like school isn't real life?"

"Okay, *non-math* life." Marianne laughed, too.

In the distance, Marianne saw some kids skateboarding. "Nice bomb drop. Did you see that?"

"Nice who huh?"

Marianne moved on. "I have to go home and study in a few minutes," she told Skyla.

"Oh. So not here? Okay, we can do it back at home." Skyla picked some clovers and twisted them between her fingers. "My house? Oh, I forgot to tell you." Skyla changed topics. "Julie has announced that Zara is 'too dramatic.' Can you believe that? She—"

"Trust me, I want to hear about this," Marianne said. "*Trust* me," she repeated. "But wait—I don't need to study for Quiz Quest anymore. Just school."

"Wait . . ." Skyla dropped the clover she'd picked. "Mr. Garcia said no to competing then?!"

Off of Marianne's silence, Skyla made her own conclusions and snapped, "Oh no, it's that you're giving up? Marianne, no. You can't give up *again*."

Marianne thought of what Mr. Garcia had said.

She had to decide who she wanted to be.

This was a good start.

"Hey." She targeted her whole self toward Skyla. "I want you to take my place on Quiz Quest."

Skyla tossed a handful of grass at her. "Yeah, sure."

"I know you were trying to not make me feel bad by not telling me how good you've gotten at school," Marianne pulled a stray grass blade out of her hair. "The As on the midterms, the honors classes, all of it . . ."

Skyla jumped in. "I just didn't see the point in talking about it."

"The point is that it's awesome," Marianne said. "*You're* awesome! Own it!" She felt that cheerleader in her come out again, the one who showed up to Regionals.

Skyla pulled her knees up and wrapped her arms around her legs. "Isn't the competition on *Sunday*?" she said. "I don't even know the rules."

"It doesn't matter," Marianne said. "Those guys deserve a win, and I want to help them get one. And even without all the practice I've had, their chances are better with you on the team."

Skyla lifted her chin from her knees. "I'm really weak in English lit, trust me—"

"That's okay," she told Skyla. "On Quiz Quest, you don't have to know everything because everybody knows something."

In the field in front of them, a bunch of kids played soccer with their parents. They had mud on their knees. One of them skidded in the dirt and fell, and a parent came to pick him up.

Marianne and Skyla watched for a moment, quiet together.

"But, Mar," Skyla said finally. "If you don't compete, you won't get the extra credit. And then?" She looked toward her, hazel eyes filled to the brim with concern. "You won't graduate. Right?"

It was Marianne's turn to pick a clover. She picked one and then another and then another and tied a clover bracelet around Skyla's wrist.

"You're my best friend," Marianne said, knotting the stems.

"Um, of course?"

"But whatever happens—high school or no high school—next year will be really different. You know? We might be doing different stuff. But I don't know . . . maybe that's okay." Bracelet complete, Marianne stood and wiped the dirt off her pants.

Skyla held her flowered hand in the air and Marianne pulled it, lifting her up.

Skyla gripped Marianne's hand, not letting go. "I know what you mean," she said. "And you're my best friend, too."

They stood at the tree together, watching the soccer. One of the kids scored a goal and the whole pack of them surrounded her and cheered.

"Woo-hoo!" Marianne yelled toward the soccer hero.

"If they let me, I'll do it," Skyla said, a grin creeping out. It was perfect.

"Ohmygod, you are going to *shine*," Marianne told her.

She squeezed Skyla's hand tighter.

Marianne pulled out her phone and made a call.

Three faces appeared.

Skyla, sitting next to her, moved out of the frame. "What do I do?" she mouthed to Marianne, who ignored her.

"Guys, great news," she told the Ermines. "We're going to win States!"

The three faces all spoke at the same time.

"Hooray!" Nina cheered.

"That's a relief, because I really liked winning the last one," Dan said.

"We have a lot to do, we've wasted a lot of valuable time," Vi said before listing off a set of goals and asking for everyone's schedules.

"Wait, wait, guys!" Marianne interrupted Vi. She pulled Skyla in closer. "Meet your new teammate. Skylaaa Raymooond!" she yelled like a sportscaster.

"It's too late for a swing," Vi said.

"No, no," Marianne explained. "She's taking my place."

Immediately, the group panicked. Nina and Vi competed for airtime, and Marianne couldn't hear a word and then Dan's voice lifted above the two of them and asked, "So Ms.

Clarke and Mr. Garcia said you couldn't compete? Harsh, man. Cruel."

"Actually . . ." And dang it, Marianne felt her throat catch. She didn't even feel sad, so why was she about to cry? "Mr. Garcia said I could. He's not so bad, I guess. And I'm—"

"No!" Nina jumped in. "No! Why?"

"I'm okay with taking the year again," Marianne explained. She tried to sound upbeat. She felt Skyla's chin rest on her shoulder.

"I probably need it, anyway," she went on. "You guys know that. I just . . . you guys helped me so much, but I'm a little too far behind. And I've seen Skyla—believe me, she's *so* good at this stuff, she learns facts in a *second*, she's got a brain like a sponge—"

"That's fantastic," Dan muttered.

"And I know I'm not, like, a 'statistics' expert, I'm, like, the exact opposite of that? But I'm positive your chances at winning are better with Skyla. So . . . I'm gonna pass on the extra credit." She paused. "I'll be okay."

She could be the heart of the team. That was who she wanted to be. The heart.

As they walked home through the field, Skyla said, "Hey, can you give me some advice on this awkward Julie-Zara situation?"

"*Yes! So* glad you brought it back up. I love people stuff. What's up?"

While they chatted, they stopped to linger by the little boys doing bomb drops until the sun began to set.

13

ON THE DAY OF the competition, Marianne sat by the window next to Lillian, who lay sprawled with her long swimmer limbs on the orange rag rug on the floor.

Marianne, after finishing her graphic novel the night before, read on in *A Tree Grows in Brooklyn*, while Lillian read a book called *Wuthering Heights*, which she said was "supposed to be romantic, but is actually horrifying."

Around 10:00 A.M., a large gray van pulled up in front of Skyla's house. It was the Ermines, taking her to Lansing.

"We'll meet you there in a couple of hours!" Skyla's dads yelled as they waved her off.

She saw Skyla glance over toward her house and so she quickly lifted the windowsill.

"Break a leg, guys!" she yelled.

"You'll do great!" Lillian hollered from the floor.

Skyla motioned her down, but she shook her head. She'd stay up there.

Maybe two eighth grades wouldn't be so bad. Marianne would meet a lot of the seventh graders and make new friends. Maybe. But that thought still didn't feel very good, and she pushed it out of her head.

The van rolled slowly by the curb and came to a stop in front of her house.

Skyla must have forgotten something.

Marianne walked away from the window.

She picked up her phone.

Unable to stop herself, she texted the Ermines:

you guys got this! vi—go for it and enjoy it! let it be fun, right? dan—this is the moment—get on that buzzer and you can WIN! you're smarter than every-one! nina—take a breath! say bye bye to the scary thoughts! it's all good! skyla—just pretend you're with me in my room doing flash cards. that's all it is.

Vi responded: im at the door.

Marianne rushed back to the window and saw that the van was still there, the door wide open.

"Huh?" Marianne said aloud.

The doorbell rang.

She heard her parents answer it. Her dad yelled, "Mar! It's for you!"

As she walked down the stairs, the sight of Vi greeted her. Her thick hair was pulled back into a large, tight bun. She wore black pants and a white T-shirt with some kind of graphic on it. And she checked her phone two times before Marianne even made it to the bottom of the staircase.

When Marianne greeted her, Vi handed her a piece of cloth.

Lifting it up, Marianne saw a cartoon ermine on the front with ETHERIDGE under it. The back read BLUME.

"I tried to think, 'What would Marianne do to prepare us for Championships?' and I figured you'd make some corny shirts."

Before Marianne could respond, Vi turned to Marianne's dad.

"Hi, Ethan." She pulled a slip of paper out of her hand. "Could you sign this, please?"

Her dad slid his glasses down to read it and then glanced back up at Vi. He pulled a pen out of his back pocket and signed. "There ya go."

"Thanks," Vi said. "Okay, get in." She turned around toward the van.

"What?" Marianne looked from her dad to Vi and back again.

"Permission slip. Come on, you're coming with us," Vi commanded.

"Huh?"

"Norah!" Vi spoke loudly over Marianne's shoulder. "Tell Marianne to grab a couple of snacks, but we'll have lunch in Lansing! Throw the shirt on," she directed Marianne.

"Simple psychological strategy," she explained. "You're not there and it's bad for morale."

Her parents peered out the door at the van and turned back to their daughter.

"What are you waiting for?" her dad asked. "You heard the girl. Get your stuff together!"

Her mom leapt up to grab some things for Marianne and started stuffing them in a tote bag. "We'll drive over later with Jason and Luis. We'll see you there!"

Marianne took the bag in her arms, still frozen by the surprise of it all, but Vi clutched her arm and pulled her toward the car.

While they were still on the path to her house, Marianne turned to Vi. "Thanks."

Vi practically tossed her inside.

The Ermines greeted her with cheers.

"Welcome back, Coach!" Dan said, patting her back.

Nina squealed and hugged her.

Skyla blew her a kiss.

Mr. Garcia turned around from the driver's seat and put the car in drive. "Now that we're all here, let's go."

***

The halls of the Lansing high school were so enormous that their voices echoed.

"Do elephants attend school here?" Dan asked as they wandered inside.

The six teams arrived two hours before the competition to prepare. After the moderators and administrators showed them around the auditorium and reviewed rules and decorum, they were served sandwiches in the cafeteria. The Ermines claimed a table and dug in.

Marianne eyed the rest of the teams. Lots of blouses and button-ups. They were the only team with T-shirts.

"Love these shirts, Vi," Marianne whispered.

"I'm starting to think they make us look unprofessional," Vi said as she texted furiously.

"You should eat something." Marianne pushed Vi's tray closer to her.

"I will, I will."

"Your parents coming?" Marianne asked, fighting the urge to read Vi's texts over her shoulder.

"My mom, yeah. My dad is on call and he had to run to the hospital," she said.

"Oh my gosh, is he okay?" Marianne put a hand on Vi's arm.

"He's a cardiologist," Vi explained, eyes stuck to her screen.

Nina snickered. "I love you, Marianne."

"Andy's coming today," Dan said before digging into his chicken sandwich.

"I'm so excited for two Dans!" Nina trilled.

Dan glared. "That's offensive to twins, please retract your statement. We are individuals."

"He's going to see the glories of public school in action thanks to you," Marianne declared, chomping on a chip.

Another team a table away burst into laughter at something. Two of the girls had their arms around each other. The teacher told a story that every kid listened to. Marianne eyed Mr. Garcia and wondered if teachers ever got jealous of other teachers.

"You were right that it's kind of, like, intimidating to see that. They all look like best friends who joined Quest together or something," Nina reported to Marianne with an eye roll.

"Yeah. No one is like us Ermines, though!" Marianne cheered.

She wrapped an arm around Skyla just to emphasize it.

"So, Skyla, what's your favorite Best Picture winner of, say, the last twenty years or so?" Dan asked her.

As they chatted, Vi remained on her phone, taking bites occasionally, her expression more glum than ever.

After lunch, their parents and family trickled in, and soon the auditorium bustled.

It was weird to see Andy walking around. He looked like a grumpy, more formally dressed Dan, his red hair combed over and slicked back like a politician's.

"Little Miss Sunshine!" Dan introduced him to the team.

Marianne whispered to Dan after, "He's going to see you *dominate* today. Remember—"

"Put his face on every opposing team's face. I got it."

"No," Marianne said. "I changed my mind about that."

"Oh, now you tell me," Dan groaned.

"I think it worked, but you don't need it anymore. You go to the buzzer now. You got this. Just have fun, Dan. You love trivia. And today? You get to trivia!" she said, and she could hear how bubbly and airy her voice sounded, but she didn't mind it that day. Who cared how she spoke?

Marianne gave him a couple of pats on the back.

"You're the best, Coach," Dan said with a grin.

Vi's mom seemed nice and said hello to everybody. She resembled Vi, but her face was more angular rather than round and full. She quickly sat down and stayed on her phone.

When her parents swooped in to find seats, waving her over to join them, Marianne spotted Lillian. And, next to her, Harper.

"Hey!" Lillian grabbed her and gave her a squeeze. "Harper, you remember Marianne, right?"

"Yeah." Harper waved. "Hey. This is cool." She motioned around the room.

Lillian beamed at Marianne and gave her a secret thumbs-up.

Marianne led her family over toward Mr. Garcia, and she took a seat next to him.

Jason and Luis settled in the row behind them.

"This is exciting!" Luis announced.

"Skyla's going to do an amazing job," Marianne told them.

 299

As round one took off, Marianne noticed Vi gave everyone high fives and pats on their back throughout. Whether it was to show the other team they weren't nervous and worked well together or if it was intended to pump up the Ermines, Marianne was proud.

"Right on, Vi," Marianne said aloud, and ignored that her parents gave each other a "She's so cute" look.

Skyla answered two questions leading to extension rounds right off the bat.

"Sensational," Marianne heard Skyla's papa whisper under his breath behind her.

Her natural calmness helped her. It seemed to help Nina, too, Marianne saw.

At the end of every round, Skyla looked toward their families and gave a little wave.

As Dan demolished the first few history questions and extension rounds, Marianne couldn't help but say out loud, *"Yes, Dan, you tell 'em!"*

"Have you ever thought about coaching football one day?" Skyla's dad joked.

"Shhhhh," an entire crowd said toward both of them.

"Sorry!" she mouthed.

She heard Lillian snicker beside her.

Nina stumbled. She answered "Pakistan" when she meant somewhere else. Marianne saw her beat herself up for it.

Skyla took over on the geography questions. She seemed to know everything about every state in the country.

Marianne saw Vi place a hand on Nina's.

Then Nina took a breath, put her feet into first position, and went all in:

Bhutan, the Nile River, the island of Luzon, Australia, the Great Lakes, 40,075 kilometers long, strike-slip faults, Tashkent in Uzbekistan . . .

The Ermines had this.

Hands shot out and buzzers buzzed and facts filled the air.

And before she knew it, the Ermines had won their first two games, leaving it down to the Etheridge Ermines and the Morningside Lions for the end-of-the-year trophy.

It was actually happening.

And they only had a half an hour to prepare.

Mr. Garcia herded them into a corner to go over strategy.

Marianne, Skyla, Dan, and Nina gathered around him.

But where was Vi?

None of them had seen where she'd gone.

"I'll find her," Marianne told the team, and she went off to search.

For her first stop she headed toward where Vi's mom sat, thinking maybe Vi had stopped to talk with her, but her mom just scrolled on her phone.

Marianne came up to her, anyway.

"Hey, Ms. Cross. Have you seen Vi around?"

Vi's mom lifted her gaze from the screen and shook her head with a polite smile. "She's not with the team? Probably in the bathroom or something."

Marianne spotted a team huddled together solemnly going over their loss and another laughing in the back of the auditorium, seemingly unbothered. She tried not to look too closely at the Morningside Lions in case it seemed like she was listening in to cheat somehow.

She left the auditorium and checked the bathrooms. No Vi.

As she made her way down the enormous hallways, she softly cooed, "Viii? Oh Viii?" like she was calling to Possum.

Finally, inside a classroom toward the end of the hall, she spotted Vi's high bun through the door window. She sat at a desk, her face indecipherable.

As the door creaked open, Vi saw her and pulled her knees up toward her neck, stuffing her face down between them like a turtle.

Vi's back bounced slightly. She was crying.

"Vi, what's wrong?!" Marianne rushed to her side and knelt down on the carpet beside her.

"It's too embarrassing. I can't tell you," Vi whimpered.

The clock above the desks read 2:09. They didn't have long.

"Hey, you're talking to the queen of embarrassment here. You think you'll faze me?" Marianne asked.

No response.

Vi's flushed face met Marianne's.

"Fine," Vi said. She pressed a couple of buttons on her cell, then handed it to Marianne.

On the screen, she saw two names: Addison and Vi.

Vi had texted multiple times over several days, but there wasn't any response from Addison. Until:

Vi: ok i know youre super busy but we are here! sooo close to getting this done. we are one step away from getting to the finals of finals can you even believe it????

Addison: thats cool

Vi: we did it!!!!!!! ok now you can tune in on the livestream! ill send you the link again. i think youre going to be so impressed w Skyla

Addison: cant sorry

Vi: oh ok

Vi: k maybe itll be up on youtube like regionals.

Addison: honestly i probably wont be able to watch it

Vi: oh

Addison: don't take this the wrong way but im just way too swamped here

sometimes its kinda hard to respond to everything you write. theres the time difference and then like im just busy here and keeping up w even like my closest friends from back home takes up so much of my time i cant really always respond to everybody and its not like im on the qq team anymore ya know?

but good luck w all of it srsly!

gtg

Marianne put down the phone.

"Did I really think Addison Schuler was my best friend? I'm so stupid," Vi said, slamming the desk and sitting up.

"Hey, don't say that about yourself." Marianne stood in front of the desk and tried to get Vi to look at her.

"I think skateboarding or student government or Quiz Quest is going to make me friends or find a 'group' or something embarrassing like that, and of course it *doesn't*." Vi closed her eyes and tears slid out in buckets. "I give up."

Marianne sensed someone at the door and saw her dad. He waved and pointed to the clock.

She turned back to Vi. They were running out of time.

"Okay, so sometimes it's tough for you to . . . like . . ." Marianne grasped for words. "Connect with people. So? What do you do if something's hard? You work on it," she assured Vi, hearing Mr. Garcia in the back of her mind.

. . . *Sit in the discomfort of not knowing, of not getting it at first.*

Vi started to cry. Sobs overtook her. She couldn't stop.

What could Marianne do?

She hopped on the desk in front of Vi and sat perched there. She would figure this out.

"And who says Addison's so great, anyway?" Marianne threw it out there. It couldn't hurt.

"She is," Vi insisted predictably, between heaving breaths.

Could Marianne tell Vi she *had* connected with people? That she and Nina and Dan were her friends? Or at least almost-friends? The start of friends? Could she say that Vi had helped her so many times, like when she'd taken her cell from her at Regionals and made her forget those cruel voices, or all the times she'd worked with her on homework and flash cards?

She should stand up on the desk, pump her fist, and give Vi the ultimate pep talk—tell Vi she was going to win today. That she had to go give the love of knowledge her all. That she should win for them, for Nina and Dan and Skyla and Mr. Garcia. She was Violet frickin' Cross, the captain of the scholars and the best teacher Marianne had ever had!

But there Vi sat, so sad, so unconcerned with winning or glory or being the best.

So Marianne did what friends do. She came to her side. She slowly guided her to standing. She said, "Hey, it's okay."

And she hugged Vi Cross with all her might.

For an instant, Vi stiffened.

Marianne repeated, "It's gonna be okay."

Then Vi let go. She cried harder, into Marianne's Ermines tee. And Marianne said, "It'll be alright," a few more times.

And over the next minute Vi's breathing slowed. She sniffled.

She patted Marianne's back awkwardly a couple of times, and she pulled away.

"Okay," Vi said. "Okay, okay," she repeated, stepping back from Marianne.

It was Vi's turn to check the clock.

"Almost time," Marianne said.

"Five minutes?!" Vi wiped her face with the black sleeve under her T-shirt. She stuffed her cell in her back pocket.

"Go time," Marianne said.

"Go time." Vi took another deep breath.

Marianne opened the door and watched Vi steel herself. She sniffled, slicked back her hair, and strutted out the door, determined.

Marianne leaned against the wall of the hallway, where her dad stood waiting for her.

"Shall we?" he said.

As they walked down the hall together back toward the auditorium, he threw an arm around her.

"Hey," he said.

"Hey," she said back.

"You're a great kid. You know that?"

**

The Ermines and the Lions were evenly matched.

"Who's winning?" her mom asked her multiple times.

Marianne couldn't say. It was going too fast.

As they reached the final minute before the timer buzzed, the moderator announced that the two teams were tied.

"Have you ever seen a tie before?" Marianne whispered to Mr. Garcia.

He hadn't.

The moderator proceeded to describe the rules of a tie game as they went into overtime.

"Can you translate?" Marianne's dad whispered into her ear.

She tried to speak as quietly as possible while Skyla, Dan, Nina, and Vi conferred, awaiting the start of overtime.

Several others in the auditorium were whispering to one another as well.

"Basically, there are no more extension rounds, just questions given to both teams. Teams can talk to each other for like ten seconds, and then each team captain holds up the answer on some paper." She still couldn't believe how much she knew about this game. She remembered Dan explaining every possible scenario to her.

"Like *Jeopardy!*" her dad said.

She nodded. "Sort of."

"So the first time one is wrong and the other is right, the team who is right wins?" he asked.

Marianne nodded. She rubbed her palms back and forth across her jeans. The tension was killing her.

She hoped there were some good history questions. She hoped there wasn't anything too tricky. She hoped one of the answers was "Misty Copeland" or "phosphorus."

The countdown began.

Both teams knew the Hundred Years' War.

Both teams knew LeBron James.

Both teams knew Joseph Smith founded the Mormon Church.

Both teams knew the Silk Road.

And then:

"Gougères often comprise which portion of a French meal?" the moderator asked in his robot-like voice.

Marianne saw Skyla's face contort in confusion. Vi mouthed "Gougères?" to her teammates. Nina bit her knuckle, her toe tapping on the floor. Dan lightly hit his forehead over and over, like he could smack the right answer out of his brain.

Both teams brainstormed.

The seconds ticked on. Nothing.

And Marianne knew it. She knew the winning answer.

Marianne almost laughed out loud but put the tips of her fingers to her mouth instead, hiding a smile.

Hors d'oeuvres.

She could still see the picture of them on her poster—the dough puffed up in a little half circle, hiding the creamy cheese within. She remembered the image had made her so hungry. She'd been excited to show it to the class and maybe make some at home one day, though she never did.

"Dessert," said the Ermines.

"Fromage," said the Dolphins.

"Incorrect," the moderator said. "The answer is an hors d'oeuvre."

Marianne checked in with her parents, who watched, expressions unchanged. They didn't remember that presentation, that story. They probably didn't remember what they'd said after, either. To them, that moment hadn't actually meant very much, had it?

The questions continued, without skipping a beat.

If she'd been up there, and they'd made it to that point, into overtime and to that very question . . . she would've won States.

She pictured her old fantasy of Quiz Quest: giving the final correct answer that won the game, the balloons and confetti falling down around her, the music playing, a bouquet of roses brought to her as all her teammates basked in her glory and her parents wept in pride. The Supreme Court judge–looking moderators saying they'd never seen anything like it before—this girl was the next Marie Curie.

But instead, there she was, in a regular old assembly room, a moderator wearing a brown suit and standing at a typical auditorium podium, the winning answer in her own head and her head alone.

Sometimes you just knew one.

And within seconds, another question flew by, and the moderator said, "Correct," tilting his head toward the Ermines. "The answer is Coretta Scott King."

Their parents and siblings and Mr. Garcia erupted in wild applause, and it was all over.

Marianne jumped to her feet. "We did it!" she yelled to Mr. Garcia over hoots and hollers.

"Yaaaay, Vi!" Marianne heard Vi's mom say. She held up her phone and took a hundred pictures.

"Da-an, Da-an, Da-an!" Dan's family chanted, even Andy.

Nina's parents clutched hands.

"*Whoo! Go Ermines!*" Lillian and Harper shouted before hugging each other.

As her team jumped up and down and grinned and shook hands with the Morningside kids, Marianne closed her eyes.

She heard someone say, "Come on up here with us, Marianne!"

And, for an instant, she could swear she felt the flutter of confetti swirl around her.

14

IT TURNED OUT THAT *A Tree Grows in Brooklyn* was a page-turner. By the end, at least. What would happen to little Francie when she became not-so-little Francie? Marianne had to know.

She got to the final two pages as they pulled up to school and five minutes before the bell would ring for the last homeroom.

"Can I just sit in here for *one* more second?" she asked her mom.

"Nope. Hop out, you. There's a line here. And good luck! We're proud of you no matter what!" her mom yelled out a half-open window as she drove off.

Marianne kept the book in front of her, reading as she headed into the front doors.

By the time homeroom began, she'd finished.

It felt sad to complete the story, like saying goodbye to someone you'd never see again.

Before her first class, while Marianne was still lost in the world of Francie, Vi cornered her between the end of a row of lockers and a door leading to the stairwell.

Marianne hadn't talked one-on-one with Vi since the competition a couple days before. They'd sat together among all the Ermines while they spent a few lunches recounting each moment of glory in detail, stood side by side as Ms. Clarke gave them a congratulations speech while posting a picture of the Ermines holding the trophy onto the school bulletin board, and blushed in unison as Mr. Garcia forced the math class to applaud their achievement.

But now Vi stood before her as if she had something she'd been aching to say.

"I lied," Vi confessed in a rush.

"Okay . . ." Marianne gripped her backpack straps, waiting for a bombshell.

"You didn't have to win in order to get the extra credit." Vi paused.

"What?" Marianne leaned forward, as if she hadn't heard her properly.

"Okay," Vi sighed. "At first, I really thought Mr. Garcia meant he needed you to win to prove you earned the credit. But then it got pretty obvious that he just meant he had to see proof you were trying, and you were *obviously* trying." Vi gripped her stack of books with both hands.

Marianne started to say something, but Vi interrupted her.

"I mean, he'd have to be a *total villain* to make you have

to win a frickin' *championship* to get the credit if you were working that hard, right?" Vi said.

"This . . ." Marianne paused, struggling for the right thing to say. "Wasn't obvious to me? You were the boss, so I figured you were, like, interpreting him for me?"

"He's not a monster!" Vi shook her head at the thought. "He's mostly just *awkward*, right?" Vi tapped her toe on repeat. "I'm sorry."

"Whoa," Marianne said. "You *really* wanted to win."

"Yes," Vi said, her tone clipped, her tapping ceasing. She adjusted her glasses and her ponytail. "I made a mistake."

"Eh, that's okay," Marianne said with a shrug.

"Really?" Vi asked.

"Yeah! You had to motivate me!" Marianne said, waving at Kylie Chen as she flitted by. What was the point of getting angry? It had all worked out in the end . . . Sort of.

"I feel pretty bad for judging Mr. Garcia so harshly, though . . ." Marianne made a "yikes" face.

Vi didn't say anything.

"Didn't Skyla do great?" Marianne beamed, changing the subject, ready to let the whole year and all its mistakes go.

"She's got real potential," Vi answered.

Marianne giggled at Vi's version of trying to be nice.

"But we've all got our strengths and weaknesses," Vi added. She paused and added almost inaudibly, "Including Addison."

"True," Marianne agreed.

"I talked to Mr. Garcia. I *insisted* he give you the extra credit despite not performing at States," Vi said with a heavy dose of passion as the hallways thinned out.

"Well, thanks," Marianne said. There was no point in discussing it. Mr. Garcia didn't fudge points and he didn't break the rules. She didn't compete, so she wouldn't get the credit. In a way, it was a relief just to know what to expect.

"Hey, Horse!" Tripp hollered as he walked by and high-fived her. "Have a great summer, you hear?"

"Hey!" she called out as he moved on down the hallway. "I'm putting a moratorium on the 'Horse' thing. That means don't call me that, 'kay?"

"Moratorium?" Vi repeated, impressed.

"It's a Mom word," Marianne said. "She uses it a lot."

"I love your mom," Vi said.

They stood together, Vi still swaying slightly.

"I gotta get to history," Marianne told Vi, stepping away. "See ya in math."

"Wait, one more thing." Vi jumped forward. She glanced around like she was about to say something secret or embarrassing. "My parents want to have some kind of celebration for the championship . . ." Vi shuffled her feet. "They want to get pizza or something, and have you guys over in our game room and stuff—"

"Game room?!" Marianne blinked. "You're so loaded."

Vi's family probably went on winter and spring break vacations every year and had one of those fridges with a water dispenser in the front, too.

"It'll probably be pretty boring," Vi went on, "but I'm inviting all the Ermines, so . . ."

"I'd love to! Shoot me a text to tell me when," Marianne said, heading off.

"Oh." Vi's eyes widened in surprise. "Okay. I mean, if you want to."

"Of course! We're friends, aren't we?" she yelled to Vi as she walked backward and hollered, "See you in math!"

And she hurried to history before the bell rang.

Behind her, she heard Jalilah Jacobs approach Vi.

"Hey, is there a Quiz Quest team at Brookdale High? Do you know how to get in?" Jalilah asked her.

Vi launched into a detailed rundown, and their voices faded behind Marianne as she arrived at class.

***

Before math, Marianne tried some visualizations. Nina had taught it to her. She told her she was practicing some meditation on a new app she got, and one of the techniques was to picture what was about to happen as if it were going the way you wanted it to go.

So Marianne imagined two impossible things. First, she pictured an A plus plus written on her test paper, surrounded by smiley faces. She visualized Mr. Garcia shaking her hand and saying, "You've done so well on the final, you didn't even need Quiz Quest in the first place. You are a hero."

Then she stifled a chuckle, took a breath, and pictured

the possible: a C plus. She wanted to pass. She imagined him saying, "We'll get it right next year, won't we, Ms. Blume?" She would finish the year unable to pass the entire class but finally earning a better test score.

Nina said to use her senses in her visualizations, but all she could think about was the slight sneaker smell in the math classroom, so she gave up and watched the second hand on the clock until Mr. Garcia announced he would pass out the final exams.

He walked past her, his stride slow and steady, and started in the back.

"Yes!" she heard Lucas Hayes bellow. "*Aced* it! Take *that*!"

"Bumping chests over grades . . ." Vi pondered a few seats behind her. "Such fascinating creatures."

Marianne twisted her torso around to face Vi. "Wait, we're not going to bump chests?"

Vi threw Marianne her signature glare, and Marianne laughed.

It was a good distraction. But she could still feel the nerves all throughout her limbs.

Mr. Garcia arrived at the corner of Kylie's desk. "Here you are," he said, placing her test down before her.

Then he handed Marianne hers. "Nice work, Ms. Blume," he said as he made his way back to his desk.

And on the top of her paper she read:

B-

No way. It couldn't be true.

Below it, Mr. Garcia had written out the point totals for all her tests and homework that semester and added it to what looked like two times—double!—the extra credit she was promised if she participated in Quiz Quest. Scribbled on the line underneath it was her point total and her overall grade in class: 72%.

Good luck in high school, it read. *Keep up the <u>effort</u>*.

Wait. This couldn't be real. Even if he'd counted her on the team for extra credit like Vi had requested of him, he'd made an error by including it twice. Hadn't he?

With some hesitation, Marianne ambled up to him.

In a low voice, she asked him if they could talk for a second, and he brought her to the corner of the classroom, beneath a poster that read *Math Is Everywhere!*, far enough away from the students' desks to have some privacy.

"Mr. Garcia, you made a mistake." She held out her test for him to see.

"Did I?" he asked, not giving the paper a single glance.

That day, he wore a bright green tie with the pi symbol decorating it. Had she gotten Mr. Garcia all wrong? Was he just truly awkward, like Vi said? Stern, trying hard to seem in charge, but unsure of himself? She had assumed *so much* about him.

Certainly, she could no longer see him in any way as hateful or mean.

Out of her periphery she saw Vi checking them out to see what was going on.

"You put the extra credit twice. See?" She pointed at her paper again. "You doubled it."

"That can't be," he said. "Settle down!" he chastised a group in the back having an animated discussion.

"No, look." Marianne held it out closer to his face. "The math is wrong."

"I doubt that, Ms. Blume," he answered her. "I'm pretty good with numbers."

He took a step back toward the front of the room, but Marianne stopped him.

"Wait. That's not okay. I didn't earn it." Marianne couldn't believe the words coming out of her mouth, but she knew they were right. "I didn't do work all fall or winter. I popped a bubble in your face. I left class. Then I didn't even compete."

Mr. Garcia seemed to ruminate on this. He put his hands in his pockets and rocked slightly back and forth on his heels. "Hmm. I've recently begun to examine the concept of point systems. They're, um . . . complicated. The trouble with them, you see, is how they don't always account for authentic *change*." His face scrunched up in thought as he added, "Obviously, I'm not the first one to consider this, but . . . ." He lifted a finger as if debating someone who wasn't there and said, "Should someone be punished for low points earlier on when they've raised their points as time progressed? It's getting harder for me to accept that."

"Huh?" she asked, still clutching the test in front of her chest.

"What I'm saying is that maybe there's some space between 'rules are rules' and just letting someone slide by. Right?" He lifted his shoulders up, his whole body asking the question. Was he asking *her*?

"No, *no*!" she found herself arguing with him, her voice rising slightly. Noticing a couple of kids check her out, she brought her tone down to a near-whisper again.

He'd finally convinced her he was right! And now this!

"Look, Mr. Garcia, you told us that you earn what you earn! And now you're saying all this stuff?!"

Mr. Garcia checked the clock behind them. He looked toward the kids. Most of them were texting or comparing tests. He took in a deep breath and let it out.

"Okay," he said. "How about a compromise?"

"Okay . . ." She had no idea where Mr. Garcia was going with any of this.

"No *extra* extra credit. But. You still earn the credit for Quiz Quest. That was our agreement, after all. Effort!"

Before she could argue with him, he added, "I think Ms. Cross over there would organize a protest on your behalf if we didn't allow for that, at the least."

And he smiled what might have been the most genuine smile she'd ever seen on him. He really liked Vi, she could tell. And why wouldn't he? Vi was so tough, so loyal.

"That's still not enough to ensure you pass my class, however," he went on. "So here's my final offer: You retake algebra this summer. Practice the concepts. *Learn* them . . . And that gets you to high school. In fact, it *prepares* you for high school. And considering you went from Fs to a B minus today, I think you'll do just fine. That is, if you're not too tired of me yet. Deal?" He held out a hand.

"Summer school?"

Marianne imagined a June spent shivering in an overly air-conditioned room under the florescent lights of Anna Etheridge Middle School while summer sport practices went on outside. She foresaw the July twilight hours spent redoing worksheets she should have done in the fall of the eighth grade, slowly mastering each step of each problem with her mom or Vi or maybe even Skyla, instead of soaking in the heat at Roseway Park.

She had once been so far behind even summer school couldn't save her.

But now it could.

Marianne clutched Mr. Garcia's hand and shook. "Deal."

Off his nod, Marianne followed him back toward his desk and stood in front of her seat.

She stared at the test.

She flipped through its pages.

"I got a B minus," she whispered to herself.

"Huh?" Kylie said.

Marianne scurried to Vi, scooting a chair out of her way to get there. "I got a B minus! On the test!" She waved the papers in Vi's face. "And do you see how many answers I got *correct*?" She flipped her hair behind her shoulder.

"Wow!" Vi exclaimed.

"*Do you know how hard I had to work to get this grade?*" Marianne nearly shouted. "I am *amazing*!" Marianne spun in place, holding the paper in the air.

"Oh my gosh, maybe next time you'll even get an *A*!" Kylie cheered, joining Marianne and Vi at the desk.

"Hey, let's not get carried away here," Marianne said. "This isn't a movie."

"Lol," Kylie said. "True."

Yeah, maybe one day Marianne would get an A. Or maybe not. Maybe she would *never* would get an A in math. Who could say? But right then? She was a B (minus) student, and that was just fine. More than fine. As Lillian might say, it was her fastest swim yet. And she felt like she'd won an Olympic gold.

"Wait, did he give you the extra credit?" Vi asked breathlessly.

"He did, he did!"

Vi exhaled and cheered.

Marianne went on: "And I'm going to summer school— which . . . blech, but okay, fine—and then I'm going to high school, and then I'm going to Hawaii and the *moon*!" Marianne performed another goofy little spin as Mr. Garcia tried in vain to calm the classroom.

But they were bubbling over with last-day excitement.

Lucas cupped his hands around his mouth and hollered out "Nice going, Blume!"

"Go, Blume!" Niko echoed him.

"B for Blume!" Jalilah whooped.

"Barely scraping by with a B minus isn't exactly something to brag about . . ." she heard Ava Hayes murmur under her breath from a couple of feet away.

"Ava, seriously?" Vi barked in her direction. "Like if she doesn't get a 4.0 she's not good enough for you? Gross."

Marianne laughed. "Give it up, Vi. Who cares what she thinks?"

"True," Vi agreed.

All the kids in the classroom chattered at full volume, and Mr. Garcia gave up all control. He sat at his desk and worked on something on his laptop, waiting for the bell that was soon to ring.

Marianne stayed next to Vi, showing her which answers she got right and which ones she didn't, and as the kids played musical chairs and switched around depending on who they were talking to, Marianne took an empty spot next to her.

"Wait, before class ends," Vi said, turning over Marianne's final so she'd stop talking about it for a second, "want to be on the Quiz team next year? There will probably be a lot more kids, so you might end up on B team at first, maybe C, but not for long, and we could really work well together, I think. I don't know if there's a role for someone to work just in a coach or captain capacity or—"

"Whoa there," Marianne said, taking a breath, turning

her face to the bright, almost-summer sun pouring in through the classroom windows. "One thing at a time."

***

The halls had emptied out except for a few stragglers, Marianne among them.

The teachers looked as happy as the kids, some already taking down a few items off their walls or desks.

Marianne knocked on Ms. James's door.

"Yes?" she heard Ms. James say from inside.

"Happy end-of-the-year." Marianne leaned against the doorframe.

"And happy graduation," Ms. James replied, shutting her desk and fiddling with a few folders on its surface.

"You heard?"

Ms. James gave an affirmative "Mm-hmm."

Marianne wondered how many students Ms. James had had over the years. Hundreds and hundreds. Thousands?

"I wanted to ask you about Francie," Marianne said. She held up her now-tattered copy of *A Tree Grows in Brooklyn*.

"Oh, did you finish it?" Ms. James lowered herself into her swivel chair.

Marianne nodded. "I like how she sees the tree in the end of the book, which grew even though it was like a weed in the concrete at first?"

"Mm-hmm." Ms. James smiled.

"And how at the same time, Francie also sees the little girl sitting on the fire escape. I'm guessing they're supposed to be, like, symbols of one another or something like that? Am I using the wrong words, or . . . ?"

Ms. James held up a hand to signal a pause. "Wait, wait, wait, this is a longer discussion. Come on in."

Marianne walked through the door and into the classroom.

"Let's start from the beginning," Ms. James said.

"Okay." Marianne placed the book on the desk and faced ahead.

"So tell me, Marianne. What did you think?"

Acknowledgments

Thank you to Connie Hsu, Megan Abbate, and Nicolás Ore-Giron for your masterful editing. All three of you were indispensable in sharpening and enlivening Marianne's story. I cannot tell you how many times I read your insights and experienced both clarity and inspiration.

Kat Kopit, Claire Maby, Andrea Monagle, and Kathy Wielgosz, thank you so much for all your hard work on perfecting the book. Thank you to Emmy Lupin and Liz Dresner for creating a dynamite cover. To the entire team at Roaring Brook . . . thank you. I am eternally grateful.

I offer my overwhelming gratitude to my agent, Melissa Edwards, who consistently provides support, wisdom, savvy, and humor. Melissa, I couldn't ask for a better teammate.

I am indebted to Sarah Kim for sharing her sensitive and incisive thoughts with me and helping me in my attempt to illuminate Dan's reality. Thank you so much, Sarah, for your time and guidance.

And thank you to Sarah Kate Sligh for helping me envision

Dan's life more fully. I encourage readers to check out Sarah's YouTube channel to learn more about life as a young person with cerebral palsy: youtube.com/sarahkatesligh.

Thank you to educators Edward Powers and Donna Vaupel for allowing me to pick your brains about the world of trivia competitions. Your generosity with your time helped me immeasurably in breathing life into this story, and in appreciating the beauty of a bunch of kids getting together to share knowledge.

Thank you to Kelly Granito and Steven Lopez for offering your insights on the art of teaching. Your students, past and present, are lucky to have such thoughtful and empathetic educators. You both epitomize the oft-repeated truth that the craft of teaching is a constant exercise in learning.

Thank you to the following educators, who range in subject from my kindergarten teacher to my theater director to the advisor of my honors thesis in college: Michele Kotowicz, Cynthia Page-Bogen, Molly Sykes Crankshaw, Jim Melby, Constance Corwin, Linda S. Hoadley, Tracy Anderson, Ellen Stone, Judith DeWoskin, Marion Evashevski, Michelle Mountain, Loretta Grimes, and Lyn Di Iorio. Thank you for sharing your gifts with me.

Mom and Dad, thank you for always caring about what I think and respecting my intellect even when my academics faltered. Mom, I'm in awe of your personal quest for education and the immense hardships you had to endure in order to learn. What a heroine you are. Dad, your lifelong passion for learning, your enormous consumption of books of all kinds, and your devotion to the field of history have long inspired me. You set a formative example of curiosity and the importance of always diving deeper into a story. Also, I'm sorry you had to put up with our math tutoring sessions for all those years.

To Margery and David Ross, grandparents extraordinaire, I can never thank you enough for the hours and hours of writing time you gave me during an incredibly difficult year. I simply could not have completed this book without you both. Thank you for your love and for such tireless and affectionate grandparenting and parenting.

Thank you to my siblings and their better halves for the support system. Michael, Lauren, Ian, Lizzie, Tom . . . You are my forever people.

Claudia Maschio, my darling niece, thank you for reading an early excerpt of *Bright* and giving me your very honest opinion. Your sharp insights delight me. And to my lovely nephews, Jacob and Oliver Young, thank you for so generously answering my random, sporadic text-messaged questions about young people!

Thank you, Jonathan, for your heart and your brilliance.

Thank you to Simone and Ingrid for being the people you are. I love every bit of you.

Lastly, thank you to every young reader who has ever written to me or chatted with me. Your lives and stories are fascinating, life-affirming, and essential.